Garrett grasped Molly's hand in his.

On the surface, the gesture was a common courtesy between two acquaintances. With the benefit of her glove as a barrier there should have been nothing to cause her alarm. But this was the first time in seven years he'd taken her hand without hesitation.

Molly liked the unexpected familiarity of the gesture, liked it far too much.

Blinking hard, she struggled to keep her composure. But his touch felt so right. Time seemed to slow, past overlaying present. And, still, Garrett held on to her.

He moved a step closer and her mind grasped one lone thought. This was Garrett, the boy who used to put her at ease when no one else could. The one who had comforted her, treasured her. Loved her.

She'd once believed that God had brought them together at the perfect time, and that the Lord's hand had been guiding them toward a common future all along.

She'd been terribly wrong. Their chance to be a couple had come and gone a long time ago.

So why wouldn't Garrett release her?

And why wasn't she insisting he let her go?

Books by Renee Ryan

Love Inspired Historical

*The Marshal Takes a Bride
*Hannah's Beau
 Heartland Wedding
*Loving Bella
 Dangerous Allies
*The Lawman Claims His Bride
 Courting the Enemy
 Mistaken Bride
*Charity House Courtship
*The Outlaw's Redemption
*Finally a Bride

Love Inspired

Homecoming Hero

*Charity House

RENEE RYAN

grew up in a small Florida beach town. To entertain herself during countless hours of "lying out," she read all the classics. It wasn't until the summer between her sophomore and junior years at Florida State University that she read her first romance novel. Hooked from page one, she spent hours consuming one book after another while working on the best (and last!) tan of her life.

Two years later, armed with a degree in economics and religion, she explored various career opportunities, including stints at a Florida theme park, a modeling agency and a cosmetics conglomerate. She moved on to teach high-school economics, American government and Latin while coaching award-winning cheerleading teams. Several years later, with an eclectic cast of characters swimming around in her head, she began seriously pursuing a writing career. She lives in Savannah, Georgia, with her own hero-husband and a large fluffy cat many have mistaken for a small bear.

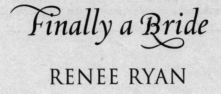

Finally a Bride

RENEE RYAN

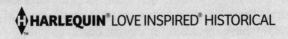

HARLEQUIN® LOVE INSPIRED® HISTORICAL

LOVE INSPIRED BOOKS

ISBN-13: 978-0-373-82987-3

FINALLY A BRIDE

www.Harlequin.com

Printed in U.S.A.

Intreat me not to leave thee, or to return from following after thee: for whither thou goest, I will go; and where thou lodgest, I will lodge: thy people shall be my people, and thy God my God.
—*Ruth* 1:16

To my beautiful, talented, intelligent, gifted daughter, Hillary Anne. You inspired Molly from the moment she showed up on the page several books ago. It's been a joy and honor to watch you grow into a loving, Christ-following young woman. You make your mommy proud!

Chapter One

Denver, Colorado, 1894

Molly Taylor Scott knew most people considered her a delightfully charming, sometimes frivolous young woman who loved being engaged almost as much as she loved the Lord. Molly would agree with this summation of her character, mostly. However, she would argue one key point.

She was never frivolous.

Especially when it came to matters of the heart. Thus, as she stood outside Denver's most exclusive millinery shop, surrounded by several would-be suitors, she treated the situation with utmost gravity.

Twirling her parasol, she gave the men her undivided attention. A rather difficult task, when one of the four seemed determined to monopolize the conversation. Molly stopped listening to the conversation as something—*someone*—exited the Arapahoe County Courthouse one block north.

Senses poised, she turned her head ever so slightly and caught sight of Garrett Mitchell moving at a clipped pace in her direction. He looked incredibly handsome today, every bit the successful attorney he'd become in the past few years.

Eyes cast forward, he made swift progress down the

lane, never once looking at Molly or acknowledging her presence. Still, her breathing quickened and her heart stuttered.

Stupid, stupid heart. An undertow of anger rolled through her. Interesting thing, anger; it signified she still cared.

She really shouldn't still care.

Not about Garrett Mitchell. Or those sculpted features framed inside dark blond hair, or that brilliant mind lurking behind the oh-so-handsome face, or that cowboy swagger that had stayed with him long after leaving his family's ranch.

Why, why, why did he still affect her so? He'd walked away from her seven years ago. *And I let him.*

Molly sighed. Better that, than give in to fresh despair.

A masculine clearing of a throat drew her gaze back to the man on her right. "Miss Scott, you must agree to attend the opera with me this evening." He took her hand and beamed down at her. "I won't take no for an answer."

A chorus of objections and counter invitations rose up from the other three in their group. Repeating his request a second time—or was it a third?—Mr. Giles Thomas gripped Molly's hand tighter and commanded her stare with an earnest one of his own.

He was not classically handsome, and he was certainly no Garrett Mitchell, but he had a pleasant enough appeal with his brown hair, brown eyes and rather ordinary brown suit.

"I'm afraid, Mr. Thomas, I must decline your lovely offer." She smiled brightly, even as she carefully extricated her hand from his bearlike grip. "Mrs. Singletary has already requested my company in her box this evening."

At times such as these Molly was ever grateful for her position as a personal secretary and companion to the most prominent widow in Denver. As if speaking her employer's name could summon the woman herself, Mrs. Singletary exited the millinery shop, her arms overflowing with her purchases.

Welcoming the interruption, and feeling guilty for waiting outside while her employer shopped, Molly set her parasol against the building and hastened forward. "Let me help you."

She retrieved the boxes, juggling the heaviest with her left hand and shifting around several more with her right. Sensing an opportunity to play the gentleman—a shade too late by Molly's estimation—Mr. Thomas and the others began snatching boxes away from her.

She stumbled under their enthusiastic efforts, careening backward. A pair of strong hands captured her shoulders and steadied her. Once she had her balance, the hands dropped away.

Head spinning, heart pounding wildly against her ribs, she barely managed to push the name of her rescuer past her trembling lips. "Garrett."

A slow, affectionate smile spread across his face. Just as quickly, it disappeared. "Molly," he said in a bland tone.

"I…that is…" She swallowed, words backing up in the throat until she thought she might choke on them. "Thank you."

"Watch your step. The footing is uneven here."

"Yes, I—"

He tipped his hat, muttered a hasty farewell and was gone.

Breathing hard, Molly blinked after his retreating back. It was always the same whenever their paths crossed. A brief moment of understanding, followed by an awkward exchange of stilted words and then…nothing but a bone-deep sense of loss that left her heart aching.

No. Oh, no. No more wallowing. No more wishing for what might have been. Molly was finished with Garrett

Mitchell and unrequited love. She was also finished with the four men still arguing over her.

Unnaturally quiet throughout her tête-à-tête with Garrett, as well as now, Mrs. Singletary eyed Molly with a speculative, almost calculating gaze. At last, as if finally finished weighing the situation, she held up a hand. "Gentleman, that's quite enough."

All four went very still, very silent.

"This boorish behavior is not helping your cause with the young lady."

Hastily worded apologies rang in the air.

"Not to me, you scoundrels." Mrs. Singletary shook her head in annoyance. "Miss Scott is the one you have offended."

And thus began another round of excuses stacked upon blame.

Only half listening, Molly nodded and smiled and generally wished to be anywhere but here. In silent understanding, Mrs. Singletary winked at her then resumed her glowering.

The expression of disapproval did nothing to hamper the woman's remarkable features. She had been a renowned beauty in her day. Her hair was still a rich, golden brown. Her face remained smooth of any sign that two decades had come and gone since Mr. Singletary had won her hand in marriage.

The argument continued, reaching ridiculous proportions, until Mr. Thomas pushed forward. "Since you have denied me your company this evening, you must allow me to escort you home now."

More disputes arose.

Again, Mrs. Singletary took control. "None of you will be escorting the lady home, for the simple reason we are not heading that way just yet."

Since the widow was one of the most powerful women

in town, not many folks were brave enough to chance her displeasure. Molly's current admirers proved no exception.

"Now, my dear, be so kind as to retrieve my packages from these young men and say goodbye."

There was a moment of jostling, followed by a bit of tugging and pushing but, *finally,* Molly was once more in possession of Mrs. Singletary's purchases.

After another flat-eyed scan of the group, the older woman dismissed the lot of them. Grumbling under their breaths, they scattered in four different directions, eventually absorbed by the noise and bustle of the busy Denver streets.

"Where to next?" Molly asked, breathing a sigh of relief. "The dress shop, perhaps?"

"Not today. I have a mind to study my hats before deciding if I need a new gown or two to match."

She considered the boxes in her hands. "Did you find anything worth wearing immediately?"

"Hardly, but I trust you will put them right soon enough."

"I'd like nothing better." Molly found great pleasure in turning an otherwise predictable hat into a new creation, with an added touch of flare all her own.

Staring off in the distance, Mrs. Singletary made a small movement of her head. "I wonder why Mr. Mitchell left so quickly after his gallant rescue."

Molly masked the falter in her step. Garrett had been especially chivalrous this afternoon. But that was Garrett simply being Garrett. He would have done the same for any woman. She was nothing special to him, not anymore. The surge of sorrow was so strong it threatened to consume her. And…and…

And Mrs. Singletary had just asked her a question. Releasing a tempered breath, Molly lifted a shoulder. "He was clearly in a hurry."

She sounded so calm, so in control. It was quite an act, when her heart was as bleak as a cold, rainy day.

"You are friends with his sisters, are you not?"

"I am."

"Hmm, very strange he didn't stick around and, I must say, quite inconvenient." Mrs. Singletary planted her fists on her hips, her gaze turning shrewd. "I have a business proposition of some urgency I had wanted to discuss with him."

Molly cast her employer a quick, baffled look. Garrett worked at Bennett, Bennett and Brand, yes, but Mrs. Singletary's personal attorney was Reese Bennett, Jr. Therefore, it seemed rather odd that the older woman would approach Garrett in lieu of her own lawyer.

"Why wait any longer?" The widow spun around and set out toward the law firm. "I shall speak with him now."

Molly trotted after Mrs. Singletary. Fingers curled into fists, she affected a placid tone. "But…" *Think, Molly, think.* "You don't have an appointment."

"I don't need one."

True. Mrs. Singletary was the law firm's wealthiest and most influential client. Appointment or not, none of the attorneys would turn her away. "Are you certain this business you have with Mr. Mitchell can't wait until later?"

"Quite certain." She quickened her pace.

Molly did the same, her stomach tied in knots, her arms growing tired under the weight of the packages she carried.

Dodging the bulk of the traffic with practiced ease, Mrs. Singletary hastened along the narrow sidewalk. A block shy of the firm, she leveled her gaze on Molly and made a most unusual request. "I would like you present when I speak with Mr. Mitchell."

"Me? I don't understand." Mrs. Singletary had never asked her to attend her business meetings before.

"It's very simple, my dear. I want to see how Mr. Mitchell behaves in your company. And you in his."

Oh, this was bad. So very, very bad. "Mrs. Singletary, you aren't playing matchmaker, are you?"

"Matchmaker, me?"

The cryptic response made Molly all the more skeptical of her employer's motives. "Why do you wish to see how Garrett and I interact with one another?"

"It's important my personal companion gets along with my business associates."

Since when? "That's never mattered before."

"An oversight on my part."

So Mrs. Singletary *was* playing matchmaker. What a disastrous turn of events! Molly must dissuade her employer from this course of action, but how? If she protested too much she would only encourage the woman. "It's useless," she muttered.

"Now, my dear, one never knows. A few false starts are no indication that we won't find our one true love eventually." She patted her hand. "The Lord has brought you into my care. I shall see you happily settled no matter how long it takes."

Molly chose not to argue. Mrs. Singletary would discover soon enough that Garrett was not the man for her. Their time had come and gone, never to be regained. Tragic, really.

She suddenly felt exhausted, and oh so lonely. Even though others had claimed to love her since Garrett, none had been any more sincere than he. Molly had given two of them a chance, going so far as agreeing to marry them.

Her greatest shame—the dark, awful secret she shared only with the Lord—was that she hadn't been the one to call off her engagements. Her fiancés had walked away from her, just as Garrett had. Nearly eight months since her last broken engagement and she couldn't help but wonder if she was destined to be alone. When all she wanted was a family of her own.

This melancholy wasn't like her. She'd always been a child of joy, of hope, her favorite Bible verse also her life motto. *He fill thy mouth with laughing, thy lips with rejoicing.*

Where was her joy now? Her laughter?

She fought off a wave of panic, and readjusted the packages in her hands. She could not give up hope, because without hope all was lost.

Secluded in his office, Garrett felt his mood take on a hard edge. He couldn't get Molly Taylor Scott out of his head.

The document beneath his hand blurred, the words a haze of black swimming atop white. He drummed his fingers on the parchment in a rapid two-finger rhythm. The sight of Molly this afternoon had been like a swift, cold wind through Garret's soul, alerting all his senses, making him agonizingly aware that they'd once been very much in love.

The bold color of her crimson gown had been a stunning complement to her raven hair, soft, creamy skin and blue, blue eyes. For that brief moment when he'd gripped her shoulders, the years had melted away and Garrett had felt the strong pull of her all over again. He'd been transfixed.

The four men surrounding her had been equally transfixed.

Hostility surged through his veins at the memory.

Rearranging the Phipps contract on his desk, he proceeded to review the legal language. A detail man by nature, he searched for loopholes others had missed, areas that might present problems in the future. Even a misplaced comma could change the meaning of a sentence and cost his client a fortune.

He was deep into the work when a knock came at the door. Concentration blown, he looked up. "Enter."

His law clerk, Julian Summers, a thin young man with ordinary features and an eager smile, stuck his head in the room. "Mrs. Beatrix Singletary has requested a moment of your time."

"She wishes to see me?" *Not Reese?* "Are you certain?"

"She requested you. And she's not alone—her companion is with her." Adam's apple bobbing, Summers sighed. "She's really quite beautiful. Miss Scott, I mean. Charming, too."

The man sounded awestruck. He *looked* awestruck, with his fidgeting hands and dazed expression. Right. Another poor, unsuspecting sap had succumbed to Molly's undeniable charm.

"Send in Mrs. Singletary. And—" Garrett's jaw tightened "—her companion."

"Very good." Summers hurried out, leaving the door ajar.

By the time Garrett crossed the room, he found the women already standing at the threshold. While Molly transferred an assortment of packages into his law clerk's care, Garrett schooled his features into a blank expression. His well-honed composure evaporated the moment Molly turned and looked at him.

His heart slammed against his ribs, his breath hitched in his lungs. *Now who's the sap?*

He cleared his throat. "Ladies, please, come in."

Eyebrows raised, Mrs. Singletary brushed past him and began a slow perusal of his office. Molly followed a step behind. Her floral scent hit him like a rough blow to the heart.

When he finally ventured to look into her face again, and she didn't quite meet his gaze, he felt a sense of validation. Though she hid her reaction behind a benign smile,

Molly was nervous in his company. At least he wasn't alone in his struggle to remain indifferent.

Affecting a bland expression of his own, he edged around her and concentrated on the task of directing Mrs. Singletary to a chair facing his desk.

While he waited for her to settle, he watched Molly wander to the lone window in his office and look out. Her shoulders were unnaturally stiff. Garrett suspected he was the cause of her tension and that wrecked him. He wanted to go to her, to tease a laugh out of her like he had when they were children.

He no longer had that right.

Adopting a relaxed demeanor for this odd meeting, he sat on the edge of his desk in front of Mrs. Singletary. "To what do I owe this unexpected honor?"

The widow set her reticule carefully on her lap and got straight to the point. "I have a mind to expand my business holdings into new areas and I want you to assist me."

He blinked at the unprecedented request. He'd met the widow only a few times, the most recent when she'd been about to invest in a lumber operation and Reese had asked Garrett to review the final contract with her.

"I see I have shocked you." She looked rather pleased at the prospect, proving her reputation as an unconventional woman with a penchant toward the outrageous.

"Why not make this request of your own attorney?"

"Reese will continue overseeing my legal matters, but I have decided that you, Mr. Mitchell, will assist me with the expansion of my fortune."

By the satisfied expression on her face, she knew she'd piqued his interest. This was just the sort of opportunity perfectly suited to his skills. "Again, why me?"

"I should think that obvious. You were invaluable during my purchase of the lumberyard."

"I merely did my job."

"No, Mr. Mitchell, you went far beyond the minimum. You have a remarkable mind for business, much like my Reginald." At the mention of her late husband, she gave a wistful sigh. "I find myself growing bored of late. I want to take more risks."

She had his attention. Although Garrett usually steered his clients into conservative investments when they solicited his advice, he'd taken considerable chances with his own finances, to very lucrative ends.

But to guide the firm's wealthiest client down a similar path was another matter entirely. "Have you discussed this with Mr. Bennett directly?"

"I have." She smoothed a steady, elegant hand over her skirt. "Once I explained the particulars of my plan, he thought my seeking your assistance a splendid idea."

Reese had said nothing to Garrett, not yet anyway. If he agreed to this, how much contact would he have with Molly? He glanced at her now and found her staring at him.

A muscle knotted in his chest.

Shifting his position, he addressed Mrs. Singletary and her very tempting offer. "What you are suggesting comes with certain dangers. You could lose a large amount of money."

"I could also make a great deal more."

A valid point. But why would a woman as wealthy as Beatrix Singletary need more money? When was enough, enough?

She answered his unspoken query with a relaxed smile. "With the additional resources I will be able to expand my charitable giving. A few of my pet projects are in great need."

Now she really had his attention. Garrett believed in doing good and being generous. *To whom much is given, much is expected.*

"Do we have a deal, Mr. Mitchell?"

He cleared his throat. "I need to discuss this with Mr. Bennett first."

"If you feel you must."

"I must." On this point, he would not relent. "Assuming all is in order, when would you like to begin?"

"Immediately." Her eyes sparkled with a shrewd light. "I will expect you to be available to me on a regular basis."

"I have other clients who require my time and attention…"

She brushed this aside with a flick of her wrist. "I'm confident you will find a way to satisfy their needs and mine."

He opened his mouth to respond, but she cut him off. "I intend for our partnership to be a success, Mr. Mitchell. As such, we must first get to know one another better. Agreed?"

He nodded. What she was suggesting would require a high level of trust between them, and that could only come with time.

"You know my companion." She indicated Molly with a hitch of her chin.

He glanced at Molly out of the corner of his eye. She'd retired to a seat by the window. She appeared serene, calm. Garrett knew better. He could feel the storm of emotion brewing beneath the surface. "Miss Scott and I are acquainted, yes."

Molly stiffened at his dry tone, but said nothing.

"Well, then." Mrs. Singletary rose and Garrett did the same. She moved through the room, idly touching random books on the shelving to her left, the stack of ledgers on her right. "Since you and Molly are…acquainted, I trust you have no objection to attending the opera with us this evening."

Molly made a soft sound of protest in her throat, barely audible but Garrett had caught it. And so, it appeared, had her employer. "You have a concern, my dear?"

"No, Mrs. Singletary. In fact…" She blessed Garrett with a sweet, sweet smile, all politeness and easygoing manner. "I look forward to Mr. Mitchell's company this evening."

They both knew that wasn't true. But he adopted her same casual attitude and said, "If Mr. Bennett has no objections, it will be my pleasure to attend the opera with you both."

Molly's smile faltered. Garrett's expanded.

"Then it's settled," the widow drawled, staring at him with that same shrewd expression as before. "I expect you to arrive at my home seven o'clock this evening."

Finished issuing her command, she headed toward the door, but not before Garrett caught sight of her satisfied expression.

His eyes narrowed. Mrs. Singletary clearly had some secret scheme she was keeping to herself. Patient, wily in his own right, Garrett would discover what she was up to, eventually.

For now, he joined her in the middle of the room. "Is there anything else I can do for you this afternoon?"

"That will be all." Head high, she swept into the hallway.

Garrett followed at a more sedate pace. Working with the widow might be just the break he needed to prove he was more than that "other Mitchell boy" or Fanny's older brother. Ever since his sister's engagement to his boss, Garrett had worked twice as hard to prove he'd been hired for his legal mind alone.

Apparently, he'd done just that, as evidenced by Mrs. Singletary's stunning offer.

Back in their younger days, Molly had understood Garrett's desire to make his own way in the world. She'd actually been the one to encourage him to pursue a career in the law. He remembered that now, and found himself softening toward her as he strolled back into his office.

When he drew alongside her and she climbed gracefully

to her feet, he took her hand without hesitation. "Until tonight," he murmured.

"Until tonight," she repeated, then tugged on her hand.

Garrett held on tight. He wasn't ready to let her go.

He'd never been truly ready to let her go.

Chapter Two

Molly had nearly reached the end of her endurance, and it was all because Garrett still grasped her hand in his. On the surface, the gesture was a common courtesy between two acquaintances. With the benefit of her glove as a barrier there should be nothing to cause her alarm. But this was the first time in seven years he'd taken her hand without hesitation.

She liked the unexpected familiarity of the gesture, liked it far too much.

Blinking hard, she struggled to maintain her composure. But his touch felt so good, so right. Time seemed to slow, past overlaying present. And, still, Garrett held on to her.

He moved a step closer and her mind grasped one lone thought. This was Garrett, the boy who used to put her at ease when no one else could. The one who had comforted her, treasured her. Loved her.

She'd once believed that God had brought them together at the perfect time, and that the Lord's hand had been guiding them toward a common future all along.

She'd been terribly wrong. Their chance to be a couple had come and gone a long time ago.

So why wouldn't Garrett release her?

And why wasn't she insisting he let her go?

Surely Mrs. Singletary would say something to him, to Molly, anything to put a halt to this endless, endless moment. But Mrs. Singletary had already moved into the hallway and was speaking to someone in hushed tones.

Molly searched for words to fill the void, but nothing came to mind. They hadn't spoken directly to one another in years, at least not in more than monosyllabic responses. All she could do now was force herself to breathe. Even that simple task proved nearly impossible.

At last, he let go of her hand and stepped back. His golden eyes swept over her, his features unreadable. Nevertheless, she found herself staring at him longer than necessary. The embroidered waistcoat he wore highlighted the unusual color of his eyes. Mitchell eyes. A warm blend of bronze, amber and gold.

Molly gritted her teeth. "Garrett…I…that is…"

His glance flicked to a spot over her shoulder. "Hello, Fanny."

His sister was here? Relief nearly buckled her knees.

"Hello, Garrett." A soft feminine voice returned his greeting, followed by a short pause. "Molly? Is that you?"

Desperate to put more distance between herself and Garrett, Molly spun around to face her friend. But she moved too fast and her legs tangled beneath her. She swayed backward.

Garrett's hands clasped her shoulders from behind. "Easy now," he whispered in her ear. "I've got you."

His low voice steadied her. She closed her eyes a moment, only a moment, and reveled in the safe feeling that washed through her. *I've got you.*

Did he know how bittersweet those words sounded?

"Molly? Are you unwell?" Fanny asked. "You've gone quite pale."

The concern in her friend's voice had her quickly opening her eyes. "I'm perfectly fine."

She stepped forward, away from Garrett, away from the burst of memories and wave of hope, and countless other emotions she couldn't seem to control whenever she was in his presence. "I merely lost my balance for a moment."

Fanny tilted her head at a curious angle. "Well, then, it was fortunate Garrett was here to catch you."

Was it? Molly made a noncommittal sound in her throat, wondering why he was suddenly right where she needed him when he'd been so determined to avoid her before today.

As if to confuse her all the more, Garrett gave an equally dispassionate response to his sister's comment.

Eyes widening, as if she suddenly realized the oddity of the two of them in each other's company, Fanny looked from one to the other and back again. Her gaze filled with unasked questions.

Molly gave a quick shake of her head, willing her friend to keep her thoughts—and questions—to herself. At least until they were alone. Of all Garrett's family, Fanny was the only one who knew how heartbroken Molly had been over his decision to leave her behind when he'd gone away to school.

"Did you need something from me?" Garrett asked his sister with the sort of gentle impatience only a devoted brother could pull off without offense.

"No. I'm here to see Reese—" she swallowed, broke eye contact, sighed heavily "—but Mrs. Singletary asked for a brief word with him."

She scowled at her brother, as if sensing he was the cause for the interruption.

He merely smiled at her, which seemed to annoy Fanny all the more. "Don't you have contracts to review, ledgers to balance, or some such work that requires your immediate attention?"

That earned her a dry chuckle. "I do."

"Then I suggest you get back to it," Fanny snapped, her tone unusually curt.

Garrett dipped his head at a curious angle, his only reaction, but a telling one from a man who never showed his inner thoughts to the world. It was obvious to Molly he was concerned about his sister. She was concerned about Fanny, too. Her friend seemed troubled about something.

As if sensing Molly was the best one to address the situation, Garrett gave a stiff nod of his head. "Ladies."

Looking perplexed, and a little apprehensive, he moved reluctantly back toward his office, as if he wasn't fully convinced leaving his sister in this state was a good idea. When he caught Molly's eye, she gave him a short nod, a silent promise to take care of Fanny. He smiled then.

And she smiled, too.

For a moment, the hostility between them faded away to nothing more than a memory.

"I'll see you later tonight," he said.

"Yes, you will."

Snatching a quick breath, he shut the door between them with a resounding click.

Molly dragged in her own swift pull of air.

Glancing at her friend to determine if she'd noticed the revealing interchange, Molly caught a look of utter distress upon Fanny's face. Something was wrong.

"Fanny?" She touched her arm. "What is it?"

"Not here." Glancing to her right, then her left, she pulled Molly down the hallway, tugging her along until they were tucked away in a small alcove off the reception area.

Molly took stock of her friend. She'd never seen Fanny so agitated, or so unhappy. Fanny was *never* unhappy. There was always a ready smile on her beautiful face, her inner light even brighter since her engagement to Reese. Fanny's amber eyes and golden hair coupled with Reese's classic, dark good looks made them a stunning pair. They turned heads wherever they went.

Molly was pleased her friend had found a good man to marry, truly she was. Except…

Right now, Fanny looked anything but the happy bride-to-be. In truth, she looked tense, confused. Worried. "Fanny? What's happened to upset you so?"

Fanny twisted her hands together at her waist, drew her bottom lip between her teeth, then sighed. "Molly, if I ask you a question you must promise to answer me truthfully."

"All right."

"How did you know when it was time to call off your weddings?"

The question dragged painful memories to the surface. She wanted to run, to forget she'd ever been engaged, but she owed her friend the truth. "I didn't actually call—"

"Was there a moment when you looked at either of your fiancés and thought he's not the one I'm supposed to spend the rest of my life with?"

Such a revealing question. "Oh, Fanny, are you having second thoughts about marrying Reese?"

"I…" Smoothing a shaky hand across her mouth, Fanny shut her eyes and groaned. "I don't know what I'm feeling. I'm confused and…and…scared."

"That's understandable. Marriage is a big step." Molly took her friend's hands and gently squeezed. "It's normal to have concerns."

"Reese is a good man, the very best." Fanny drew in a shuddering breath. "He gets along with my family, and I with his. But…"

"But…" Molly urged, letting go of Fanny's hands.

"It's nothing." She crossed her arms at her waist. "I'm simply feeling weighed down over the wedding. The planning is getting out of hand, and I don't want to let anyone down."

What an odd choice of words.

"You could never let anyone down." It wasn't in her friend's personality. "Everyone adores you, Fanny. Reese most of all."

And why wouldn't he? The woman was sweetly beautiful, well-educated, kind at the core. She never bent the rules, never made a mistake, never took a wrong step. Best of all, she'd met her counterpart in Reese.

"Your fiancé is fortunate to have you," Molly said, believing it with all her heart. "You're perfect for one another."

"Yes." Fanny nodded, then quickly looked away just as her eyes began to water. "So everyone keeps telling me."

Yet another odd choice of words.

"Fanny, whenever I have a tough decision to make, and need to organize my thoughts," she began, desperate to help her friend, "I apply a simple formula to determine if I'm making the right choice."

"You always were gifted at mathematics." Sniffing softly, a shadow of a smile on her lips, Fanny swiped at her eyes. "All right, Molly, I'm listening. What's your latest formula?"

"Well, there are only four variables to this particular equation." There were always only four. "First, start with prayer. Next, spend quiet time in the Bible. Number three, trust the Lord's guidance. And, finally, most important of all, follow your heart."

It was sound advice, Molly realized, a simple yet profound formula she needed to apply to her own life, especially now that it seemed her path would cross Garrett's on a regular, nay daily, basis.

Step one. Start with prayer.

That's exactly what she planned to do.

After carefully, firmly, resolutely shutting his office door in Molly's face, Garrett had only one desire. Forget he ever touched her.

Battling unwanted emotion, he sank in the chair behind his desk and shut his eyes against the memory of Molly in his arms. The images came anyway. Both times she'd lost her balance, he'd instinctively reached for her, steadied her. The move had been as natural as taking his next breath. And for those brief moments, they'd been closer than they'd been in years, mere inches apart.

A mistake.

Memories long forgotten reared up, twining through the present, calling to mind all they'd once shared. Even now, the lingering scent of jasmine and sandalwood teased his senses, making him yearn to sweep Molly back into his arms, to start anew, to—

He cleared his throat.

Work. Garrett needed to concentrate on work, and not on Miss Molly Taylor Scott and what could never be again.

Rolling his shoulders, he repositioned the Phipps contract in front of him and picked up where he'd left off, halfway down the third page. Unfortunately, focus eluded him. And this time, it wasn't only Molly that plagued his thoughts. Garrett couldn't ignore the anxiety he'd caught on his sister's face.

Fanny was not a woman prone to worry. She was a happy sort, always quick to smile, quick to laugh, ready to organize the next party. Something had clearly upset her. Garrett had to trust she would share whatever was bothering her with Molly. And that Molly would come to him if anything was truly wrong.

Nothing's wrong.

Fanny was a grown woman of twenty-two, her future all but set. In six weeks' time she would pledge her life to a good, decent man who cherished her beyond reason. Reese was everything Garrett could wish for his sister.

Nothing's wrong, he told himself again and put Fanny out

of his mind. Along with her beautiful, confounding friend. And all the other distractions battling for his attention.

He studied the words on the page, one sentence at a time, went on to the next and then the next. He pulled his focus in tight, filtered out everything around him. Garrett liked working alone, liked having only himself to count on—and to blame. Best that way. Less messy. Less complicated.

Focus, he ordered his wandering mind.

And he did just that, absorbing the legal language on the page as if it were as fundamental as air. It was exacting, meticulous work, and he let it consume him. This was why he'd come back to Denver—to work for this firm, overseeing business contracts, drawing up others.

Or so he told himself.

But that wasn't completely true. He'd turned down a better position in St. Louis, one more suited to his skills, so he could be near family. He'd missed them. He'd missed…

No one else. Just his family.

Focus.

Once he was satisfied all was in order, he gathered the pages, stuffed the entire document inside a leather satchel and set it aside for his meeting tomorrow with Phineas Phipps.

He stood and rounded his desk, set on addressing the next pressing issue on his agenda—Mrs. Singletary and her unprecedented request.

Before he made it across the room, two hard raps came at the door, no more, no less. Reese's signature knock.

"Excellent timing." Garrett opened the door with a swift pull. "I was on my way to your office to discuss Mrs. Singletary's business proposition."

For a long moment the other man said nothing. He didn't move, didn't blink. The unnatural stillness in his stance was completely out of character, as was the cold silence.

Was he disturbed over Mrs. Singletary's proposal? If he

was, it would be out of character. Reese never begrudged another attorney's chance to further his career. *What's good for one of us in this firm,* he said often, *is good for all of us.* That philosophy was one of the reasons Garrett had joined the firm six months ago.

No, Reese shouldn't have a problem with Garrett assisting the widow in the expansion of her business holdings. Something else had to be wrong. "Reese—"

"Come with me."

Garrett nodded, even as his boss turned and headed down the hallway in swift, ground-eating strides.

Once they entered his office, Reese glanced over his shoulders. "Shut the door behind you."

Garrett did as requested.

In silence, the other man moved behind his desk and sat. His brow creased in utter confusion, he clasped the back of his neck, circled his head and sighed heavily.

"Problem?" Garrett asked.

Reese's jaw tightened. "You could say that."

"Something to do with the firm?"

"No. I…" He trailed off, glanced out the window then back to Garrett. "I just spoke with Fanny." He didn't expand. He simply leaned back in his chair, eyes locked on a spot just over Garrett's shoulder.

Sensing he wasn't going to like what came next, he remained tactfully silent. But when Reese continued blinking at nothing in particular, Garrett pressed for more. "What did my sister have to say?"

Reese closed his eyes for a second and then opened them, his gaze sharply focused on Garrett now. Anger. Pain. Bafflement. All three glared out at him.

Garrett braced himself.

"Fanny broke off our engagement."

"She…no." Garrett exhaled roughly, completely astounded by the news. "That can't be right." He must have misunderstood, must have heard wrong.

"I assure you, it's true."

"But…" Garrett struggled for words. "She's happy, really happy. She told me so." Just the other day. She'd jumped into his arms and said, *Oh, Garrett, I'm the most blessed woman in the world.*

What had changed since then?

Something. Something she hadn't shared with him. "What did Fanny say, exactly?"

Reese scrubbed the back of his hand across his mouth. "It wasn't what she said so much as how she said it. She was upset, on the verge of tears. I'd never seen her like that, so…" He shuddered. "Emotional. She's always been a steady sort, solid, even-tempered. I can't fathom what's put her off like this."

None of what Reese said sounded like his sister. Not the Fanny that Garrett knew, at any rate.

"I asked her what was wrong," Reese continued, "told her we'd work it out, together. 'That's what couples do,' I said. It was as if she didn't hear me. Or maybe she didn't want to hear me." He shook his head. "She just kept babbling, on and on and on, her words tumbling over one another. I could barely keep up."

This time, Garrett spoke his thoughts aloud. "That doesn't sound like Fanny."

His mind kept returning to that particular point.

"No, it's not," Reese agreed. "She said we didn't add up, those were the exact words she used." He shook his head again. "We don't add up, as if our relationship was nothing more than a mathematics equation that needed solving."

Garrett's blood turned cold. Ice-cold, but he remained silent, letting Reese talk.

"We don't add up?" Reese pressed his lips into a grim line. "What sort of convoluted math was Fanny using?"

Garrett knew. God help them all, he knew.

How many times had he sat, mesmerized, as he listened to Molly applying one of her "formulas" to a personal problem? He used to find her process of applying mathematical equations to life's troubles charming.

He wasn't charmed now.

Garrett only had himself to blame for this disaster. He should have followed his instincts and spoken with his sister himself, rather than trust Molly to handle the problem.

"You and Fanny will work this out," he said, determined to see it come to pass. "This is probably just a case of cold feet on her part."

"I'm not so sure." Angry shock leaped into Reese's gaze. "She said she had to follow her heart." Shadows swirled around his eyes, dark and dangerous. "Follow her heart," he repeated, spitting out the words one by one. "What's that supposed to mean anyway?"

"I have no idea," Garrett admitted, feeling uneasy and puzzled over the phrase. Something tickled at the back of his mind, a distant memory, but he couldn't capture the thought fully so he focused on what he could address. He would find out what was going on in his sister's mind, from the source herself, sooner rather than later. In the meantime…

"Reese, don't give up on Fanny. I'm sure she'll be back, maybe even later today, retracting everything she said."

"I don't know, Garrett." Reese inhaled a ragged breath. "She sounded quite convinced she was making the right decision."

Perhaps. Perhaps not.

Garrett would know more once he spoke with Fanny.

Naturally, he'd make certain she was all right first, and would determine she wasn't hiding something about Reese that none of them suspected. If all was in order, and this turned out to be just a whim on Fanny's part, well, then, Garrett would take it upon himself to talk some sense into her.

For now, he kept his face blank, even as he struggled with the suspicion that Molly's interference may have played a role in this debacle. It was very likely that somehow, with her own brand of twisted logic, she'd influenced Fanny to break off her engagement—as she'd done twice herself.

If he was right, if he found out Molly had said or done something to cause Fanny to beg off, Garrett wouldn't let her off easily. She wasn't going to smile and simper and charm her way out of this one.

No. This time, Molly would answer to him.

Chapter Three

Molly found her parasol precisely where she'd left it earlier in the day, leaning against the building outside Mrs. Singletary's favorite millinery shop. Breathing a sigh of relief, she picked it up and backed away.

"Oh." She found her progress halted by a wall of solid muscle. *"Oh."*

She jerked forward, stumbled awkwardly, dropped the parasol.

A familiar pair of hands secured her balance with a firm but gentle hold.

Molly froze, stunned by the realization that she knew who had a hold of her. Garrett.

Garrett. Even if he hadn't prevented her previous fall earlier in the day, she recognized the clean, woodsy spice of his shaving soap.

Before she could thank him, he turned her slowly to face him.

Their gazes locked.

Her mouth went dry as dust. He was so unbelievably dashing, standing with that relaxed looseness he'd earned from years of riding the range on his family's ranch.

They continued to stare at one another.

The bristling intensity of the moment seemed too deep

to fathom. Garrett had a look on his face she hardly recognized. He was absolutely…furious. Furious, with her.

But why? What had she done?

Nothing, that's what, which meant he was upset about something else, something that couldn't possibly have to do with her. And yet, he was glaring at her as though she'd done him precise harm.

She lifted her chin, refusing to cower. Or be the one to break the silence first.

"What? No suitors clamoring for your attention this afternoon, no hordes of men enthralled by your startling wit?" He looked her over with an insolent, thorough glance. "You're losing your touch, Molly."

The aggravation in his voice slid a chill across the base of her spine. What had brought on this dark mood of his? Since when did Garrett care if she had admirers? So shocked by his behavior, it required several attempts before she could respond calmly. "I don't know what you mean."

"Don't you?" His lips twisted. "We both know you take great delight in leading men around by the nose, then casting them aside when you're through with them."

"I most certainly do not." Now he was just being mean. And that wasn't like Garrett, past or present.

Why this antagonism? It seemed so…so…personal. There hadn't been anything personal between them in years.

As the daughter of a seasoned lawman, Molly knew when to stand and fight, and when to beat a tactical retreat. The latter was in order, but Garrett still held her.

"Let me go," she whispered, keeping her voice free of emotion. "Please."

His hands abruptly released her. Palms facing forward, Garrett stepped back, though he kept his gaze locked with hers, watching her closely. "Where's Mrs. Singletary?"

"Having tea with a friend."

"Ah." The answer seemed to satisfy him, but the anger was still there, simmering just beneath the surface.

She found her own anger rising to meet his. "I fear I am one full step behind. Tell me." She kept her voice even, her tone as cool as his. "What have I done to offend you?"

Pulling in a deep breath, he looked away. She saw the conflict in him, the rough tug of emotion he struggled to keep under control. He shifted his stance. Shadows from the awning overhead curtained his face, hiding his eyes from her now.

"Fanny has broken off her engagement with Reese."

"She—" Molly's hand flew to her throat "—*what?*"

"You heard me."

No. No, no, no. That couldn't be true. It just couldn't. Thinking back to their last conversation, she sought to recall every word that had passed between them.

What had she said to her friend? Surely, Fanny hadn't misunderstood her advice. "I need to speak with her."

She set out down the sidewalk.

Garrett stopped her with a light grip on her arm. "She won't see you." He released his hold when she glanced pointedly at his hand. "Even Callie can't get her to come out of her room and talk this over rationally."

This was awful, absolutely terrible and so unlike her friend.

"Oh, Fanny," Molly whispered softly. "What have you done?"

"What do you think she's done? She's followed your lead."

Garrett blamed her for this? "I would never wish the pain of a broken engagement on anyone, not ever."

"Is that so?" He didn't seem convinced. "Then why did Fanny tell Reese that their union didn't…*add up?*"

His words wrapped around her, replacing her previous

sense of outrage with bone-deep guilt. "She…she actually said that, that she thought they didn't…add up?"

"Let me guess." Garrett towered over her, glaring down from his superior height. "You gave her one of your formulas to apply to her situation."

Molly stiffened, but didn't deny the accusation. She kept her head high, while her mind raced back to the alcove in the law firm.

You're perfect for one another, she'd said to her friend. Fanny had agreed quickly, perhaps a bit too quickly. And then she'd said something altogether off-putting. *So everyone keeps telling me.*

Such a revealing response, and yet Molly hadn't made the connection, not completely.

"What was the equation you gave her?" Garrett asked, his voice disturbingly patient. "I need to know exactly what you said if I'm going to fix this for her."

Molly lifted her chin even higher. "I gave her a simple equation, with only four variables."

"Four variables," he repeated, his gaze softening for a split second as he inched closer. "Only four, like always?"

"Yes, like always."

Her stomach did a slow, spiraling somersault. She remembered the times they used to walk the rugged land, hand in hand, discussing their plans for the future. It hurt to realize how close they'd once been and yet how far apart they were now. Their chance at happiness had come and gone, in its place only long intervals of loneliness.

"What were the variables?" Not waiting for her answer, he stepped back, looking pensive. She'd seen him like this too many times not to recognize that he was in planning mode.

At least his anger had dissipated a bit.

Sighing, Molly wrapped her arms tightly around her waist. "I told her to start with prayer."

"A wise beginning," he admitted, a bit reluctantly if his grudging tone was anything to go by.

"Then I said she should spend time in the Bible."

"Sound advice." He released a jagged breath. "And the third variable?"

"Trust in the Lord's guidance, of course."

"Of course." He almost smiled at her then, not quite but almost. It gave her the courage to continue.

"And, lastly," she squared her shoulders, "I told her…"

She broke off, pressed her lips tightly together and looked away, because now she knew why Fanny had broken off her engagement with Reese.

Clearly, her friend had been far more upset than she'd let on, and Molly hadn't seen it. She hadn't recognized that Fanny was deeply confused. In pain. Alone with her terrible doubts and concerns.

If only she had recognized the truth.

Would it have made a difference? No, she would have given her friend the same advice.

"Molly." Garrett's voice dropped to a whisper. "What was the fourth variable you gave my sister?"

She fought back a wave of sorrow, and maybe a little envy, knowing that Fanny had adopted the one part of the equation Molly had failed to apply to her own life.

Twice, she'd convinced herself the final variable wasn't important. Twice, she'd lied to herself. Twice, she'd suffered the utter humiliation of abandonment by a man who had proposed and claimed to love her above all others.

"I told her to—"

"The exact words, Molly. Your exact words."

"I said." She stared into Garrett's handsome, severe face with nothing but regret washing over her. "Follow your heart."

Follow your heart.

Only as Molly pronounced those three perplexing words

did Garrett realize why he'd been so uncomfortable hearing them in Reese's office. She'd given him the exact same advice seven years ago, when he'd struggled over whether to become a full-time rancher like his brothers, or pursue a career in law.

Both avenues had appealed, for very different reasons. One had meant the comfort and safety of the known, of family. The other had called for a leap of faith, but had promised freedom from forever being labeled as that "other" Mitchell boy.

Although he was satisfied with his choice—now—Garrett had been torn back then. Molly had methodically broken down each choice with him, calling on Scripture to reinforce various points. In the end, she'd left the decision up to him, with one final word of advice. *You must follow your heart, Garrett.*

Follow his heart? What did that mean anyway? He still wasn't sure.

If Molly had given him any indication she wanted him to stay home, he would have become a rancher in a heartbeat. No regrets. But she hadn't asked. She'd let him walk away from her, and all the plans they'd made in secret.

You didn't ask her to come with you, either. You didn't ask her to wait for you.

No. She was supposed to fight for him, for them. But she hadn't. So he'd left. Angry, hurt, miserable.

Pride. He'd had more than his share back then, probably still did. A trait he had in common with the lovely woman staring up at him.

Long day, he thought, rubbing a hand over his face. Long, never-ending day full of too much emotion and too many memories.

"Thank you, Molly. I appreciate your honesty."

She opened her mouth to respond.

But Garrett wasn't finished. "You have lent me considerable perspective on the situation."

She sucked in a ragged breath, pushed it out inside a humorless laugh. "Have I, now?"

Her sarcasm made him wince. Stuffing his hands in his pockets, he selected his next words carefully. "You can't deny that your formula influenced Fanny's decision."

"You still blame me for her actions?" Her eyes narrowed to tiny slits. "After I just explained what I said to her?"

"I'm not blaming you…" He paused. "Not directly, at any rate. I'm merely pointing out your role in this unfortunate event."

"My role in this unfortunate event." She repeated his words very calmly, very deliberately through *very* tight lips.

Where was his finesse, Garrett wondered, his superior use of the English language? Exhaling slowly, he tried another tactic. "I've always believed, Molly, that one of your greatest gifts is your power of persuasion."

Her eyes filled with skepticism.

"It's true. Most people—" *men especially* "—can't help but be swayed by your…" He searched for the right word. "Influence."

Garrett certainly had never been able to resist her charms. He'd thought of her often over the past seven years. Even now, softened by their common purpose, he couldn't take his eyes off the girl he'd once loved more than his youthful heart could bear.

"My…*influence?* You make me sound as crafty as Samson's Delilah, or Potiphar's wife at her most calculating. Or maybe—" she advanced on him, her jaw tight, her eyes flashing "—you think me as devious as Jezebel."

Sarcasm. Hurt. So much of both were there in her narrowed gaze, in the stiff angle of her shoulders.

"It's not a bad thing, you know, swaying people to your way of thinking." For the most part, that's how Garrett made his living. "Every person who meets you is better for the experience."

"Even you, Garrett?"

"Especially me." He prayed she heard the sincerity in his tone, the truth in his words. He never regretted loving Molly. He only regretted losing her, regretted not doing enough to win her heart once and for all.

"Look, what I'm trying to say is…" What? What was he trying to say? "I'm sorry for implying your words persuaded Fanny's behavior in this matter. My sister can be stubborn when she gets something in her head."

"That's certainly true." A beat passed. And then another. "Apology accepted."

She lifted a careless shoulder as if the matter of his distrust was of little consequence, but the sadness in her eyes gave her away.

"Molly—"

"Stop talking, and let me think how to help Fanny."

Yes, perhaps it was best to hold his tongue. For now.

He watched—in silence—as she wound a lock of shimmering black hair around her finger. Round and round and round. Until this moment, Garrett hadn't allowed himself the luxury of looking at her, to *really* look at her without interruption and without thinking too hard about the consequences. She was still so beautiful, her features as delicate as a porcelain doll, as precious as fine china. There ought to be a law against that sort of beauty walking freely about town.

He cleared his throat.

The gesture seemed to spur her to action. Without another word, she set out in the direction of the boardinghouse where Fanny rented a room with their other sister, Callie.

Garrett followed, determined to prevent Molly from doing—or saying—something rash in the heat of the moment. Catching her in two long strides, he moved directly in her path.

She gave him a pointed look. "You are in my way."

"I know." He widened his stance.

"Ah." Hands fisted at her sides, she jerked her chin at him. "I see you are in one of your stubborn moods."

"Not even remotely." In fact, he was trying very hard to remain calm, to think of Fanny, only Fanny. A nearly impossible feat with Molly standing so close, looking up at him with those big, striking, blue, blue eyes. Eyes that turned his brain to mush, still, after all these years.

"Let's both try to be reasonable here." He softened the suggestion with a smile.

"Reasonable?" She sniffed. "I'm not sure that's possible." But instead of continuing on her way, or expanding on her words, she leaned toward him, ever so slightly, eyes blinking rapidly up at him. She had more to say, he saw it in her troubled gaze, and knew he wasn't going to like it.

Still, he waited, fascinated by the display of emotion on her face, the exotic curve of her lips, the slight tilt of her head. It was his turn to lean forward.

Step back, he told himself. *You didn't come home for this. You didn't turn down the job in St. Louis for her.*

He remained frozen on the spot, the sights and sounds of the busy street all but ignored, because this was Molly. *Molly.*

His first love. His only love.

The beautiful girl who had never truly been his.

For a split second he was slung back in time, when things were simpler between them and they could read each other's thoughts. He moved a bit closer. Closer, closer...

He froze.

What was he doing? What was he *thinking?* He was descending on Molly, as if he was going to kiss her, out in the open, on a busy street, where anyone could see them if they were paying attention. Someone was always paying attention.

As if coming to a similar conclusion, Molly frowned, shifted to her left and resumed walking.

Garrett followed again, this time a few steps behind.

A block later, they arrived at Mrs. Agatha's Boardinghouse for Women. An unassuming structure, the house was as plain as its proprietress. The three-story home, painted a dull gray, reminded Garrett of a woman's dormitory on a college campus.

Like any housemother, Mrs. Agatha had strict rules of conduct for her residents. That, among other reasons, was why the family had been happy enough to see Fanny and Callie settle here while they worked at the Hotel Dupree, Fanny as a concierge and Callie in the kitchens.

Had it been wise to allow the girls to move off the ranch? Not that anyone could have stopped them. Well-educated, far too worldly after returning home from school out East, both had claimed they didn't fit on the ranch anymore.

Molly, on the other hand, fit perfectly on the ranch. She fit just as well here in Denver. In truth, she fit everywhere, anywhere. He'd forgotten that about her, forgotten her ability to blend in wherever she went, and befriend whomever she met. Her inner light drew others to her. Garrett was no exception.

Heart lodged in his throat, he watched her stare up at the boardinghouse's entrance. "We should formulate a plan," he said, mainly to break the silence between them.

Although she'd given no indication she was aware of his presence, she didn't seem surprised he'd spoken. "Oh, Garrett, I thought I was encouraging her when I gave her my four-step formula. Now, I'm not so sure. Then again—" a sigh leaked out of her "—if Fanny doesn't love Reese enough to want to marry him, then maybe, *maybe* she's making the right decision."

Was she speaking from experience? Had Molly broken her own engagements because she hadn't loved her fiancés enough to spend the rest of her life with them?

A pleasing thought, to be sure, one that sent an unexpected surge of relief spreading through him. Satisfaction, too.

Focus, Garrett. This isn't about you, or Molly, or the past. "The important point is that my sister has changed her mind about Reese and we need to find out why."

"Agreed."

A rare moment of solidarity passed between them and they shared a brief smile. Turning as one, they commandeered the steps leading into the boardinghouse together. They progressed side by side, their movements perfectly in sync with one another. For an instant, they were back at a place of deep understanding, where words weren't necessary between them.

The sensation brought on a spurt of hope, nearly breaking through Garrett's cynical heart. Problem was he relied heavily on his well-honed cynicism to keep him from making a mistake. A mistake, such as, say…drawing Molly's hand into his and forgetting all about their tumultuous history.

Don't do it, he warned himself. *Not a single glance in her direction.* He lasted an entire three seconds.

Then, he turned his head.

She stole his breath, just as she had when he was a boy. Feeling boldly nostalgic, he reached out.

And…

Closed his hand over hers.

Chapter Four

Molly sucked in a breath, torn between tightening her grip around Garrett's hand and yanking free of his touch. With him this close, holding on to her oh so casually, every sense was heightened to alarming proportions. Smells became stronger, colors brighter, sounds louder.

It was always this way with Garrett, she realized, despite the years of turmoil standing between them. Sadly, she couldn't remain detached, not with his fingers tenderly entwined with hers, and his masculine, woodsy scent wafting over her.

Her throat constricted.

Panic reared.

Despair threatened.

She really, really needed to distance herself from the tall, handsome man who thought the worst of her one moment, and then pointed out her strengths the next. The same man who'd so easily walked away from her seven years ago.

Your time to be together has come and gone, she reminded herself. *The Lord has a different plan for you both.*

Precisely. No use wishing for what might have been at this point.

Let him go, she told herself.

Instead of pulling free, she clutched her fingers around his a little tighter. A dreaded show of weakness, to be sure.

When Molly paused at the entrance, and spared a look at their joined hands, Garrett finally released her. Yet he didn't go far. As she entered the house and climbed up to the third floor where Fanny and Callie shared a room, Garrett kept close, only one step below. At least he didn't touch her, or try to hold her hand again.

Small blessing, that. But then he did something equally disturbing. He placed his palm at the small of his back, gently guiding her forward.

Unbearable longing sharpened in her throat, and something else, something equally awful, something that felt like wistfulness.

Your chance to be together has passed. Why couldn't she remember that important fact?

Frustrated with herself, with him—with them both—she treated him to a fierce scowl. He dropped his hand.

Molly resumed her ascent.

This time, Garrett joined her step for step. From beneath her lashes, she took in every angle of his once-beloved face. He'd changed. Gone was the lean, almost lanky physique, replaced by broad shoulders, long legs, corded muscles and sun-bronzed skin. The latter was proof he spent time outdoors, working on the family ranch when he made the trip home.

"Through with your inspection?" he asked in an amused tone.

She suppressed a sigh. "Must you be such a…a…man?"

"I'm not sure how to answer that."

"It was a rhetorical question."

"Naturally." A grin spread across his lips, teasing, almost flirtatious.

Telling herself the flutter in her stomach was due to physical exertion, she completed the rest of the climb. The moment her foot hit the third-floor landing, she whirled to face him again.

With him two stairs below, they stood nose to nose, neither moving, neither breathing. One shift on her part, one step on his and their lips would touch. Bad, bad idea.

She lowered her gaze.

He pressed his fingertip beneath her chin and applied gentle pressure until she looked him in the eye once more. "What's wrong?"

Did he really have to ask?

"Molly." He spoke her name on a whisper, his gaze full of remorse. "I'm sorry I accused you of encouraging Fanny to break her engagement."

"Are you?"

"Beyond words." He leaned over her, all six feet two inches of him, and rested his hand on her shoulder. "But I'm thankful we're together now."

Was he? "Why?"

"With the two of us working in tandem we'll uncover what's really behind Fanny's decision to break up with Reese."

He spoke with such confidence, as if they were a single unit, a team, stronger together than apart. She thought of a favorite Bible verse from Ecclesiastes, the one she'd once dreamed would be recited at their wedding. *Two are better than one; because they have a good reward for their labour.*

It was hard not to sigh, but Molly had a lot of practice controlling her emotions around Garrett. "I'm glad, too."

She spoke the simple truth.

He pulled his hand away from her shoulder. As before, they turned toward the door as a, well, a single unit. *Two are better than one.*

She gave in to that sigh, after all.

Rolling his shoulders, Garrett lifted his hand to knock. The door flew open before he made contact.

"At last, you've come." Callie, the older of the two sisters by a year, spoke directly to Molly. She hadn't noticed Garrett yet. Or perhaps she'd chosen to ignore him for now.

Either way, Molly did her best to smile at her friend.

In return, Callie gave her a shaky lift of her lips. The gesture didn't quite reach her eyes. Upon closer scrutiny, Molly noted her friend looked uncharacteristically ruffled. Her pretty, oval face was flushed. Her green eyes, usually so bright, were dimmed with worry, and her hair was in disarray, with several blond locks fluttering around her ears.

"Is Fanny still in her room?" Molly tried to hide her concern behind a bland tone.

Callie nodded her head in resignation.

"Well, then, let's see if we can coax her out of there."

"I'm not sure I'll be of much help." Something uncomfortable shifted in Callie's eyes. "She's not feeling especially charitable toward me at the moment."

"Not to worry, Cal. When Molly said *we*—" Garrett stepped forward, drawing his sister's attention "—she meant her and me."

"Oh. Right. Garrett…you're back." Callie's shoulders relaxed, then stiffened again. "Wait. Now wait just a minute. You and Molly are here…" Her gaze darted between them. *"Together?"*

Her reaction came as no surprise. Still, Molly shared a look with Garrett. He flattened his lips in a grim line. She did the same. They drew a collective breath.

"Oh, honestly, Callie." She choked out what she hoped was a mild, casual laugh. "Garrett and I have done nothing out of the ordinary by arriving here together."

"I beg to differ." Eyes wide, Callie divided a look between them. "It's completely out of the ordinary for you two to be together, under any circumstances."

Well, yes, that was true. But still…

Molly flicked a glance at Garrett. Quiet, calm, expression impassive, he appeared perfectly willing to let her carry the conversation.

So be it. "For Fanny's sake, Garrett and I have agreed to join forces—this once."

Molly emphasized the last two words, reminding herself she had a point to make. A very large point. It wouldn't do for Callie, or Garrett, or even Molly herself, to assume matters between them were resolved simply because they shared a common purpose here today.

Too much stood between them—spoken and unspoken—hovering under the tense surface that she was taking great pains to ignore.

As was Garrett.

Molly glanced at him again, arched an eyebrow, waited.

He shot her a half smile then, finally, addressed his sister directly. "The point isn't that Molly and I have arrived together, but that we have come to speak to Fanny. Not you."

Callie scowled at her brother, opened her mouth to speak then clamped her lips shut and sighed. "Then you better come with me."

She entered the suite. Garrett and Molly followed her inside.

Narrow and cramped, the tiny foyer barely had enough space for all three of them, especially with Garrett's larger-than-life aura stealing all the available air.

Thankfully, Callie continued into the front parlor without breaking stride. Molly joined her, pleased to discover the room was still as warm and cozy as she remembered, welcoming even, much like the women who called this tiny space home.

The large, overstuffed furniture and flowered wallpaper offered a pleasant contrast to the stark, whitewashed beams in the sloped ceiling. Off to the left was Callie's bedroom. The room next to it belonged to Fanny.

Pushing past both women, Garrett strode to Fanny's closed door. He banged with two hard raps.

No response.

"Fanny, open up." He knocked again. "It's Garrett."

Still no response.

Frowning, he stared straight ahead with a narrowed gaze, as if by sheer force of will he could make Fanny obey his command.

"I brought Molly with me." Male frustration rolled off him in waves, but his tone remained conversational. "She's eager to speak with you."

More silence.

"Fanny."

"Go away, Garrett." The muffled reply came from just behind the door, as if Fanny had her forehead pressed to the wood.

He fisted his hand again, drew in several breaths then uncurled his fingers. Muttering to himself, he began pacing. A black weight seemed to settle on his shoulders.

Molly tried not to watch him move, tried not to see the boy she'd once loved inside the man he'd become. It was hopeless, of course. Whenever Garrett was near, she rarely saw anything but him.

She tracked his progress through the room. The hint of a swagger clung to him as naturally as the year-round snow on the mountain peaks. Garrett's cowboy upbringing was written all over him, as natural as the innate integrity and strong sense of family all the Mitchell brood possessed.

"I don't know what's gotten into my sister," Callie whispered to Molly in a low tone, her gaze tracking her brother's movements. "She's acting irrational. And I…that is, I…"

Letting her words trail off, she pressed her lips tightly together, sighed unhappily.

Garrett's feet ground to a halt. "What have you done, Callie?"

She took a shuddering breath. "It's not what I did. It's what I said."

Molly touched the other woman's arm. "I'm sure it wasn't anything too terrible."

"Oh, it was bad all right. I really upset her. But I don't regret a thing I said, not one thing." Callie lifted her chin in an unexpected show of rebellion. "Someone needed to talk some sense into that stubborn girl. Why not me?"

"What did you say to her, Callie?" Garrett's voice held remarkable patience, even though his eyes grew dark with banked emotion.

"I said—"

"She told me I'd made a grave mistake." The reply came from the open doorway where Fanny stood glaring at her sister. Eyes red-rimmed and puffy, she wrapped her arms around her waist in a defensive gesture. "She warned that if I didn't ask for his forgiveness, I would lose Reese forever."

That didn't sound too terrible, Molly decided, especially since it was partly true, assuming Fanny still loved Reese.

"She also called me…" Blinking rapidly, Fanny's bottom lip trembled. "Stupid."

Oh, dear.

"I didn't call you stupid." Callie snorted in disgust. "I said you were *stupid* to let Reese go."

At this, Fanny's eyes glazed over, giving her a lost, dejected look. Tears wiggled to the edges of her thick lashes but she bravely held them in check.

"Reese is a good man." Callie jammed her hands on her hips, her earnest tone emphasizing her words. "He's decent and loyal. You won't find another like him."

"If he's so wonderful, you marry him."

"He wants you, Fanny. It's you he's in love with." Callie took a step closer. "Can't you see the blessing in that?"

"Can't *you* stay out of it?"

The two squared off, nose to nose. Standing there, staring at one another with an identical turbulent expression in their eyes, the similarities between the sisters were impossible to miss. They were of a comparable height, equal build, and tilted their heads at a common angle. Although Fanny was considered the great beauty of the family, Callie had her own appeal, less pronounced perhaps, but there all the same.

Before Molly could intervene, Garrett moved between his sisters.

A head taller than both, he placed a hand on each of their arms. "Is there something you aren't saying?" He addressed Fanny directly. "Something less than honorable we should know about Reese?"

"What?" Both women gasped simultaneously and ripped free of his hold.

Unmoved by their shocked response, Garrett persisted. "Has Reese done something to make you question his character, Fanny? Has he hurt you in any way?"

"Hurt me? No, Garrett. *No.* How could you ask such an awful thing?"

"How could you even suspect something so vile?" Callie's outrage matched her sister's. "You won't find a better man than Reese Bennett, Jr."

Despite being outnumbered, Garrett showed no remorse over his line of questioning. If anything, he seemed to grow fiercer, looking very much like a protective older brother. "If Reese has hurt you, Fanny, and you're protecting him for some reason, you need to tell me. If he—"

"Don't you dare utter another word."

Ignoring the warning, Garrett opened his mouth. Fanny cut him off again. "Reese has always behaved above reproach. He's the best man I know. He's absolutely—" a sob slipped out of her *"—perfect."*

She made the word sound ugly, which only managed to rile her sister all the more. "If Reese is so wonderful,"

Callie challenged, "then why break off your engagement with him?"

Fanny lowered her head. "I have my reasons."

"Which are?"

"None of your business."

The two went toe-to-toe again.

"Callie, step back." Sighing, Garrett gently edged her aside then focused solely on Fanny.

Speaking slowly, calmly, as he would to a spooked horse, he whispered words of encouragement, all the while pressing for details. But no matter what he said, or how he said it, she refused to respond.

His voice dropped another octave. "Can't you see I'm trying to help you?"

She promptly burst into tears.

Wincing, he glanced at Molly. A mix of resignation and uneasiness flickered in his eyes, a look that read utter masculine helplessness. Garrett had never been good with female tears, especially when the crying woman was someone he loved. It was another trait he shared with his brothers.

"Fanny, please. Don't cry." He pulled her into his arms, patted her back awkwardly. "Everything's going to work out."

She muttered something incomprehensible into his shoulder.

He closed his eyes a moment. "No, you're not alone in this. You have your family, your friends and, of course, the Lord. You can lean on us."

"It's not that simple."

"It can be, with a little trust on your part." He set her away from him, but kept his hands on her shoulders. "Help me to understand what's made you change your mind about Reese."

"I already did. He's—" she released a choking sob *"—perfect."*

Garrett chuckled mildly. "We live in a fallen world. No man is perfect."

"Reese is," Fanny whispered glumly. "Even worse, he thinks I'm equally perfect."

There was that word again, spoken in that same dismal tone. So telling, so illuminating.

Garrett captured Molly's gaze over Fanny's head. At his arched eyebrow she arched one of her own. Didn't he understand what his sister was saying?

Molly certainly did. She understood what it meant to fall short of others' expectations. And now, she knew what she had to do.

"I want to speak privately with Fanny," she said, looking pointedly at Garrett then widening the arc of her gaze to include Callie.

Callie immediately started to protest, but Molly cut her off with a firm shake of her head. She expected Garrett to balk, as well. He simply stared at her in measured silence.

Memories settled over her, her mind returning to a time when he trusted her without reservation. What would it be like to have him rely on her again, if only a little?

"Perhaps that's not a bad idea," he acknowledged, setting Fanny away from him, "but only if that's what you want."

Fanny nodded. "Yes, I want to speak to Molly. Alone."

Despite being dismissed, he was calm, stoic, full of uncompromising integrity and strength. "If you continue down this path—" he took his sister's hands in his, held her stare "—others will have to be told of your decision."

"I'm well aware of that."

"All right, then." He released her and settled his gaze on Molly. "Walk me out."

Before she could respond, he hooked his arm through hers and ushered her onto the third-floor landing. "She's hiding something from us, something important."

Perhaps. Perhaps not. Molly would know more once she spoke with Fanny.

"If this is merely a matter of cold feet—"

"It's more than that."

"I'm afraid you're right." Garrett rubbed the back of his neck, shifted his gaze to meet hers. "Since she's made it perfectly clear she doesn't want to discuss this with me or Callie, I'm counting on you to uncover the truth."

"I'll get her to talk," she promised.

"I believe you will." He turned to go then swung back around. "I'll expect a full report later this evening."

"This evening?"

"We're attending the opera together. With Mrs. Singletary." He punctuated the statement with a frown.

At his gloomy expression, Molly bit back a smile. Garrett hated the opera. Actually, he disliked all forms of theater, while she reveled in the drama of any production that required a stage and a troupe of performers.

Their vastly different opinions had been the source of their first argument. And, if memory served, the provocation that led to their first kiss.

Refusing to dwell on *that* thought, she cleared her face of all expression and became graciousness itself. "You'll get your report. I won't leave out a single detail."

His eyes widened.

Oh, honestly. Did he think her completely incapable of agreeable behavior? Even after their unspoken truce?

Insulted, she pivoted around and, without uttering another word, left him to stare after her retreating back.

Let him think whatever he wished about her abrupt departure. Molly had a friend in need. At the moment, nothing mattered more than that.

Chapter Five

Garrett grimaced at the look he caught on Molly's face, right before she turned her back on him. He'd offended her, somehow, when that hadn't been his intent.

Rather than demand an apology, as she would have done in the past, she simply walked away from their conversation. Head high, chin tilted at a jaunty angle, she showed no real signs of temper. Yet, when she shut the door behind her with a firm click, her message was unmistakable.

Garrett was dismissed.

Torn between exasperation and amusement, he tunneled his fingers through his hair.

The afternoon was turning out to be a strange one. Indeed, nothing was as expected. There was Fanny with her uncommon tears and drama, Molly with her lack of either. In a matter of hours, his well-ordered, predictable world had tilted slightly off-center.

As if matters weren't confounding enough, Callie joined him on the landing, a frustrated scowl on her face. "I've been banished from my own home."

"Don't look so tragic, Cal." Her annoyance sent a slow smile curving across his mouth. "You earned your dismissal."

She visibly stiffened. "I most certainly did not!"

"No? You were unusually harsh with our sister. That's not typical of you."

With exaggerated dignity, her spine snapped straighter still. "I don't regret my behavior here today."

He held silent for effect.

"All right, yes." She gathered in a tight breath, let it out slowly. "I suppose I could have been more delicate in my delivery."

"You suppose?"

Her lower lip wobbled. And then—God save him—her eyes filled with tears. Just what the afternoon needed, another bout of unchecked female emotion.

Too much for one day.

If he were a wise man, Garrett would head down the stairwell, exit the boardinghouse and just keep walking.

He remained firmly in place, watching Callie, waiting for her to pull herself together. Unlike Fanny, *this* sister wouldn't welcome any outward show of sympathy from him.

After a moment of eye blinking and steady breathing, she morphed into the cagey fighter he knew her to be—and smoothly turned the conversation back on him.

"You and Molly, overly polite with one another, acting as if there's no history between you. I want an explanation. A real one, this time."

Holding on to his patience, barely, he rubbed a hand over the stubble of a late-day beard coming in. "Haven't we been through this already?"

"Yes, and we'll continue to revisit the topic until I get a reasonable answer out of you."

Of that, he had no doubt. Once his ornery sister had an idea in her head, she never let go. "It's just as Molly said earlier. We joined forces for Fanny's sake."

"How very noble of you both."

A portion of his patience edged into annoyance. "Save

the sarcasm, Callie, it's not helping, nor is it productive. In fact—"

She talked right over him. "I can't think of a time in the past six months since you've been home that I've seen you and Molly in the same room, much less conversing with one another beyond monosyllables."

She was right, of course. Since taking the position at Bennett, Bennett and Brand, Garrett had made every effort to avoid Molly, and she him. With both of them working toward a common goal, they'd reaped remarkable success, managing to circumvent one another as efficiently as possible.

That had changed today. Even without Fanny's situation to bring them together, Mrs. Singletary had tapped Garrett to work with her directly. Which meant he and Molly would cross paths far too often.

He exhaled sharply.

"Garrett, I asked you a question."

Another ripple of annoyance shred what little patience he had left. "No, you made a statement."

She rolled her eyes. "I see you're going to be difficult. So let me speak frankly."

"Never a good idea," he muttered.

She ignored the barb. "Why—no, *how*—did you and Molly end up arriving here together? The truth, Garrett. I won't accept anything less."

Short of muzzling her, he might as well give his tenacious sister what she wanted. "It's not complicated," he explained. "When you and I couldn't talk Fanny out of her room, I went in search of Molly."

"Because?"

"I wanted answers and I thought she had them."

"Why would you think Molly knew any more than we did?"

"I believed she'd been the one to influence Fanny's decision."

Callie gasped. "You didn't actually accuse Molly of such a terrible thing?"

He shrugged. "Her history speaks for itself."

"Garrett, Garrett, Garrett." Callie shook her head in obvious disapproval. "You really don't know her at all."

Oh, he knew her. Or rather, he thought he knew her. He wasn't sure anymore. And that left him even more agitated than before. If he'd been wrong about Molly in this situation, was he wrong about her in other ways as well? Was he prejudging her unnecessarily without gathering all the facts?

"Maybe I don't know her as well as I thought," he conceded.

With far too much perception in her gaze, Callie studied him out of narrowed eyes.

Garrett braced for one of her lectures. But she surprised him by switching topics again. "What are we going to do about Fanny? I can't bear to watch her ruin her life."

This abrupt change of subject gave Garrett pause. Callie was trying to tell him something, something personal, perhaps. But what? What was going on inside that complicated mind of hers? He could simply ask, but he suspected she wouldn't answer him candidly.

Besides, the day was slipping away and he had a lot of work still to do.

"We can't help Fanny until we know more," he said reasonably.

"I guess not." Callie released a resigned sigh. "Let us pray Molly can convince her to see reason."

He nodded.

But then Molly's words came back to him with alacrity. *If Fanny doesn't love Reese enough to want to marry him, then maybe,* maybe *she's making the right decision.*

Pulling out his watch, he flipped open the lid and read the time. "I need to get back to the office." He refocused on Callie, then glanced around the darkened landing. "Will you be all right if I leave you here alone?"

Her withering glare was answer enough. Right, his mistake—Callie was a grown woman of twenty-three, more than capable of taking care of herself in her own home.

"I'll try to stop by again soon," he said. "If not later this afternoon, then tomorrow at the latest."

"Will you speak to Reese after you return to the office?"

"I don't know. Perhaps."

Her eyes went cool, accusatory.

"Stop looking at me like that. For all I know, he might have already left for the day." Though Garrett doubted it. Reese was nothing if not dedicated to his work.

Maybe she's making the right decision...

He heard Callie say something more, something about his duty as an older brother to his hurting sister, but Garrett had already started down the stairs. He waved a hand in farewell, exited the boardinghouse. And just kept walking.

"It occurs to me," Molly said to Mrs. Singletary as they awaited Garrett's arrival in the blue parlor later that evening, "that a night at the opera is an odd place to begin your business association with Mr. Mitchell."

The more she thought on the matter the more she realized how truly out of character the request had been. There could be no opportunity to discuss their plans, or any other business for that matter. That left one glaring reason for the invitation.

Mrs. Singletary was, indeed, playing matchmaker. With Molly and Garrett as her current victims, er...beneficiaries.

Molly stifled a groan. She couldn't fall for Garrett again. She'd given far too much of herself to him once before, only to suffer unspeakable heartache. There'd been no letters once he'd gone away to school, no contact when he'd come home on breaks and certainly no cause to hope he'd change his mind about them.

As time and distance had brought healing, Molly had moved on with her life. Or so she'd always thought. Today had shown her that a part of her would always belong to Garrett. He'd been her first love, her first kiss, her first *everything.* There was no erasing that sort of shared history.

However, that didn't mean she was willing to open her heart and let him trample on it again.

"Nonsense, my dear, his joining us this evening makes perfect sense."

Did it? Molly had her doubts.

Calm as you please, Mrs. Singletary picked up her enormous cat and set the animal on her lap. Weighing in at nearly twenty pounds, Lady Macbeth's fluffy black-and-white fur spilled over the edges of the chair.

While stroking the cat's back, the widow slid a look at Molly out of the corner of her eye. "Aside from getting to know the young attorney better, this is an opportune time for you and Mr. Mitchell to become more comfortable in one another's company."

Decidedly *uncomfortable,* Molly's stomach dipped at the prospect of spending the evening with Garrett. She was already on edge after her conversation with Fanny. Her friend had explained herself in excruciating detail, sharing reasons Molly understood all too well. And that brought her back to Mrs. Singletary's frustrating, albeit well-meaning, interference in her life.

"You want me to become more comfortable with Mr. Mitchell, nothing more?"

"It's as simple as that."

Possible. But not probable.

Unable to stand still any longer, Molly moved restlessly through the elegantly decorated room. She wove a path around the brocade furniture and randomly placed tables adorned with priceless trinkets. Her footsteps caught the rhythmic ticking of the large grandfather clock Mrs. Singletary had purchased on her last trip to London.

Unfortunately, the slow, soothing cadence did nothing to ease Molly's agitation. "Why is this so important to you?"

For all intents and purposes, she'd called her employer's bluff. Would Mrs. Singletary admit to her plan now, or continue to play coy?

"I saw the stiff way you two interacted with one another this afternoon. If Mr. Mitchell and I are to work closely together, it's essential you and he smooth out your differences before we begin."

Molly should have guessed the observant woman would have noticed the charged atmosphere in the man's office. "Garrett and I aren't at odds with one another, if that's what you're implying."

It was shameful, really, how familiar Molly had become with lying in the past few months, a flaw that didn't speak well of her character. She should draw up a formula for cleansing her jaded soul. She would spend more time in the Word, of course. And—

"So it's *Garrett* now, not Mr. Mitchell?" The other woman smiled craftily, her dark eyes warm and full of steely purpose.

Oh, Mrs. Singletary was a slick one. Unmistakable resolve was in her eyes now, just behind that matchmaker gleam. "It's not that I don't appreciate what you're trying to do, but I—"

"What is it you think I'm trying to do, dear?"

"You are attempting to help me find my one true love."

"Am I?" The question sounded as smooth as cream wrapped inside the woman's innocent tone.

"Mrs. Singletary, please, no more pretense." Molly pinched the bridge of her nose. "You have made no secret of the fact that you believe every person has only one soul mate."

"I do indeed believe that, yes," she agreed without an ounce of remorse. "But in my observation, only a blessed few find one another on their own. Most couples need a nudge in the proper direction."

Not Molly and Garrett, for one very simple reason. "We are not one another's soul mate."

"Do you deny having feelings for the man?"

"I've known him all my life," she hedged, swiveling away and taking another turn around the room. "Of course I care about him. He's the brother of my dearest friends."

"That's not what I meant, and you know it."

Absorbing the fact that the older woman cared enough to want to see her happily settled, Molly stopped walking and closed her eyes. She adored Mrs. Singletary, truly she did, and was ever grateful to be in her employ. But this madness had to end.

"You are focusing your efforts in the wrong direction. Garrett and I will never be more than friends."

Mrs. Singletary arched a brow. "You seem convinced. Is there more to the story you aren't telling me?"

Oh, there was definitely more. But Garrett would be arriving any moment. Molly couldn't risk him walking in during a retelling of their tumultuous past.

"Mrs. Singletary, I can't…I'm not…" *Think, Molly. There has to be a way to forestall her matchmaking attempts.* "That is, I'm not ready to find my one true love."

To her utter humiliation, tears welled in her eyes.

"Oh, my dear girl." Mrs. Singletary set the cat on the floor and hurried over to pull Molly into her arms. "I've upset you."

Molly wanted to push free of the widow's hold. She wanted to claim she was fine, just fine.

But she wasn't fine at all.

Her discussion with Fanny had reminded her of her own failures, of all her lost dreams and vanquished hopes.

She felt so terribly alone, exposed and raw. Vulnerable, even, as if God Himself had abandoned her.

Sensing Molly's fragile state, Lady Macbeth rubbed against her leg, a purring, furry ribbon winding around the hem of her dress.

Still holding on tight, Mrs. Singletary gave her a little squeeze. "I would never push you into another romance if I didn't believe you were ready."

"I'm *not* ready."

"Oh, but you are. You only need a little courage and a bit of faith. God has a distinct plan for your life, and I'm determined to see it come to pass."

The tears in her eyes trickled to the edges of her lashes. She refused to let them fall. Not in the company of this woman, or anyone else.

It was her own fault she had to bear this secret pain in silence. She'd let everyone believe she'd been the one to break her engagements. As a result, even her own family feared she couldn't follow through on a promise.

This, she decided, this lack of faith in her character was what came from telling lies. Lies born of pride.

"Molly." Mrs. Singletary set her away from her. "As the Apostle Paul advises, we must strain toward the future, rather than dwell on the past."

"I never look back."

She braced for a lightning bolt, a crash of thunder, something to show God's displeasure in her. She heard nothing but the incessant ticking of the clock. Slow, melodic, sounding very much like a name. *Gar-rett. Gar-rett. Gar-rett.*

How would she bear seeing him tonight? In his company her mind wanted to relive old regrets.

There had been moments this afternoon, when he'd stood so close and she'd caught his familiar scent, that she'd felt a spark of hope. The encounter had brought back memories, memories she'd shoved to the dark corners of her mind.

"I will ask you this only once, my dear, and then we won't speak of it again." Mrs. Singletary reached out and grasped both of her hands. "Are you absolutely certain you won't have a problem with Mr. Mitchell working with me, here, in this home?"

"Of course not." Determined to make her words come true, she added with more conviction, "You've chosen well. Garrett is the most capable man I know. He won't let you down."

It was the simple truth. Garrett met all of Molly's criteria for a man of integrity, her formula deceptively simple. He had to be a devoted follower of the Lord, good at heart, brilliant of mind, authentic to the core.

"I would never wish for you to be unhappy." The widow squeezed Molly's hands. "I've grown quite fond of you."

Molly smiled, really smiled. "And I you."

"You would tell me if you were uneasy with this arrangement?"

"Absolutely." She inwardly cringed, reminded yet again how quickly fibbing had become a part of her character. Thankfully, she was spared from further soul-searching when Mrs. Singletary's manservant, Winston, entered the room.

Standing at attention, he made his announcement with a dignified flourish. "Mr. Garrett Mitchell has arrived."

"Thank you, Winston." Mrs. Singletary released Molly's hands. "Please send him."

He sketched a bow. "Very good, madam."

The moment the butler turned, the clock began chiming the hour.

Of course Garrett would arrive on time. Trying not to sigh, Molly shut her eyes and battled a wave of emotion, only to open them again and find him striding across the ornate rug. He headed straight for her, his golden, tiger eyes unreadable in the dim light.

Trapped in the moment, she drank in the sight of him. He'd shaved recently, his face free of stubble now. He wore elegant evening attire, perfectly appropriate for a night at the opera. The pristine white of his starched shirt stood in stark contrast to the black of his tailored coat and vest.

Halfway across the room, his eyes captured hers. *And held.*

An unwelcome jolt of longing crawled up her spine and landed in the center of her heart.

Molly's reaction was the same whenever he was near. Her mind raced. Her thoughts scrambled.

Her vision blurred.

This evening, she had no route of escape, no pressing matter awaiting her in another part of the house.

She was trapped, good and truly trapped.

Panic reared, morphed into a far more complicated emotion. Anticipation. Something different flickered in Garrett's eyes tonight, something that spoke solely to her. Something she didn't dare name.

The questions were there, too, questions about his sister's situation. He wanted to know what Fanny had confessed to Molly in private.

He wasn't going to like what she had to relay. But would he understand?

She briefly wondered if she could withhold the information from him, and decided the point was moot. If Garrett Mitchell wanted answers, he would get them. His resolve to help his sister was just that strong.

Because of that, Molly's fondness for the man went up a notch, putting her heart at greater risk than ever before.

Chapter Six

Caught inside Molly's stare, Garrett nearly tripped over his own two feet. Exquisite in a gown of dark blue silk and silver lace, the modern cut emphasized her trim figure, while the unique color combination made her eyes take on a full shade lighter than usual. The effect was striking.

She was stunning from every angle. The exotic curve of her lips, the shy tilt of her head, called to him.

He took a step closer.

When he nearly stumbled again, he broke eye contact and looked down. A monster ball of black-and-white fur had taken up residence at his feet, hindering further progress.

The creature looked like a cat. But Garrett had never seen one quite so large. Or so fat. A moment more of staring through that mean, narrowed gaze, and the animal crouched low. It swished the fluffy plume of a tail, crouched lower still, danced on its hind quarters and then...

Launched its massive body into the air, landing smack in the middle of Garrett's chest.

He staggered under the blow, arms instinctively wrapping around the mound of fur. After his own awkward dance, Garrett caught his balance. Frozen in place, he and the beast eyed one another for a taut moment.

A slow blink on his part, another swish of the bushy tail on the cat's and then the purring began—loud, guttural, uninhibited.

"Garrett Mitchell." Smiling broadly, Mrs. Singletary peered around his shoulder. "Meet Lady Macbeth."

The widow had named her pet after one of the most heartless female murderers in all of fiction? Wary now, he angled his head and studied the enormous cat with careful focus. Certainly big enough to be a killer.

Did she have the heart of one, too?

Mrs. Singletary answered his unspoken question on a laugh. "Any mouse in a two-mile radius is doomed."

"Ah." He chuckled along with her. "So the Lady earns her keep."

"And then some." This last statement came from Molly, spoken in an amused tone as she reached around him and scratched the cat behind the ears. "She likes you."

Trying to decide if that was a good thing or not, Garrett shifted the animal in his arms.

The purring took on an unrestrained edge.

"She *really* likes you."

Arms overflowing with giant kitty, he answered in his best philosophical tone. "I guess we can add cat wrangler to my list of various talents."

"So it would seem."

They shared a laugh. It felt surprisingly good to enjoy the moment with Molly, like old times. But as those big, expressive blue eyes held his a moment too long, his breath clogged in his throat. The impact of all that beauty was like a gut-punch.

"My sweet girl doesn't usually like men." Retrieving her cat, Mrs. Singletary looked from him to Molly and then back again. "You are a rarity, Mr. Mitchell."

Sensing an undertone in her words, Garrett's smile tightened. "Am I?"

"Of course. My cat is an excellent judge of character, don't you agree, Molly?"

When she sniffed in response, Garrett's shoulders stiffened.

Mrs. Singletary laughed outright.

"I wish to leave for the opera at once." After a quick kiss to the cat's head, she set the animal on the floor then retrieved her reticule off a nearby table. "I prefer to arrive early whenever possible."

"Whatever you desire." Garrett gave her a short bow of his head. "I am your humble servant for the entire evening."

"Wonderful."

He offered her his arm, turned to Molly and, after only a slight hesitation, offered her the other. "Shall we?"

They left the house in companionable silence.

Not more than a half hour later, Garrett escorted the women into the recently finished Tabor Grand Opera House. They entered from Curtis Street, straight into the rotunda with its impressive stained glass roof. The newly finished building was an architectural marvel.

After speaking to several people she knew, Mrs. Singletary indicated they could continue into the lobby. A large chandelier lighted their way across the well-laid parquet floor. Thanks to several more social opportunities for the widow, it took considerable time to maneuver their small party into the main auditorium.

Eventually, they passed through the main area and climbed the stairwells to the top tier of the theater where she'd secured a box.

As they settled in the crimson plush chairs, Garrett took the seat between the two women and looked around. Paintings and murals decorated the entire theater. Senses overloaded, he shut his eyes and concentrated solely on the sound of the orchestra tuning their instruments. Recognizing several notes, he winced in dread.

Hoping he was wrong, he looked at the playbill in his hand. A groan shot past his lips. Perfect. Just perfect.

The traveling opera troupe was set to perform *The Barber of Seville,* absolutely the worst tale of love and deception ever composed. The convoluted story was Molly's all-time favorite and—*ironically*—the source of their infamous first argument as a couple.

Their mutually heated words slammed through his mind. And, then, because he was a man after all, his thoughts leaped to the end of their verbal tussle, straight to that remarkable kiss. The first for them both.

Lost in the memory, he glanced over at Molly. She was staring back at him. With a wry twist of his lips, he lifted the playbill and pointed to the title of the opera.

Her pupils instantly dilated, but it was her cheeky half grin that told him all he needed to know. She remembered their argument as well as he did. And the concluding kiss.

His heart tripped.

They were in tricky, dangerous territory.

The precise place they both liked best.

Mind stuck somewhere between past and present, he leaned forward. Molly did the same. He might have said her name. She might have whispered his.

He moved his head a fraction closer to hers, and—

A masculine clearing of a throat stopped his pursuit.

Attention averted, Garrett swung around to look at the curtained entryway. Two men, both impeccably dressed, stood in the halo of light pouring in through the slit behind them.

Garrett knew one of them by name, reputation and, more importantly, by his recent connection to Molly.

The other had been among her suitors this afternoon, the one who'd continually taken her hand in his and spoke to her with far too much familiarity for Garrett's liking.

The evening only needed this added dramatic twist.

It's going to be a long night, Garrett thought glumly. And the screeching Italian hadn't even begun.

Molly rose to her feet at the same time as Garrett. Her stomach dipped to her toes, then whipped straight to her throat and stuck.

Swallowing several times, she concentrated on the man to her left. Marshall Ferguson. Her former fiancé, looking exceedingly elegant in his evening attire. He'd even managed to tame his unruly, blond hair into neat, orderly waves.

Eyes on his handsome face, Molly braced for the change in her heartbeat, for the sickening roll in her stomach, for... *something.* She felt nothing, nothing at all, not even a quickening of her breath.

Odd. Wasn't she supposed to feel a physical response to seeing him again?

As though he were equally unmoved, Marshall looked at her with a benign smile on his lips. He didn't speak, nor did he try to move deeper into the box. He just stood at the entrance, waiting for someone else to break the silence.

Garrett didn't do the honors.

Mrs. Singletary didn't, either.

Molly couldn't. Because, well, Marshall wasn't alone.

There, beside him, stood Mr. Giles Thomas, dressed, for once, in black rather than his customary brown. Even more disconcerting, a look of disapproval pinched his ordinary face into a rather unattractive scowl.

"What is the meaning of this?" demanded Mr. Thomas in a voice full of outrage. "Miss Scott. You told me you were attending the opera with Mrs. Singletary, and yet here you are with—" he stabbed a finger at Garrett "—him."

Oh, honestly.

Did he not see Mrs. Singletary standing beside them, looking...amused? The widow found this situation funny?

Molly frowned.

"You will not speak to Miss Scott in that tone of voice." Tightening his jaw, Garrett took a step forward. "Have I made myself clear?"

"Now see here, who are you to go ordering me about?"

"Mr. Thomas." Mrs. Singletary shifted into view, diverting disaster with the move. "And Mr. Ferguson. I say, how very good of you both to stop by my box this evening."

The two addressed her in return—Marshall with genuine regard, Mr. Thomas with a much more fractious attitude.

Unaffected by his rudeness, the widow chattered away, oh-so-casually moving between him and Garrett. When she took a breath, she wrapped her fingers around Mr. Thomas's arm and led him toward the exit.

At the curtain's edge, she mentioned her most sincere wish for a glass of lemonade before the show began, and would he be so kind as to accompany her?

The request was a subtle one, sly even, with the result of leaving Molly alone with Garrett *and* Marshall.

Wondering at the motivation behind such a tactic, Molly forced down her nerves and performed the introductions. "Garrett Mitchell, I'd like you to meet Marshall Ferguson."

"We know one another," they said in unison.

Garret offered his hand to the other man. "Marshall."

"Garrett."

They shook respectfully.

If Molly wasn't mistaken, Garrett was decidedly tenser than their visitor. Marshall, on the other hand, was as cool and unruffled as ever. She'd always liked that about him, had appreciated his ability to negotiate any situation with steady calm, no matter how emotionally charged.

He was a good man, wise enough to see that they were better friends than future spouses. Knowing he was right, Molly felt the shame of self-reproach. She should have never agreed to marry him in the first place.

"I understand the banking business is treating you well," Garrett said into the silence, taking charge of the situation.

Marshall nodded, smiled. "It's been a good year for you, too, or so I hear."

They fell into a discussion over silver mines, railroad stock and water rights. Content to listen, Molly noticed how well the two men seemed to get along, as if they were friends.

Not a surprise; they had a lot in common. Both were handsome, well-educated, at the top in their choice of careers.

Like Garrett, Marshall also came from a large, happy, gregarious family. The oldest of eight children and the only male, if Molly had married him she would have acquired seven younger sisters on the spot.

Melancholy roiled through her, making her question whether she missed the girls more than she missed Marshall.

What did that say about her?

Certainly nothing good.

"Molly." Marshall took her hand and brushed his lips across her gloved knuckles. "You are looking well."

"Thank you," she said. "It's good to see you looking so well, too."

And, oh, wasn't this remarkably civil? Molly standing between two of the three men who'd rejected her.

Still smiling, Marshall released her hand and took a step back. As he glanced at Garrett, then back to her, a light of understanding glimmered in his gaze.

"Well." He took a breath. "I'll leave you two to enjoy your evening together."

Another quick inhale and he was gone.

Expecting Garrett to make some remark about the scene they'd endured with her ex-fiancé, Molly waited.

He said nothing.

When he still didn't speak, she heaved a weighty sigh. "He thought we were here, *together*. You didn't correct him."

"Neither did you."

No, she hadn't.

Shifting to a spot directly in front of her, Garrett lifted her chin with a gentle finger and searched her face. One beat, two, on the third he said, "It had to have been difficult for him to see you with another man, yet he didn't appear upset."

How did she respond without revealing her secret shame? Of course Marshall hadn't been upset to see her with another man. She was easy enough to forget once she was no longer in a person's life—the quintessential "out of sight, out of mind" syndrome incarnate.

Her own mother, a busy prostitute and madam, had consistently left her in someone else's care. Until she'd died. At which time, Molly had been shipped off to live with her miner father. When he'd died five months later she'd been sent to Charity House, a home for prostitutes' by-blows, where she'd lived with her older sister, Katherine.

From the start, Katherine had taken on a mother's role in Molly's life. She'd been so successful, many had believed she *was* Molly's mother, Molly included.

Despite the safe, loving home her sister had provided, after all that shuffling about as a young child, Molly still felt a little apart, separate, as if she didn't fully fit in anywhere.

As she wrestled with these thoughts, Garrett took her hand and pulled her back to their seats.

"Molly." His tone gentled. "Everything I know about Marshall Ferguson tells me he's a good man."

"He is a very good man."

"Then tell me why you broke off your engagement with him."

"Because…" She chewed on her bottom lip, thinking through her answer, trying to decide how much of the truth to reveal and how much to withhold. "Marshall didn't believe I loved him."

With nothing showing on his face, Garrett sat back in his chair. Was he remembering their final argument the day he'd left for school? He hadn't trusted her feelings for him, either, had claimed her love for him was tangled up inside her love of his family.

The truth was Garrett hadn't loved *her* enough, not the other way around. The same had been true of Marshall, and Bart Williams before him. All three men had walked away from her, without a backward glance.

"Was Marshall right?" Garrett asked, his voice barely audible over the din of the theater. "Were your feelings for him…lacking?"

She couldn't lie, not to Garrett, not about something this important. "Yes."

"I see."

But she could tell he didn't see. He didn't see anything at all.

She wanted to explain herself, *needed* to explain herself, but Garrett spoke first. "Since we're on the topic of broken engagements, did Fanny reveal her reasons for jilting Reese?"

Molly shivered at the shift in his mood. He was so, so distant. She looked away, flinched at the sound of laughter ringing out from the seats below them. Glancing over the railing she saw that the theater was filling up quickly.

The show would begin soon.

Not soon enough.

"Yes, Fanny told me everything."

Relief crossed Garrett's face and he rolled his shoulders. "Why doesn't she want to marry Reese?"

Here came the slippery part, the part that hit far too close to home.

"She claims he doesn't know her and, worse yet, doesn't especially want to know her." The words spilled out of her mouth, tumbling over one another, taking on a personal meaning despite every effort to remain detached. "She believes he loves the image of her, not Fanny herself."

To his credit, Garrett didn't immediately respond, but considered her explanation in contemplative silence. "If that's the case," he began. "If Reese doesn't know the real Fanny, then whose fault is that?"

"Fanny's," they said as one.

Molly sighed. "From what I understand, Reese has very specific requirements for a wife. And up until recently Fanny has played the part to perfection."

"It's a problem easily remedied. All she has to do is stop playing the role and let him get to know her real self."

"You think it'll be easy for her to change his perception of her, at this late date? From a young age, Fanny has been considered the pretty daughter, the adored sister and then, most recently, the treasured fiancée. She's—"

"Played all those roles admirably," he finished for her. "And not without benefits."

"True." Yet Molly understood the pressure Fanny felt, the burden that came with being labeled one way as a girl and unable to break free of that image as a woman.

Some people—*most people*—saw what they wanted to see and never bothered looking beyond that initial impression.

Molly knew what it meant to wear a role others had set upon her shoulders. She also knew the burden of falling short of loved ones' expectations.

At least Mrs. Singletary saw her for who she was, now, today. Not the little girl whose mother had been a highly paid prostitute, or the abandoned child living alone in a mining camp with only a threadbare blanket for warmth, or the woman who used mathematical equations to prevent emotion from ruling her heart.

She wanted to explain all this to Garrett, and thought maybe he would finally hear her. At one time, he'd known her better than anyone.

Unfortunately, the outer curtain swung open with exaggerated fanfare, filling the box with a burst of light and noise.

"Well, now." Smiling broadly, Mrs. Singletary bustled in and moved hurriedly to her seat. "I hope you two found something to talk about in my absence."

Garrett answered for them both. "Indeed, we did."

"Excellent."

As if the widow had planned her arrival down to the second, the moment she sat down, the orchestra played the first notes of the overture.

The lights dimmed. The curtain began its ascent.

Molly leaned forward, pressed her hand to her heart and lost herself in her favorite romantic tale of love in disguise.

Chapter Seven

After two hours of sitting through excruciating agony, Garrett's ears throbbed. He'd nearly reached the end of his endurance, yet the heavyset woman playing Rosina continued shrieking out her heart's most secret desires.

Awful. Truly terrible.

The soprano's voice grated as it reached an octave unfit for dogs. Her overuse of the dramatic was nothing short of criminal, while her command of the Italian language was questionable at best. In Garrett's estimation, the only saving grace was that the opera was drawing to a close.

The final notes could not come soon enough.

How did anyone find this tedious form of entertainment enjoyable?

Glancing at Molly, he caught the tragic sigh sweeping out of her, noted how her gaze was riveted to the stage. Her eyes were two pools of watery emotion, demonstrating just how much the evening's performance moved her.

That unbridled reaction *moved* him.

He wasn't sure why he did it, couldn't fathom what had gotten into him, but he reached over and clasped Molly's hand.

She turned her head and gave him a tremulous smile.

That look, it brought out all sorts of inconvenient emotions. Tenderness, longing, a need to protect. He wanted to drag her in his arms, beat off the competition and slay her every dragon, whether real or imagined.

He didn't have the right. Not anymore.

Perhaps he never had.

He'd walked away from her—*from them*—because he'd realized it wasn't him she loved but his family. Oh, she'd liked him well enough, had even cared for him. But Garrett had never accepted the status of second best, not in anything, and especially not in Molly's heart. He'd so wanted to be wrong about her lack of feelings for him. But when she'd failed to ask him to stay home with her, he'd regarded that as proof she didn't love him in the same way he loved her.

After time and distance, he'd begun to look back and wonder if he'd been wrong, if he'd misjudged her feelings for him. Then, his suspicions had been confirmed when both of her fiancés also came from large, happy, loving families like his.

Garrett must keep that in mind, or he would never be able to keep much-needed distance between him and Molly.

Then why was he still holding her hand?

And why, if her heart had never truly been his, was she clutching his in return?

The screeching came to an abrupt halt. *Praise God.*

A pause, a moment of poised silence and then…

Applause exploded throughout the auditorium.

The clapping grew louder, and louder still, all but vibrating on the air and shaking the rafters.

Wrenching her hand free, Molly jumped to her feet and joined in the audience's enthusiastic response to the performance.

Garrett and Mrs. Singletary remained seated.

The widow swung her amused glance in his direction. "Not a fan of the opera, I take it."

"Not even a little."

They shared a smile.

She leaned in closer, her voice lowered to a hushed whisper. "And yet, here you are."

Garrett held her stare, his face a cool mask wiped free of all emotion. "You requested my presence."

"Do you always put your clients' needs above your own?"

"Not always, no." He waited a beat. "However, you can't deny my being here this evening served a mutually satisfying purpose for us both."

Her lips twitched as she tried to contain her smile. "I dare to ask, what is this mutually satisfying purpose?"

"You wanted to see how I handled myself in a social setting, and I had no objection to appeasing your curiosity."

"I'm wounded." She let out a tinkling laugh that belied her words. "You think me that calculating?"

A smile was his only answer.

"Well, yes. I suppose I am a bit calculating." She winked at him. "But only a little."

She made to continue, but Garrett spoke over her. "We both know you are a woman who cares not one fig what others think of you. Thus, no matter how I handled myself this evening, you would have retained my services if you so desired."

"Very shrewd." She relaxed back in her chair and snapped open her fan. "But, tell me, Mr. Mitchell, what was *your* reason for attending the opera this evening? Don't pretend you didn't have one."

After assuring Molly's attention was still fastened on the stage, he answered. "I merely wished to get to know you better."

The enthusiastic applause continued as the cast trooped out onto the stage, one at a time, the least important role first.

"Did you succeed in your goal?"

"I did." Yet, he still hadn't discovered the widow's true reason for seeking his counsel in the first place. He was good at sniffing out a lucrative venture, and calculating the odds of success. But so were others in this town.

He had an idea why she'd chosen him, and it had little to do with advancing her fortune. Increasing her charitable giving was a worthy goal, but there was something else driving the widow's actions. He would know more once he gathered additional evidence.

"I believe, Mr. Mitchell, you are not being completely forthright."

That made two of them.

"You had another reason for accepting my invitation this evening. One that was strictly..." The widow's gaze slid past him, brushed over Molly, then slid back. "Personal?"

Well, well. Mrs. Singletary had just revealed her hand and proved herself far more conventional than most realized.

The woman was matchmaking, evidently assuming that by simply throwing Garrett and Molly together as often as possible they would fall in love.

He nearly called the widow out on her scheme, but knowledge was power *only* if wielded with wisdom. And caution. Caution was key. For now, Garrett decided to bide his time. And watch to see what Mrs. Singletary's next move would be.

The applause died to a low roar.

"Wasn't that magnificent?" Molly spun around to smile at him, her eyes shining with awe.

She sighed appreciatively, the soft sound dreamy and very, very appealing.

Garrett was slung back in time.

Molly used to look at him like that, used to sigh over him like that. Against his better judgment, he allowed himself to bask in her unguarded adoration, as if she only had eyes for him.

This moment isn't real, he told himself. *She will always hold a portion of herself back.* He knew this. Accepted it. And yet his pulse sped up anyway.

The evening in Garrett's company wasn't turning out to be as dreadful as Molly initially feared. Despite expectations to the contrary, his presence had actually added to her overall pleasure.

When he'd taken her hand during the final song of the opera everything in her had simply stopped and sighed.

The moment had been perfect.

Although she knew he would disagree, the opera had been equally perfect. The production had met every variable in Molly's formula for engaging entertainment—colorful costumes, superb acting, wonderful music and dazzling drama.

Ah, yes, the drama. Even now, an hour after leaving the opera house, Molly shivered in remembered delight.

Still humming with pleasure, she wanted Garrett to take her hand again, wanted to feel his warmth spread through her gloves. But he sat on the opposite side of Mrs. Singletary's formal sitting room, conversing with the widow in low, even tones. He paid Molly no heed whatsoever.

A flare of frustration swirled in her stomach. Garrett had cooled considerably toward her since arriving back at the house.

There he sat, oh so relaxed, with his legs stretched out before him, perfectly at home on the fragile brocade-covered settee. He should have looked ridiculous, surrounded by the frills and lace of the room. Instead, he was masculinity personified, all hard angles, broad shoulders and sharp features.

The attractive boy had grown into quite a handsome man.

Molly appreciated why the cat had been instantly smitten

and thus decided to let him into her stingy world. Curled up beside him, eyes closed, chin on her paws, Lady Macbeth allowed him to rub her ears. The animal allowed *no one* to rub her ears.

Molly drew in a shaky breath.

Man and cat made quite the homey picture.

From beneath her lowered lashes, she continued watching Garrett interact with Mrs. Singletary. He was good with people, always had been, his easy manner encouraging them to let down their guard. Mrs. Singletary seemed to be no exception, as she candidly regaled him with stories from her youth.

"I'll admit growing up in a mining camp was an unconventional, often dangerous upbringing," she said after a particularly harrowing tale about losing her way in a mine shaft at the age of seven. "I learned the value of hard work and the importance of seeing a job through to its completion."

Considering her with thoughtful eyes, Garrett moved his hand to the cat's back and ran his fingertips along her spine. "Those are valuable lessons for any child."

"Quite so."

He continued his lazy stroking of the cat's fur. She thumped her tail rhythmically against his leg in blissful feline approval.

"I'm curious, Mr. Mitchell." Mrs. Singletary leaned forward to snare a tiny cake off the tray her housekeeper had brought in earlier. "What was it like growing up on a ranch like the Flying M?"

"It was hard, physical, often grueling work." A line of concentration formed between his eyes. "The day started at sunrise and ended at sunset."

"Sounds exhausting. No wonder you became a lawyer."

He moved a shoulder. "Every season had its challenges, but there were rewards, too. As you yourself said, there's satisfaction in a job well done."

"True, true." She went for another cake. "Tell me about your family."

"Not much to tell." He uncrossed his ankles, readjusted his position, crossed them again. "We're like most families. We work hard, band together in times of need, turn to God when all seems hopeless and praise the Lord for our many blessings."

"How lovely." For a brief moment, she looked overcome with sadness. A trick of the light? Molly wondered.

"How many brothers and sisters do you have?"

"There are seven of us."

"And where do you fall among them, agewise?"

Thunder rumbled from somewhere in the distance. He briefly looked toward the sound, his gaze as distant as the mountain peaks beyond the balcony. The question wasn't a hard one, or particularly probing, yet he seemed slightly disturbed by it.

"I'm the middle boy. Logan and Hunter are the oldest, barely a year apart in age. Then there's me, followed by my two sisters. The twins, Peter and Paul, bring up the rear."

The widow absorbed this information a moment, giving Molly a chance to do so, as well. There was something in the way Garrett had grouped his brothers and sisters— two by two—that gave her new insight into his childhood.

Why had she not made the connection before?

Garrett had been the odd man out in his family, much as Molly had been hers. Though she adored her younger brothers, they'd always been closer with one another than with her. Part of that, she knew, had to do with their considerable age differences. Ethan was a full six years younger than Molly, and Ryder almost eight.

"So every child in your family had a partner, so to speak, except you."

Looking taken aback, Garrett stilled his hand and said, "I guess that's one way of looking at it."

Slitting open an eye, the cat butted her head against his open palm until he resumed his petting.

"You must have been terribly lonely."

"Lonely?" He laughed. "Not even remotely. I was surrounded by cows, horses, dogs. *People.* My younger siblings were always underfoot. The older ones constantly dished out orders. Then there were the ranch hands, my parents and…"

His words trailed off and his eyebrows furrowed together. His chest rose and fell over and over again. "Well, hmm…"

The poor man looked poleaxed. Molly desperately wanted to go to him. She wanted to smooth away that look of shock on his face, wanted to tell him she knew what it meant to be surrounded by people, even people who loved her, and still feel alone.

Perhaps that had been the reason they'd gravitated toward one another as children, at least initially. Although neither of them had recognized it at the time, their mutual loneliness had helped them form a strong bond.

"You weren't without a partner," she blurted out. "Not when I was around."

Oh, my. She'd just said that out loud.

Garrett gave her a slow smile reminiscent of the amusing, clever boy always ready to tackle their next adventure.

"That's certainly true. I was always a willing participant in whatever scheme you'd cooked up." He spoke so simply, with such confident nonchalance that her heart skidded to a stop. "What I never understood, though, was why enlist me in your plans at all? Why not ask Callie or Fanny to join you?"

Didn't he know? "You were far more daring than your sisters." She gave him a saucy smile. "And five times more fun."

His lips twisted at a sardonic angle. "We did have fun."

They stared at one another a moment, both apparently lost in memories of better days, when their time together had transcended words. She was aware of the same warm, curious pull she'd always felt every time she was near him.

She remembered the day when they'd suddenly, unexpectedly, gone from friends to something…more.

Her visit to the Mitchell ranch had started as all the others before. She'd climbed the steps onto the front porch ahead of her family, set a little apart—a little *alone*—and had marched straight toward Garrett.

By the time she'd reached out, took his hands in hers and said, "Garrett, my dear, dear friend," her feelings of friendship had turned into love.

The transformation had happened that quickly.

He'd been equally struck. Or so he said. Yet, three months later he'd walked away without a backward glance.

"Am I to understand…" Mrs. Singletary cleared her throat. "You two were close as children?"

Close? The word didn't begin to describe their relationship back then. Even before they'd fallen in love, their connection had been deeper than mere friendship, as if God Himself had drawn them together—one reckless adventure at a time.

Exhausted, laughing until it hurt, they would cook up their next plot. They also discussed life's most perplexing problems. Sometimes Garrett would help her design a formula for her latest concern, at others he simply listened as she worked out the particulars on her own.

They'd discussed spiritual matters, too, everything from whether or not animals went to heaven to more complicated topics such as predestination and why God allowed injustices in the world.

Molly's love for the Lord had been strengthened during those conversations, her faith secured.

"Yes, we were—" Garrett smiled at Molly "—close."

"Ah" was the widow's only response. However, the satisfied look she divided between Molly and Garrett spoke volumes. She now had all the ammunition she needed to continue her matchmaking scheme.

Molly went statue-still. She could feel her cheeks flaming as words backed up in her throat.

Equally silent, Garrett focused on the cat's thick fur. After a moment, he lifted his gaze. "I should go." He unfolded his large frame and stood. "I have an early appointment in the morning."

All politeness and gentlemanly manners, he took Mrs. Singletary's hand and placed a kiss above her knuckles. "Thank you for an enjoyable evening. It's been…enlightening."

"For me, as well." She set her hand on the arm of her chair and peered at him, a question in her eyes. "I trust you found an opportunity to discuss my business proposition with Reese this afternoon."

He let out a low sound of agreement. "If you still wish to expand your financial empire and increase your charitable offerings, I will gladly offer my assistance."

"Excellent. Most excellent, indeed." She pushed gracefully to her feet. "We'll begin our preliminary discussions tomorrow morning, at ten o'clock sharp. Come here prepared to work."

Although he didn't show any outward reaction to this imperious command, he did, however, say, "I'm afraid that won't be possible. I will be unavailable until early afternoon."

A beat of silence followed this statement.

The two regarded one another, neither balking, neither giving way.

At last, Mrs. Singletary smiled. "Tomorrow afternoon will be fine."

Garrett's head tilted in a slight bow. "Very good."

At his flat tone, the widow's smile turned into a hearty

laugh. "I believe, Mr. Mitchell, you and I will get on quite well."

"You may count on it."

"Then I will say good evening."

He responded in kind, shot Molly a brief farewell from over his shoulder and strode toward the door.

Molly watched him go, a sense of relief relaxing her shoulders. The evening hadn't been so bad. She and Garrett had survived their time together.

Ah, but Mrs. Singletary wasn't through with them just yet. "Molly, be a love and escort our guest to the door."

As the two young people exited the room, Beatrix Singletary clasped her hands together in delight. She couldn't be more pleased with her choice of suitor for her sweet companion.

Garrett Mitchell was smart, shrewd and nobody's fool. His steady nature was a perfect foil for Molly's less predictable one. Their individual strengths and weaknesses would balance out one another perfectly.

His calm to her storm.

Her feistiness to his more guarded personality.

Beatrix was going to enjoy watching them fall in love. Not that their road to happiness would be a smooth one. Those two stubborn souls were going to fight her every step of the way.

She looked forward to the challenge.

She had little else to look forward to these days. Tears misted in her eyes, a far too often occurrence of late.

Her thoughts turned to her deceased husband and the loneliness she battled daily. "Oh, Lord, I miss my dear, dear Reginald." She squeezed her eyes shut. "So terribly much."

A large, silky paw swatted at her skirt.

Sniffing away her melancholy, Beatrix smiled down at her treasured feline and refocused on her plan. With the

Lord's help, and a good nudge from her, two worthy young people would unite their lives together in holy matrimony.

"I give them less than a month before they succumb to the inevitable. What say you, my lady?"

The cat gave her a skeptical meow.

"Very true." She picked up her baby and cuddled her close. "We better keep a close eye on those two. Left to their own devices, there's no telling what missteps they'll take."

Her course set, she headed to the stairwell to indulge in some necessary spying.

Chapter Eight

Garrett released a slow, steady breath. The gesture reduced the tension between his shoulders not one bit. Given a choice, he'd prefer to see himself out. He desperately needed the time to clear his mind. Talk of his childhood had left him feeling uneasy.

Now, his head was full of a time when he'd thought his future would always be linked with Molly's. Beatrix Singletary was a crafty one, purposely guiding him mentally—and emotionally—through the past, with Molly by his side.

Garrett didn't appreciate the widow's machinations. He didn't appreciate the way she'd made him question why he'd come back to Denver, wondering if Molly had been a small part of his reasoning. He refused to consider the possibility for even a moment. Instead, he focused his frustration on Mrs. Singletary.

Subterfuge and trickery were no way to begin a business relationship. Her unhanded tactics went against everything he believed about good Christian behavior.

Let a man's yes be yes and his no be no.

There were several solutions to the problem. He could walk away from his agreement with the widow. Or he could follow the Biblical model and confront the widow directly.

The first would be taking the easy way out. He'd never

been one to choose a path simply to avoid discomfort. That left the other, more straightforward route. He made up his mind to speak with Mrs. Singletary about his concerns when next they met—in a respectful manner, of course. Using a clear, succinct argument he would ask her to cease her matchmaking efforts at once.

In the meantime, there were a few things he and Molly needed to get straight.

"Hold up a minute." Taking her arm, he gently steered her into an alcove surrounded by an assortment of potted plants. It was a fairly secluded spot, perfect for a private conversation. "We need to talk."

She pivoted to face him. "I know."

"Mrs. Singletary is playing—"

"Matchmaker." She completed his thought for him. Then, with an ironic lift of her eyebrows, she added, "With you and me as her—"

"Intended victims." Garrett finished Molly's statement, and earned a droll smile for his efforts.

He felt his own lips twitch. They'd always been able to complete one another's sentences. Time and distance should have put up a metaphorical wall between them.

But no, they were still as connected as ever.

Not sure how he felt about that, he rolled his shoulders and refocused on Molly. "When did you figure out her—"

"Plan?" She shrugged. "I had my suspicions this afternoon. But I didn't know for certain until tonight, after the opera. Her questions about your childhood were too specific. It was as if she were leading you to a particular memory. And when she asked about our relationship, well, she clearly—"

"Revealed her intentions?"

Molly nodded, paused, looked as if she had more to say.

Garrett held his tongue, waiting for the rest.

But she remained as silent as he.

"Molly—"

"Garrett—"

They both heaved a sigh.

He pressed a fingertip to her lips, holding off whatever else she'd been meaning to say.

Her eyes danced with amusement. Garrett felt his own lips lift in a smile. How many times had they struck this exact pose, for this very reason?

Too many to count.

Garrett's gut churned with a sensation that felt stronger than affection, deeper than fondness and more than a little complicated for his peace of mind.

He dropped his hand. "We need to put an end to this madness before it goes any further. I'll speak with Mrs. Singletary tomorrow."

"I'll speak with her as well," Molly offered. "Except… there might be a problem."

She pulled her bottom lip between her teeth, and a thoughtful expression spread across her face. "I'm afraid, no matter how forthright we are with Mrs. Singletary, simply asking her to desist won't deter her."

Garrett tilted his head back, eyebrows raised.

"Once the widow sets her mind on something, she doesn't give up until she accomplishes her goal."

An admirable trait. *In business.* Irritation rippled and his tone turned sharp. "She can't force us to fall in with her scheme merely because she's decided we suit."

"Garrett, you mustn't hold her resolve against her." Molly touched his sleeve, her tone earnest. "Mrs. Singletary means well."

Molly would know better than he. "Nevertheless, I won't be forced into—"

"Feeling something you don't feel?"

"That wasn't what I was going to say." He felt plenty. That was the problem. He could easily fall for Molly again.

She would reciprocate, he saw it in the way she leaned toward him, in the way her eyes filled with a soft, gentle emotion. He'd seen her stare at him like that before often enough.

They would be good together. For a time. But Garrett would accept nothing less than Molly's whole heart.

And *that* she couldn't give.

"I won't be forced into a romance that neither of us wants," he declared, his tone grave.

She opened her mouth. Shut it without speaking. Then, an all-too-familiar twinkle filled her gaze.

Garrett's breath caught.

"How about—" Molly batted her long, dark, beautiful lashes at him "—we give her what she wants?"

Shock had him taking a step back. "*What?* No."

"Garrett Mitchell, I'm disappointed in you. What happened to the bold, daring boy I used to know?" She pursed her lips then let her gaze wander over him, slowly, confidently, a familiar challenge in her eyes. "Where's your sense of adventure?"

His reaction to her goading was not rational. Standing before him in all her feminine glory was the thrill-seeking girl he'd once loved with all his heart. The one he'd happily accompanied into all sorts of trouble. She might have been the mastermind behind their schemes, but Garrett had always been the first to take action.

He closed his eyes against the unwanted memories sliding into place, smooth and effortless, urging him to forget he was a responsible attorney now, with a reputation to uphold in the community.

"Think about it," she suggested in that sly, taunting voice he still heard in his dreams. "If we allow Mrs. Singletary to believe her plot is working, we maintain the control."

He allowed his own gaze to wander over her, slowly, confidently, with equal challenge. "Let me get this straight.

You want us to pretend to fall in love so we can control Mrs. Singletary's matchmaking efforts?"

Her logic was flawed. It *had* to be flawed. But, at the moment, with her floral scent teasing his nostrils, he couldn't figure out exactly how.

"Don't you see? If we enter a courtship knowing how it ends, no one walks away hurt."

Someone always walked away hurt. The day he'd boarded that train for Boston had been the lowest of his life. He couldn't go through that again. He *wouldn't* put himself in a position for that sort of pain again.

"If your employer won't listen to reason, I'll refuse to work with her." Warming to the idea, he gave a firm nod. "It's the simplest solution. Quick, efficient and…" He shot Molly a pointed look. "Honest."

"Yes, yes." She brushed his comment impatiently aside with a flick of her fingers. "You do realize she's already made up her mind? You quit now and all you'll do is throw away an excellent opportunity to advance your career. Mrs. Singletary, on the other hand, will devise countless other ways to throw us together. She's very clever."

She wasn't the only one, he thought. Still, the widow hadn't amassed a large fortune by giving up in the face of opposition. That made her a formidable foe, and left them with few options. "I fear you may be right."

"Of course I'm right, you silly man." She tapped him playfully on the chest. "Come on, Garrett. Pretending to fall in love won't be so horrible. It might even be fun."

That remained to be seen. The fact that he wanted to kiss that teasing smile off her lips warned him to step back. Instead, he moved a fraction closer.

Obviously taking his silence for ascent, Molly beamed. "We'll set up a list of rules. That way we'll leave no room for misunderstanding when it's time for us to go our separate ways."

Garrett found himself actually contemplating the absurd idea. If he went into a courtship with Molly knowing the end would eventually come, perhaps...*yes, perhaps*... he could finally put the past behind him and move on with his life.

"You've convinced me. And just to show you how magnanimous I can be, I'll let you set the first rule, or rather the first variable. We'll treat this venture the same as one of your formulas."

The playful light in her eyes dimmed. "After what happened with Fanny this afternoon, you would trust one of my formulas?"

He winced at the unmistakable hurt in her tone. "It wasn't you, or your formula, that changed Fanny's mind about Reese."

"You think not?" She seemed to want more from him.

"You offered good, solid advice." He touched her sleeve, let go almost immediately. "I'm sorry I accused you otherwise."

"Thank you." Her smile returned, slowly at first, then came at him full force. "I appreciate you saying so."

His chest felt unnaturally tight. His breathing became short and thick and painful.

Was he actually agreeing to enter into a pretend romance with this woman? "Go on, Molly. Assign the first rule of our so-called courtship."

She thought for a moment, her eyes full of something he couldn't quite name. Mischief, yes, but something more, something that urged him to let down his guard, to take a chance, to forget all about correctness and simply...let...go.

Perhaps this wasn't a wise idea, after all.

"If we're going to do this," she said before he could find the words to beg off, "we do it right. No half measures. That's the first variable. We go all in."

"All in?"

"You know, like always, we jump into this venture with everything we've got, no holding back. Anything less and Mrs. Singletary will know we're only faking."

Garrett's chest cinched tighter. No good would come of this. And yet, he found himself saying, "Agreed."

Her entire countenance brightened. "Your turn. Set the next rule."

He swallowed, reminded himself this game of theirs was a means to an end, a way to regain control of a slippery situation that could easily get out of hand. "When we're in Mrs. Singletary's presence, we make every effort to watch one another when the other isn't looking."

"Very clever," she said. "I like that one a lot."

He did, too, especially since he already engaged in the practice. No matter how hard he tried to remain unmoved by Molly, he found himself watching her. Often. Almost all the time.

"Your turn," he said, swallowing.

"Let me see." She planted her hands on her hips, tapped her toe on the marble floor. *Tap, tap, tap.*

A mischievous light flickered across her gaze.

Garrett's heart sank. He knew that look. Trouble. She was about to throw them headlong into *trouble.* And not the good kind. Best to put an end to her shenanigans right now.

"No, Molly." He spoke very slowly, very deliberately. "Whatever you're thinking, stop right there."

She gave him a cheeky grin. "Variable number three—"

"I'm serious." He was also doomed. *Doomed.*

"Variable…number…three."

Garrett struggled to even out his breathing.

"We let Mrs. Singletary discover us kissing."

Madness. Utter madness. He'd never recover. He'd enjoy every minute—oh, yes, he would—but wasn't that the problem? This venture wasn't about fun. It was about control.

Rigid control. Holding tight to control, as he did in every area of his life.

Someone had to be the voice of reason. And that someone was him. He opened his mouth to set this woman straight, but Molly took his hand and pulled him close.

Every thought vanished from his mind.

"We should start now," she suggested in that sassy voice he'd dreamed about for far too many years after leaving home.

"Absolutely not."

She tugged him closer.

"Molly, no."

"Consider it practice."

They didn't need practice. Not this kind. "I'll set the third variable."

"It's already set." She took his other hand, wrapped both of his arms around her waist.

He froze. His fingers slowly flexed, once, twice. Then, he simply…let…go and relaxed his hands on her lower back. He was actually going to do this. He was going to kiss her.

There had to be a prayer to prevent this sort of disaster.

At the moment, he couldn't think of one. He couldn't think at all. Reaction took over and he tugged her closer still.

She lifted on her toes and placed her lips near his ear. "She's watching us. On your immediate left."

As if to confirm her words, Garrett heard a soft rustle of silk. Glancing out of the corner of his eye, he caught Mrs. Singletary ducking behind an oversize planter.

Something spread through him, something that made him feel reckless, and far too much like the daring boy he'd once been.

Mrs. Singletary wanted a show? He'd give her a show.

Heart thudding in his chest, Garrett blinked into Molly's

blue, blue eyes. A mistake. He felt the air constrict around them, as if some invisible force was pushing them together.

"Might as well make this look good…" he murmured, lowering his head toward hers.

Molly nestled deeper into Garrett's embrace as if she'd been waiting for this moment all her life, as if she'd been waiting for him all her life.

Not too far from the truth.

This is just pretend, she reminded herself. A ruse to keep Mrs. Singletary from pushing them into a relationship neither of them wanted.

Or rather, a relationship one of them didn't want. Molly didn't have quite the same aversion as Garrett seemed to have.

His head lifted slightly away from hers.

Had he changed his mind? Was he not going to kiss her, after all? The thought no more materialized than his mouth closed over hers.

A sigh worked its way up from the bottom of her toes and stalled in her throat.

Why did this kiss have to feel so…right?

Only pretend.

A clock chimed from somewhere in the house, announcing the hour. Midnight. The start of a new day.

A new beginning, a new—

Garrett broke the kiss and stepped back. Nothing but air stood between them now.

And a whole lot of history.

Molly gulped. "I…" She lost track of what she'd intended to say.

What could she say?

That their kiss had felt real? That this *moment* felt real?

At least Garrett looked as shaken as she felt. But then he

gave a slow blink, visibly fought off a shudder and cleared his expression completely. "That should convince her."

Oh. Yes. They'd put on this little show for Mrs. Singletary's benefit. "Is she still watching us?"

His gaze darted to a spot over her shoulder. "Yes."

Looking quite weary, he gathered Molly against him. He was going to kiss her? *Again?*

But they still had to decide on variable number four. Although...since they were already here...

She slid her arms around his neck.

Anticipation welled up in her and she closed her eyes. Waited.

Instead of lowering his lips to hers, Garrett pressed them against her ear.

"Your employer is a blatant eavesdropper."

His voice sounded amused.

Her heart plummeted and she forced out a short laugh. "We all have our weaknesses."

"Is that so?" he whispered in her ear. "What's your greatest weakness, Molly?"

You. This. Us. None of which were responses she cared to share with him. Ever. "Who says I have one?"

He laughed softly, the sound rumbling from deep within his chest. "Oh, you have one, possibly even two. But right now you're safe to keep them to yourself." He unwound his arms from her waist. "She's gone. Good night, Molly."

He pressed a brief kiss to her forehead and left her standing alone in the entryway, her heart in her throat, her breathing hitched.

Before she could review any of what had just happened between them, Mrs. Singletary called out her name.

Molly turned at the sound. The widow had moved to the second floor and now hovered over the balcony, innocence exemplified. "Before you run off to bed, I'd like a quick word. Join me in the drawing room, will you?"

"Of course."

Head fuzzy, knees weak, Molly commandeered the stairs at a slow, steady pace. When she entered the drawing room, her employer ushered her into the empty seat beside her.

At the same moment Molly sat, Mrs. Singletary took her hand. "You, my dear, have not been completely honest with me."

She softened the reproach with a gentle smile.

"No, I suppose not." Wasn't withholding pertinent information the same as lying?

"You allowed me to think Mr. Mitchell was nothing special to you, that he was merely the brother of your friends." She released Molly's hand. "But you both admitted here tonight that you were once close. I wonder. Just how close were you?"

Realizing further evasion was useless, Molly skimmed a stray hair off her face. "We were in love. But it was a long time ago. Seven years, to be exact."

"Young love can be very…trying."

"Though we'd been friends first, we didn't fall in love gradually, nothing so simple. It was as if lightning struck. We were really good as a couple, even better than we'd been as friends. But what had started out strong—" a shiver moved along her spine "—ended just as quickly."

"So it ended badly." It wasn't posed as a question, but Mrs. Singletary seemed to be waiting for an answer.

"That would be an accurate statement." If she'd been the whimpering type, she would do so now. The horrible words they'd flung at one another were as fresh in her mind as when they'd first been uttered. "There was so much anger between us."

She could admit that now, could own up to the fact that she'd been full of hurt and pride, as unwilling to ask Garrett to stay as he'd been to ask her to become his wife and leave town with him.

What if he'd have asked?

Would she have gone with him?

Yes.

Maybe.

She didn't know. God help her. She didn't know.

A sob stole up her throat. She pressed her lips together to prevent its exit.

"Molly, don't torture yourself like this. You were only a child at the time."

"Not that young. We were both old enough to know what we wanted out of life. I wanted Garrett. He wanted to make a name for himself, prove he was equal to his older brothers. I encouraged him to go away to school. And he did. Without me."

"Did you promise to wait for his return?"

She shook her head. "I wanted *him* to ask *me*. I thought he might. I really thought he would. But he didn't. He just… left."

"Did you ask him to stay?"

"No." She shook her head again. "He needed to leave so he could make his own way in the world. I couldn't ask him to choose between me and the future I believed the Lord was calling him to."

Mrs. Singletary touched her arm. "Do you still love him?"

Did it matter? She'd been so hurt, so lonely after Garrett had left, she'd accepted two offers of marriage. Two terrible missteps.

Garrett had made none.

"It's too late," she muttered half to herself.

"It's never too late," Mrs. Singletary said gently. "I know all might seem lost, but I truly believe the Lord has a very special plan in store for you. One He's already set in motion. You will soon be happily settled."

What a wonderful, hopeless thought.

"Perhaps I'm not capable of loving with my entire heart," she said, revealing her darkest fear in that smattering of words.

"Oh, Molly, you dear, dear girl." Mrs. Singletary pulled her into her arms and held tight. "You are a beautiful, treasured child of God, full of kindness and compassion and, yes, love."

Molly laid her head on the widow's shoulder and sniffed, the ache in her throat making words impossible.

"As you yourself always say, we love because God first loved us," Mrs. Singletary reminded her. "You should listen to your own advice."

A spark of hope ignited, the flame nothing more than a glowing ember. "You really think I'm capable of loving a man the way you loved your Mr. Singletary?"

"I have no doubt." She set Molly away from her, stared intently into her eyes. "I'm going to make you a promise, my dear. One I have every intention of keeping."

Not sure what to expect, Molly gave a vague smile.

"Upon my word, your next engagement shall be your last."

Chapter Nine

Calling himself all kinds of fool, Garrett entered the newly renovated Hotel Dupree with a hard shove to the heavy, ornate door. His feet felt unnaturally leaden as he slogged into the large atrium recently added to the majestic building.

His thoughts in turmoil, he shifted his gaze to the right, to the left, back to the right. But no matter how much he studied the elegant lobby, his mind refused to settle.

Was it any wonder?

When he'd left for work this morning, his life had been on a calm, predictable course. His sister had been engaged to a good, decent man and Molly had been exactly where she belonged. In the past.

A mere handful of hours later, Fanny was no longer engaged to Reese, Molly was back in Garrett's life with a vengeance and he'd lost a large portion of his renowned control.

One kiss, one soul-twisting, ill-thought-out kiss, and his guts were tied up in knots within knots. He'd gone years without experiencing the sensation. He'd planned to go several more. Say, fifty.

He should have taken the job in St. Louis.

Riding the edge of temper, he moved deeper into the lobby, noted he had the area to himself.

Good. He wanted to be alone. He was used to being alone. He *liked* being alone.

Regardless of what Mrs. Singletary had intimated with her adroit line of questioning, Garrett was comfortable with his own company. He was a thinking man by nature, or was now, best suited to putting words on a page and unraveling complicated legal language.

He squared his shoulders and veered in the direction of the elevators, perfectly content to face the rest of the evening *alone*.

He hardly noticed the rich fabrics on the furniture he passed by, or the expensive mahogany paneling on the walls, or the polished marble floors beneath his feet.

Overall, the hotel's décor was too lavish for his taste. A men's boardinghouse would have suited his needs just fine, but as an associate in a prestigious law firm he was required to project a certain image.

Eventually, Garrett would buy a house of his own. Not yet, though. A house needed a family. And a family started with a wife. Garrett had no intention of marrying anytime soon. Of course, if Mrs. Singletary had her way, he'd be married off in a month, and his future bride would be Molly.

Molly.

At one time, she would have been his pick, too.

You are not going to fall for her again, he told himself firmly. *You came home to be near family, not Molly.*

Not Molly.

He nearly had himself convinced when he caught sight of a familiar blond head bent over the reception desk. "Fanny?"

She lifted her chin, grimaced. "Hello, Garrett."

Her eyes were as sad as they'd been this afternoon. And he felt just as helpless in the face of all that pain. Frustration made his voice sound hollow. "What are you doing here?"

"I should think that obvious." A similar hint of annoyance flattened her tone. "I'm working."

Her answer only increased his confusion. "At this hour?" He dipped his hands in his pockets. "You never take the evening shift."

Her shoulders moved in a gesture of careless indifference. "The new owner is arriving in a few days. I thought I'd get the books in order."

"It couldn't have waited until tomorrow?"

"No."

He held her stare.

"Oh, all right, if you must know." She placed her pencil carefully on the counter. "I couldn't bear another moment in the boardinghouse. The walls were closing in on me."

There was something in her eyes, something that looked like suppressed anger mixed with equal parts frustration and female impatience.

"Did Callie go too far, say something she shouldn't have?"

The question set off Fanny's temper like a match to a tinderbox. "She's convinced I'm making a mistake." Her shoulders slumped forward. "What does she know about mistakes? Callie always does the right thing and makes the right decision."

So had Fanny. Until today. "Take a break," he urged.

She hesitated a beat. Then her expression closed. "I can't…I'm really busy." She picked up her pencil and concentrated on the ledger beneath her hand. "Everything must be in order for Mr. Hawkins's arrival."

"He isn't due for several days yet, you said so yourself." Garrett gentled his tone. "Come on, Fanny. Give me a couple of minutes."

She twirled the pencil between her fingers and sighed impatiently. "You're not going to let this alone, are you?"

"No." It wasn't the Mitchell way. They went at problems

head-on, no pulling punches. As a whole, they were honest to a fault. *Let your yes be yes and your no be no.* "We can talk right here if you'd like."

"Not here. Over there." She pointed at a spot behind him. "Near the windows facing the mountains. Just let me tell my manager where I'll be."

"Good enough."

Not one for cooling his heels, another Mitchell trait, Garrett made his way to the area she'd indicated. Although covered in an elegant brocade pattern of swirling golds, greens and blues, the chair he chose was surprisingly comfortable.

He fought back a yawn. It had been a long, eventful day.

Fanny joined him just before he nodded off. She sat in the chair directly facing his.

"I attended the opera this evening with Molly," he said without preamble, stretching out his legs. "She told me a little about what's going on with you."

"And she told *me* about Mrs. Singletary's business proposition." Fanny angled her head, switching the focus to him.

He decided to let her. For the time being.

"I take it tonight was a trial run," she said. "An attempt, of sorts, to see if you met the widow's expectations."

So many ways to respond, he decided to answer with a one-shoulder shrug.

"Did you pass her test?"

He gave a sardonic snort. "Oh, I passed."

But not for the reasons Fanny intimated.

"I'm glad." Fanny's eyes filled with sisterly pride and affection. "You've earned this chance to prove your value to your firm."

He thought of Mrs. Singletary's machinations tonight, the ones that had nothing to do with his position at Bennett, Bennett and Brand. "The coming days should prove interesting."

And then some.

"What about you and Molly?" Fanny asked in a deceptively innocent voice. "Are you two going to be able to bear one another's company on a daily basis?"

His mouth thinned and, not for the first time that night, he struggled to even out his breathing. He and Molly had certainly found themselves in each other's arms quickly enough, and now they were set to begin "courting" soon, perhaps even tomorrow.

"Molly and I have come to an understanding." And that was all he planned to say on the matter.

"I'm glad. Oh, Garrett, I'm so very glad for you both." Fanny covered his hand with hers. "It never felt right, you know, the way you two avoided one another at family gatherings, pretending the other didn't exist."

Perhaps not.

"I'm not here to talk about Molly and me. I want to talk about you, Fanny." He pulled his hand out from beneath hers and placed his on top. "Tell me what I can do to help you through the next few days."

Her eyes narrowed. "You're actually offering me your support."

"Is that so hard to believe?"

"You're not going to tell me it's my own fault I'm in this position, and that I'm making a mistake?"

"Are you making a mistake?"

"No." She choked out the word. *"No,"* she repeated with more conviction. "Reese deserves to marry a woman who is more than a pretty, perfectly coifed addition to his home."

"You're more than that, Fanny. Much more."

"I wish I could be certain." A look of stark fear filled her gaze. "What if there's nothing behind my pretty face, proper manners and exquisite sense of style? What if my beauty is all I am?"

Eyes wide, her hand flew to her mouth, as if she hadn't meant to speak so plainly.

"You're more than a pretty face," Garrett reiterated, not sure how to convince her that her thinking was flawed. Fanny was smart, funny and accomplished. She was even fluent in four languages.

Looking miserable, but steadier now, she lowered her hand from her mouth and pressed it to her stomach. "I have to find out, Garrett. I have to discover who I am underneath the veneer I've presented to the world all my life."

"You should tell Reese what you just told me. You might be surprised what you discover. He's a good man, Fanny, one of the best I know."

She buried her face in her hands. "I never meant to hurt him."

"Maybe not. But, Fanny, you did. And now he deserves an explanation. It must come from you."

"I know. I know." She lowered her hands and drew in a calming breath. "I'll speak with him tomorrow."

"That would be wise." Garrett sat back. He could have said more, probably should have said more, something about the need to tell the rest of the family her final decision.

But first, she needed to speak with Reese. He might be able to change her mind. If that's what they both wanted.

"Thank you, Garrett. For listening and not judging me." She gave him a watery smile. "You're a good brother."

"'Bout time you said so."

She laughed at that, as he knew she would. "I know you're feeling out of control and confused, but Molly gave you sound advice. Turn to God, Fanny, pray for His guidance and all will turn out well."

"You may be right."

"I am right."

Laughing through her tears, she swiped her fingers across her cheeks. "If you and Molly can come to an understanding, then surely Reese and I can, as well."

Garrett gave a noncommittal response, not sure if his relationship with Molly was the model Fanny should be emulating.

They might have come to an understanding tonight, but that didn't mean he and Molly had put their differences behind them.

Or had they?

Garrett thought about how easily she'd slipped into his arms less than an hour ago, how right she'd felt there. And then there was that kiss. When their lips had met, it felt more like a step toward the future rather than a journey back to the past.

Perhaps he and Molly were on the road toward a new relationship, a more mature one.

Would it last?

Only time would tell.

Molly woke the next day with gritty eyes and an aching head. She'd snatched a few, restless hours of sleep in the wee hours of the morning, just enough to restore her common sense. But not enough to erase Garrett Mitchell completely from her thoughts.

As if to torture her, his image slid through her mind once again. Groaning, she flipped onto her stomach and covered her head with her pillow.

Why had she come up with the idea of a fake romance with the man? Only trouble lay down that road, and not the kind either of them wanted.

Still, she couldn't help but admit that she was excited. Today she and Garrett would begin their courtship, or rather their *pretend* courtship.

Filled with anticipation, she tossed off the covers and scrambled out of bed. After months of wallowing in despair she felt like her old self again, as if her joy and laughter were returning. No matter the reason, the change was a good one, and cause for gratitude.

Thank You, Lord.

Dressing for the day, her fingers trembling just a bit, Molly donned a lavender dress with silver trim and mother-of-pearl buttons on the bodice. She was just securing the laces on her matching ankle boots, when Mrs. Singletary popped her head into the room.

"Good morning, dear."

Molly leaped to her feet. "Am I late for breakfast?"

"Not at all." Her employer smiled with genuine affection, then narrowed her eyes as she studied Molly's face more closely. "You didn't sleep well?"

Guilt skittered up Molly's spine. As Mrs. Singletary's companion it was her job to worry about the widow, not the other way around. "I slept splendidly."

"If you say so." Much to Molly's relief, Mrs. Singletary didn't argue any further. She simply turned around and headed down the hallway without a backward glance.

Molly followed her into the morning room. The housekeeper had already delivered a tray laden with pastries, coffee and a soft-boiled egg for each of them. As they did most mornings, they tucked into the meal in companionable silence.

Halfway through, Mrs. Singletary made her first request of the day. "I need you to run an errand for me this morning."

Molly stopped chewing.

"After you finish your breakfast, of course. Go on, dear. Continue eating."

She obligingly swallowed, then took another bite of pastry. The sweet, creamy filling was a delightful surprise. She'd been expecting fruit.

"You mentioned an errand?" she said, lifting the pastry for another bite.

"I need you to run some papers over to the law firm."

Molly's hand froze. Mrs. Singletary was sending her to the law firm, when she'd never done so before. "I thought Garrett said he wouldn't be available until this afternoon."

"I wasn't referring to him." An amused smirk lifted the corners of the widow's mouth. "The papers are for my other attorney, Mr. Bennett."

"Oh…of course."

Not quite able to hide her satisfaction in Molly's telling mistake, Mrs. Singletary's smirk turned into a cagey grin. She looked very pleased with herself. "Are you going to finish your pastry, dear?"

"Pardon me?"

The widow pointed to the confection in Molly's hand.

"Oh." Her cheeks heating, she took another bite.

"Now. About the hats I purchased yesterday." The widow smoothly changed the subject. "I'm thinking we will need additional ribbon to make them presentable. You will make the necessary purchases on your way home from the law firm."

"It'll be my pleasure." Molly fell into the discussion with ease, mulling over colors, widths and potential styles with the widow. She suggested several changes to each hat, most of which Mrs. Singletary approved.

When they came to a point of contention, her employer bowed to Molly's judgment. "I'll let you make the final decision."

They finished their breakfast on that happy note.

Setting her napkin aside, Mrs. Singletary rose from her chair and smoothed out her skirt. "The carriage is waiting for you outside. Winston has placed the papers you are to deliver on the seat. I can't stress enough that they are of the utmost importance. Make sure you put them in Mr. Bennett's hands directly."

"Yes, Mrs. Singletary."

"Off you go, now." She gave Molly a brisk wave of her hand. "We'll begin work on the hats once you return."

Fifteen minutes later, dressed for the cold mountain air in a warm, serviceable coat and thick woolen gloves, Molly climbed into the waiting carriage.

She tried not to get too excited over the possibility of running into Garrett at the law firm. He'd claimed he had an appointment this morning. There was a good chance she wouldn't see him at all.

Oh, please, Lord, let Your will be done. If I'm meant to see Garrett this morning let it be so.

As prayers went, it was simple and, admittedly, selfish. She repeated the request several more times, muttering the last one aloud and with great feeling.

"Put your signature here." Garrett pointed to the line at the bottom of the page. "And here." He indicated the same spot on the duplicate copy.

While Phineas Phipps scrawled his name with unnecessary flourish, Garrett swallowed back a sigh of relief. The older gentleman, with his shiny bald pate and overfed belly, was a difficult client on a good day, impossible all the others. Their meeting this morning had fallen among the latter.

Garrett's head pounded with tension. He discreetly drilled a hole in his temple in an attempt to relieve the pressure.

Although he'd assured Mr. Phipps that he'd addressed every one of the man's concerns, the successful miner had reviewed every clause. Twice. Consequently, their meeting had lasted an hour longer than necessary. Prepared for this eventuality, Garrett had scheduled his morning accordingly.

"I appreciate your attention to detail, my boy." Mr. Phipps straightened. "I'm quite pleased with the result."

"As am I." Garrett had perfected every bit of the language himself.

He gathered the pages together in two separate piles, keeping one on his desk and handing the other to his client. "This is your copy."

Taking the stack, Mr. Phipps finally cracked a smile. The gesture revealed a gold incisor made from his personal stock. "I thank you, again. You do your family name proud."

Trying not to react to the indirect mention of the man's friendship with his father, Garrett discarded his first response, and reminded himself why he'd chosen to work in Denver instead of any number of other cities. "Allow me to walk you out."

He led the way to the reception area, caught Mr. Summers's eye and gave the man an imperceptible nod. His clerk disappeared inside the cloakroom. He reappeared almost immediately with Mr. Phipps's topcoat and hat.

While he helped his client into the superbly tailored outerwear, Garrett noticed a familiar carriage draw to a halt directly in line with the front door. He knew that petite frame exiting onto the sidewalk, noted that she was alone.

Like well-trained soldiers, the hairs on the back of his neck stood at attention.

"Good day, Garrett."

He managed a nod. "Good day, sir."

As Mr. Phipps exited the building through the door on the right, Molly entered through the one on the left.

She paused on the threshold and blinked rapidly, as if her eyes weren't yet accustomed to the change in light.

This gave Garrett a chance to study her uninterrupted. She wore no hat, which was unusual for her and a welcome change. The lack of adornment allowed him to take in the soft slope of her cheek, the tiny bow of her mouth and the perfectly arched eyebrows.

His mouth went dry as dust.

The dull gray coat she wore would make most women

look dowdy. However, on Molly, the bland color allowed her inner light to shine. She was dazzling, her stunning face as bright and welcoming as the sun peeking out of a dingy cloud on a cold, blustery day.

Her vision seemingly adjusted, she entered the large reception area where Garrett stood unmoving, his gaze still transfixed on her. When she saw him, her footsteps halted and her mouth formed a perfect *O*.

His own mouth compressed into a grim line.

He'd been kidding himself all morning, imagining he was immune to this woman's charms. He doubted he would find any level of peace in the coming days. Not with him openly courting her. *Uh...pretending to court her.*

He needed to get that straight in his mind.

Setting strict parameters to their relationship should have given him a sense of control. A ridiculous illusion.

Caught in the snare of her gaze, Garrett admitted the truth to himself at last. He still had feelings for Molly.

And they had nothing to do with friendship.

Chapter Ten

I'm still besotted with Molly?

Garrett recoiled at the possibility. He'd had seven years to come to his senses, seven long, lonely years to forget she'd ever been in his heart. He came home to be near his family, he reminded himself.

He was tired, working on too little sleep. Surely that explained his visceral reaction now.

Right. He'd moved on, he assured himself, put the past behind him. Yet when he spoke, his voice rasped with emotion. "Hello, Molly."

"Garrett." His name sounded like a soft whisper wrapped inside that same, achingly familiar tone she'd adopted last night. "I hadn't expected to run into you this morning. I believe you said you had an appointment?"

He nearly smiled at the knowing look she leveled over him. "The gentleman just left."

"Ah. I see." She rolled her gloved hands over on another, again and again and again. She was nervous.

And he was confused. "Why are you here, Molly?"

Her eyes widened at his abrupt tone.

He repeated the question more gently.

"Mrs. Singletary sent me to deliver these papers to her attorney." She lifted the leather satchel hooked around her wrist. When he reached for it, she drew it out of reach. "These are for Mr. Bennett. I'm to deliver them into his hands, personally."

His eyebrows pulled together. "Mrs. Singletary has never sent you to deliver correspondence before."

"I think," she lowered her voice for his ears only, "she hoped we would run into one another."

Indeed. "Beatrix Singletary is a very determined lady."

"Very."

They laughed together, the sound reminiscent of better days, when laughing had come easier for them both.

"Come on, then." He took her hand without thinking, as he would have done when they were children. "Reese is in his office. I'll take you back myself."

She curled her fingers around his. "I appreciate your assistance."

As they passed by the reception desk, Molly's steps slowed. "Good morning, Julian."

The clerk's face turned bright red. "Goo—good morning, Miss Scott." He swallowed several times, sending his Adam's apple bobbing up and down. "It's always a pleasure to see you."

"And you, as well."

Garrett almost felt sorry for the poor love-struck fellow, but not enough to release Molly's hand. Now that he had hold of her, he wasn't letting her go.

Not until he absolutely had to.

Savoring the feel of her hand in his, Garrett readjusted his grip, waited for her to finish her conversation with his clerk, then pulled her into the hallway leading to Reese's office.

After only a few steps, Molly tugged him to a halt. "Before we continue, I was wondering. Have you spoken with Reese today, you know, about…Fanny?"

"I tried." Garrett turned to face her. "He wasn't in a talkative mood."

"Pity."

"I had better success with Fanny."

This seemed to surprise her. "You spoke with your sister this morning?"

"Last night."

Her brow wrinkled in confusion.

"At the hotel," he explained. "She'd taken the night shift."

"She never works the night shift."

Garrett lifted a shoulder. "She claimed she wanted the distraction."

"Now that makes sense."

They fell silent.

"Thank you, Molly."

She angled her head at him. "For what?"

"For explaining Fanny's point of view so succinctly last night." He took her other hand and pulled her closer. "I was able to have an honest conversation with her, and I think it might have helped."

"Oh, Garrett." Molly's fingers braided themselves through his. "That's really good news. Whatever happens next, she needs to know her family will stand by her."

"I'm only one Mitchell," he pointed out.

"The rest will come around. You'll make sure of it."

Her confidence in him did strange things to his insides. His gut churned with unexpected longing, and an unexpected emotion: hope.

"You don't have to continue holding on to me when no one else is around." She tugged her hands free. "Our agreement doesn't require us to act as though we're falling in love when we're alone."

"Right." He'd have to think about that some more, when his head was clearer. Didn't seem right, somehow, not touching her. And if it didn't seem right that meant there was a flaw in the logic. A flaw in the logic meant a loophole somewhere.

Garrett always found the loophole.

In the meantime, he directed Molly down the hall once again.

In thoughtful silence, she studied the portraits of mature, stodgy-looking men lining both walls. Most of the likenesses belonged to lawyers with the last name Bennett.

The final portrait on the right stood out from the rest primarily because of the youthful features. With his black hair, dark, serious eyes and stern expression, Reese Bennett, Jr. looked overly determined, as if he wouldn't rest until the job was done to his satisfaction.

The artist had captured Reese's essence seamlessly. Garrett would have enjoyed welcoming the man into the family.

A few more steps and he knocked on his boss's door.

"Enter," came the reply from within.

Wanting to announce her properly, Garrett stepped in the room ahead of Molly.

Reese looked up from his desk. His eyes appeared even more tired than they'd been this morning. In fact, dark shadows had taken up residence beneath his lower lashes.

"You need me for something?"

"Mrs. Singletary's companion is here to see you."

Reese stood. "Send her in."

Garrett waved Molly into the room.

"Miss Scott." Reese moved out from around his desk and approached her. "What a nice surprise. I wasn't expecting you this morning."

"I hope I'm not intruding."

"Not at all." Reese's eyes lit with genuine pleasure. "You are always welcome in this office."

"I'm glad, but I won't keep you long. I've brought you

these." She handed over the satchel. "Mrs. Singletary told me to deliver them to you personally."

"And now you have." Reese finally smiled. "Thank you."

"You're welcome. I'll leave you to your work." She turned to go.

"Miss Scott?"

She glanced at him over her shoulder. "Yes?"

"How is…" He shook his head, as if he were at a complete loss for words. A rarity for the always controlled attorney. "That is…I wanted to know if Fanny is…never mind." He drew in a ragged breath. "Have a good day, Miss Scott."

Molly lingered a moment longer, turning to face Reese directly instead of taking her leave. She released a sigh. "Mr. Bennett, you should know, Fanny never meant to hurt you."

"I never doubted that for a moment." He raked a hand through his hair. "I wouldn't want to think she's suffering. If you see her before I do, Miss Scott, would you let her know I'm worried about her?"

"Consider it done."

"Thank you." Reese swept his gaze over to Garrett. "Did you need anything else?"

"Not at the moment. I'll see Molly out."

Leveling his shoulders, Reese nodded. "Very good."

Garrett escorted Molly into the hallway and shut the door behind them with a soft click.

"He's sad," she said simply.

"I caught that."

She continued staring at the shut door, pondering the wood with thoughtful consideration. "But not heartbroken."

How could she know that? Garrett wondered.

"No," she said, confirming her assessment with a firm nod of her head. "Definitely not heartbroken."

Garrett felt his eyebrows travel to his hairline. "He seemed upset to me."

"Oh, his pride is hurt." Her gaze stayed glued to the door. "He's also embarrassed, baffled and definitely concerned for Fanny's welfare. But his heart is still fully intact."

Again, Garrett wondered at her confidence. "How can you know that for certain?"

"I—" she lowered her gaze "—just…know."

Molly could feel Garrett's eyes on her. The rational thing to do would be to continue down the hall, out the door and straight into Mrs. Singletary's waiting carriage.

Unfortunately, when it came to Garrett Mitchell, Molly rarely did the rational thing.

"Stop it," she said to him.

"Stop what?"

"You're thinking so loud it's hurting my ears."

He chuckled.

Oh, he thought this was amusing? She turned to face him, caught his smile and went instantly on the offense. "Want me to tell you what you're thinking?"

His smile disappeared. "Not particularly, no."

She advanced on him, just a step, enough to make her point.

From the way his mouth thinned, she knew she'd succeeded.

"We used to be able to read one another's minds," she said.

"I remember."

She advanced another step.

His lips twisted at a wry angle, but he held his ground. Stubborn man. She'd always liked that about him.

"You're thinking—" she tapped a fingertip to his chin "—that it's a shame Fanny and Reese won't be getting back together."

"Not even remotely close." A corner of his mouth lifted. "Of course, you already know that, don't you?"

Oh, she knew he wasn't thinking about his sister. Or Reese. Or the work he still had to complete before his meeting this afternoon with Mrs. Singletary.

No, Garrett was thinking about her, wondering if Molly had broken her fiancés' hearts and that's how she knew Reese had escaped a similar fate.

"The answer to your question is no."

He quirked an eyebrow.

"No," she repeated, fighting off a sudden wave of humiliation. Why was she telling him this? Why this compulsion to share her secret?

Because this was Garrett.

"My former fiancés were not heartbroken after they broke off—" She stopped herself, realizing her mistake a shade too late. "I mean, after *I* broke off our engagements."

For a long, tense moment, he went utterly still, his eyes locked with hers. "You just said *they.* Molly, did you end your engagements? Or did they?"

Oh, boy. Was it time? she thought. Time to give up the charade? Time to face up to the fact that she'd allowed the people closest to her—including Garrett—to believe a lie?

"Tell me the truth."

"I...that is, *we*..."

"Wait. Let's talk in my office where we won't be disturbed." He tugged her into the room and closed the door behind them.

Alone. They were completely, utterly, irrefutably alone. The smells of parchment and ink and something purely male wafted on the air, driving home the point that it was *just the two of them,* not a single other person to see—or hear—them.

There were a lot of ways the next few minutes could go, all of them troublesome. Especially since Garrett looked decidedly grim as he hovered over her, his gaze dark and unwavering. They hadn't had this much uninterrupted eye contact since he'd left for school seven years ago.

Making a sound deep in his throat, he leaned forward, his handsome face full of intensity and resolve.

Glory. That was one determined man looking at her.

She hated not knowing what was going on inside his head, hated wondering if this was the end of her carefully constructed charade.

"We're going to do something we've put off for far too long." His voice came out grave. "No more stalling, no more avoiding the inevitable."

He looked so serious.

"It's time we had a good, long…"

Her heart skipped a beat.

"…talk."

And another.

"When I say *talk,* Molly…" He pushed slightly away from her. "I mean I want you to tell me about your engagements."

"We really don't have to do this now."

"Yes, we do."

Oh, please, Lord. Anything but this. Anytime but now.

She couldn't bear the thought of expressing her hidden shame out loud. Not to Garrett.

Anyone but him.

Smiling tenderly, as if understanding her trepidation better than she did herself, he reached up and smoothed a stray strand of hair off her forehead. "No judgment, Molly, no condemnation. I want the truth. I *need* the truth."

She watched him slide the lawyer in place and shivered in dread. "Oh, Garrett, please don't ask this of me."

"Do you think it'll be easy for me to hear about you and those other men?"

"I…I don't know. Will it?"

"Not in the slightest. But it's long past time we stopped

avoiding one another and settled this like two grown, mature adults." He spoke in a tone that denoted friendship first, always, *forever.* "That's it. I'm setting variable number four, right now."

"You…what? I don't understand."

"Our pretend courtship," he reminded her. "We haven't come up with the final parameter."

When she simply blinked at him, he placed his hand on her shoulder. "Your formulas always have four variables. We've only agreed to three."

How could she have forgotten something so crucial?

"Variable number four," he said with none of the playfulness of the night before. "We talk honestly about the past, no matter how much it hurts. We hold nothing back, no hedging, no glossing over important details."

She said nothing. She couldn't. He'd left her speechless.

"And once we've cleared up any misunderstanding between us, we'll never speak of the past again. Agreed?"

"I…" He was right. They needed to have this conversation. But did they have to discuss this now? She needed time to prepare.

"Molly? You with me on this?"

She released a shuddering sigh. "Yes."

"Good, but we aren't going to have this conversation here." He reached around her and twisted open the door.

"We aren't?" Dare she hope for a reprieve?

"You shouldn't be shut in a room with me longer than a few minutes at a time, not without the benefit of a chaperone."

"You're worried about my reputation?"

"I am."

How…sweet.

And completely unnecessary. For all intents and purposes, she had no reputation worth protecting. She was the daughter of a prostitute-turned-madam. She'd been raised by a sister many still believed to be her natural mother. People who knew the truth about her parentage also knew her real father had been a down-on-his-luck miner who'd squandered his life savings on a gold rush that had come to naught.

Even without all those strikes against her, she had two broken engagements behind her. "My reputation isn't my greatest concern."

"It's important to me."

And wasn't that just like Garrett? A gentleman to his very core.

He ushered her back into the hallway. "What are your plans for the rest of the morning?"

Hope for that reprieve returned. "I'm supposed to purchase additional ribbon for Mrs. Singletary's new hats."

"Exciting." His tone said otherwise. Molly fought back a smile. Garrett disliked shopping almost as much as the opera.

"Mrs. Singletary is expecting me to go straight home afterward."

He didn't respond right away as he guided her through the reception area and out onto the sidewalk. The cold air whipped across her face, chaffing at her cheeks. She huddled deeper in her coat.

The busy street bustled with activity. The shout of vendors' cries joined with the high-pitched voice of a mother telling her brood to settle down as they crossed the street.

Garrett took her arm and led her toward the waiting carriage. "Have an early lunch with me before you proceed to the millinery shop."

She balked. She'd really rather not… "Mrs. Singletary will be wondering where I am."

"Once he's dropped us off, I'll send the carriage driver to tell her where we are." He grinned. "She'll understand why you're late when she finds out who you're dining with."

He had a point. "She'll think it a great coup," Molly admitted reluctantly.

"Superior line of thinking. Now, up you go." He handed her into the carriage before heading over to speak to the driver, presumably to explain the change in plans.

Moments later, the carriage dipped under Garrett's added weight as he joined her inside and settled in the opposite seat facing her. Seemingly lost in his own thoughts, Molly took the opportunity to gather hers.

Barely five minutes into the process and the carriage drew to a stop once again.

"We're here."

She pushed aside the green velvet curtain and peered out the window. "Where, exactly, is here?"

"The Brown Palace." Garrett exited the carriage first, then helped her onto the sidewalk. "We might as well enjoy the best food in town while we have our conversation."

"You sure you don't want to change your mind about this?"

"I'm sure."

"It was worth a try," she muttered.

He cracked a smile. "Valiant effort, indeed." He waved her forward. "After you."

Sighing, Molly braced herself for the interrogation…er, the discussion that lay ahead. As soon as they entered the main dining room they were escorted to a table with the kind of deference reserved for favored customers.

Apparently, Garrett dined at The Brown Palace regularly. Did he bring his clients here for lunch?

Other young ladies?

She plopped into her chair without her usual grace.

Lifting an eyebrow, he picked up a menu. "Any idea what you want to eat?"

"You seem to be familiar with this restaurant." She

paused, smoothed out her tone, continued, "Why don't you order for us both?"

"All right." While Garrett told the waiter they'd each have the chicken and dumplings, Molly looked around.

Rivaled only by the Hotel Dupree, The Brown Palace was considered the height of fashion, the dining room no exception. Bone china graced every table. Engraved silverware was spread out at her fingertips. Even the finely dressed patrons added to the rich, expensive air.

Finished with her inspection, she waited for the waiter to disappear then swung her gaze back to Garrett. He was watching her intently, staring actually. Now that they were alone, he took her hand and twined their fingers together.

There was a look of tenderness in his gaze that made her slightly uneasy. How dare he look at her with all that affection, as if she mattered to him, as if it had been difficult for him to walk away from her?

A second time today, she went on the offense.

And cut straight to the heart of their rift. "You weren't much of a letter writer."

Seemingly indifferent to her accusatory tone, he lifted a shoulder. "Who is at seventeen?"

At least he wasn't pretending to misunderstand her meaning. "You managed to write your parents."

"I wrote my mother, actually, and I seem to remember sending one letter to her ten."

In his defense, that sounded like a boy at that age. Both of Molly's brothers were attending school in Boston. Neither had written in months.

That still didn't make Garrett's silence any less painful. Feeling vulnerable, and hating herself for it, she fought the urge to yank her hand free. "Why didn't you write?" she demanded.

"I didn't think you wanted to hear from me." He gave her a long look, perhaps challenging her to deny his words.

How could she? She hadn't wanted to hear from him. Not in the initial days after his departure, at any rate. She'd been too angry, too hurt. Then, her anger had turned to regret, which had morphed into unspeakable grief. How she had longed for a letter from him.

One letter, that's all she'd wanted.

What would she have done had he written?

Would she have answered? Or would her pride have been too strong?

She would never know.

"No, Garrett, I didn't want to hear from you. At first." She stared down at their linked fingers, remembered their agreement for total honesty and decided to give him the rest. "I didn't want to know how happy you were at school, how happy you were—" she swallowed "—without me."

Chapter Eleven

For a brief moment, Garrett considered Molly's words in silence. He kept his eyes trained on hers with unwavering resolve. Even when she gritted her teeth and fisted her free hand on the table, he held her gaze.

She stared right back, a silent accusation in her eyes and something else, something that spoke of sorrow, loss.

Clearly, this conversation was hard on her. Well, she wasn't the only one struggling with painful memories of their parting. He nearly ended their discussion right then, but reminded himself he was a Mitchell. Mitchells didn't run from difficulty, they faced it head-on.

He simply needed to remove his emotions from the equation and address their issues as an objective outsider.

No easy task.

The man he was now might understand why Molly hadn't wanted to hear from him after he'd left home. But the heartbroken, lonely boy of seventeen wanted no part in this discussion.

Garrett banished that prideful, lovesick kid from his mind and spoke with the honesty he'd requested of her. "I was miserable, especially in those early months." *Those early years.*

"You seemed happy enough to me." She snorted indelicately, a sure sign of her annoyance. "Your mother let me read your letters."

He readjusted his hold on her hand, but didn't let go. "All right, I was content. With school." *Honesty, old boy.* "But only school. Outside of class I was cheerless and lonely. I desperately missed…"

You.

He should tell her that, but he couldn't seem to push the truth past his lips. He'd missed Molly as much as a drowning man missed air. In fact, he'd nearly quit school ten times that first year, had even packed up once and headed to the train station.

But he'd stopped himself just short of boarding when he remembered her heart hadn't been his. It had belonged to his family.

"I missed home," he said at last, reluctantly releasing her hand when she tugged on it. "And you, Molly. I missed you most of all."

She dropped her chin, but not before he caught sight of her expression. Solemn. Grave.

Unhappy.

"I missed you, too," she whispered, looking up as she said the words. "So very much."

Not enough to wait for him, he thought with a pang, not enough to keep from falling in love with another man. *Two* other men.

And with that horrible thought he remembered the reason for his offer of lunch. "Tell me about your engagements, Molly."

She brushed a wisp of hair off her face. "What do you want to know?"

Everything. Nothing. "How did they start?" He swallowed past the thickness in his throat. "Why did they end?"

For a moment, she studied her curled hands as though

all the answers were in her fingertips. Then, she looked back up.

And straight into his eyes. "I need to explain my state of mind after you left first."

"All right."

As she opened her mouth to continue, their food arrived. There was a moment of jostling and rearranging of silverware before the waiter set the plates on the table. Straightening, he turned to Garrett and asked if they needed anything else.

"Thank you, no. That'll be all for now."

"Very good, sir." The young man glanced at Molly, stared at her a shade past polite.

She smiled. He smiled back, blinking rapidly, his gaze more than a little glassy-eyed.

Garrett cleared his throat.

The waiter hurried off.

For several moments, their food went untouched.

Molly set her palms on either side of her plate and leaned forward, her voice raw with emotion. "I was dreadfully lonely after you left."

Garrett's throat burned at her statement. When he spoke, his own voice came out rougher than usual. "Is that really how you felt?"

Every report from his mother had said otherwise.

"I know that probably doesn't make sense to you. I was surrounded by family and friends, after all. And I put on a good show. But no matter how hard I tried, I couldn't find joy in anything, or anyone." She lifted her hands in a helpless gesture. "It was as if a large, gaping hole had taken up residence in my very soul."

"Some would call that grief."

A sad smile played across her mouth. "They'd be right."

"Yeah, they would."

Losing Molly had felt like a death, as though he'd lost a

vital part of himself. He supposed he had. Molly had been more than a trusted friend, more than a confidant. She'd been his whole world. His entire life had revolved around her, around them.

And now, she was telling him she'd felt the same. Had he been wrong when he'd accused her of loving his family more than him?

"Oh, Garrett, try to understand. There came a point when I became tired of feeling sad. I wanted to feel whole again." She fixed her blue eyes on him and his heart broke at what he saw in her gaze. Sorrow. Regret. Guilt. "I *needed* to feel whole again."

He kept his face calm, even as he struggled with two undeniable, shocking truths. Molly's love for him had been real. And he'd hurt her terribly. "I'm sorry."

Acknowledging his apology with a brief nod, she continued. "I kept busy at first, attending plays, the opera. Church on Sundays. I also helped out at the Charity House School in my free time. I taught arithmetic, mostly."

He smiled at that, thinking about her gift with numbers and how much she loved children, and they her.

"I'd barely turned eighteen when Bart Williams took notice of me."

Garrett inhaled sharply at the name of her first fiancé, a man he'd once considered a good friend.

"I was flattered by all the attention he lavished on me, a little dazzled even." She picked up her fork, rolled it around in her fingers. "He was so much more sophisticated than most boys his age, well-educated and already running his family's store on his own."

True, Bart had been settled in his life by then. He'd known the course it would take when he was still in short pants. He'd also known Molly belonged to Garrett.

"Bart asked me to marry him after only three months of courting."

Something dark and furious moved through Garrett. Good old Bart hadn't wasted any time securing Molly's favor. Some friend.

This was your idea, he reminded himself again. "Go on," he urged.

Molly set the fork on the table and sighed. "I was shocked by his proposal. I didn't give him an answer right away. In truth, I kept putting him off."

"Why was that?"

"Because of you."

He blinked at her answer.

"You were home for Christmas, and I thought…I don't know…" She ran a fingertip across the fork tines. "I thought maybe enough time had passed and that we might be able to—"

"Reunite?"

She lifted a shoulder. "You weren't interested."

Oh, he'd been interested. But he'd also been angry she'd allowed Bart Williams to court her. Molly was supposed to have waited for him, Garrett thought. She was supposed to have been pining for *him*.

"You wouldn't even speak to me," she reminded him. "I tried, you know."

Yeah, he knew.

He shifted uncomfortably in his seat, recalling his actions that Christmas break. He'd been intentionally rude to Molly. His pride had been stronger than his sense, his heart still raw and bleeding. *No excuse,* he told himself.

"When Bart pushed for an answer, when he said I was the best thing that ever happened to him, I accepted his proposal." She shut her eyes a moment. "I liked being wanted, Garrett. And, well, he made me feel special, less—"

"Lonely?"

"Empty," she corrected.

"Did you love him?" Garrett wasn't sure he wanted to

know the answer, hadn't realized he'd been holding his breath until she responded with a firm shake of her head.

Her answer sent a shock of satisfaction through him, until he noted that her eyes had become two pools of watery distress.

"It's taken me a long time to realize my mistake," she confessed.

Garrett cocked his head back in inquiry. "What mistake?"

"I should have never accepted Bart's marriage proposal." Her eyes were huge and mournful. "I sought comfort from a human relationship instead of turning to the Lord to heal my pain."

Her honesty humbled him. And so he paid it back with some of the same. "I understand, Molly. I sought comfort in school, and then in work."

"That's different."

"It's exactly the same." Instead of turning to God for comfort during those dark days of loneliness and grief, Garrett had buried himself in work. Perhaps he still did. The thought didn't sit well. "So what happened between you and Bart?"

"He realized I didn't love him." She twisted her hands together in her lap. "He broke off the engagement. Marshall gave the same reason for ending our relationship, as well."

"Let me get this straight." Garrett felt his shoulders tense. "Both of your fiancés begged off, not you?"

"That's what I just said."

He understood her exasperation, recognized it as the same sensation running through him. "Why did you let everyone—" *me, especially,* "—believe you were the one to break off your engagements?"

"Does it matter?"

He jerked his head in a nod.

"Pride," she said simply.

Fair enough. But there was a portion of her story she'd left out, a portion that would always haunt him if he didn't seek the truth now. "Would you have married either man if they hadn't begged off first?"

Gaze tracking away from his, she didn't answer right away. Then, she nodded, looking as miserable as he'd ever seen her and, yeah, that made two of them.

Garrett squeezed his eyes shut for a second and then opened them. Too many emotions struggled for a foothold. Anger. Pain.

Jealousy.

He experienced far too much of the emotion in the past seven years, both then and now. He remembered the ache in his gut when he'd heard about Molly's engagements—both of them—and the joy he'd felt when he'd heard she'd called them off.

Except…she hadn't called them off.

She'd planned to follow through with her promise.

Why did that have to hurt so much?

"Garrett." Her voice trembled as she spoke his name. "I praise God every day that Bart and Marshall came to their senses. I'm *glad* I didn't marry either man."

And now he could add relief to the other emotions warring inside his head, mind-numbing relief.

"I should have never agreed to either proposal." Tears welled in her eyes. Tears she valiantly fought back with several hard blinks. "I'll have to live with that shame for the rest of my life."

"Molly. I'm sorry." He reached across the table and touched her arm. "I'm sorry your engagements didn't work out."

But that wasn't entirely true. The only thing he was sorry about was the sadness he saw in her gaze now. "As my mother is fond of saying, God's plan for our lives is always better than our own, even if we don't see it at the time."

"I always did like your mother. Your father, too." She gave him a sweet smile. "All your family, for that matter."

He kept his response short, but sincere. "I like your family, too."

She smiled at that, nodding in agreement.

"Working as Mrs. Singletary's companion has been a blessing. I might not have taken the position if my parents hadn't insisted."

He heard the love in Molly's voice as she spoke of her parents. Although her "mother" was actually Molly's half sister and Trey Scott was not her natural father, they'd loved Molly as their own. Their advice would have come from the heart.

"I'm pleased you took the job, too." To his surprise, Garrett really meant that. Had it not been for Mrs. Singletary's unprecedented interference in Molly's life, including her matchmaking efforts, then Garrett would still be avoiding her, and she him.

Instead, they'd come to an understanding they wouldn't have accomplished on their own. He could almost call Molly a friend again. *Except friends don't dream of kissing one another.*

Perhaps *friend* wasn't the right word.

He ran his fingertips down to her hand and brought her knuckles to his lips. "I wonder why she picked me for you."

Molly's cheeks turned a becoming pink. "She believes we're each other's soul mate, but we're too stubborn to admit it. Apparently, we need a nudge in the proper direction. By her."

Garrett's chest felt extra tight, compressing until he was forced to take a large pull of air or suffocate. "At least we're on to her game."

Relaxing for the first time since they'd arrived, Molly turned her palm around to meet his. "And that puts us in control."

"I do like being in control."

"I know."

His smile came quickly, as did hers.

This time, when the years melted away, Garrett didn't resist the shift in mood. He simply set out to enjoy a new level of kinship between him and Molly. Not as the children they'd once been, but as the man and woman they'd become.

Perhaps he'd come home for this—*for her*—after all. Perhaps the compulsion he'd felt to take the job at Bennett, Bennett and Brand had been the Lord's nudging and not his own doing. Perhaps he and Molly could find a way to start over, without the past standing between them.

Uncaring that the food had grown cold, he picked up his fork, dug into his chicken and dumplings.

"Garrett?" a familiar baritone called out from behind him.

"That you, little brother?" came another, equally familiar voice.

With deliberate slowness, Garrett set down his fork.

What were the odds that Hunter and Logan would turn up at The Brown Palace, in the middle of the day, when he and Molly were tentatively finding their way back to one another?

Just this once, Garrett had assumed he had Molly all to himself. But no.

Resigned, he rose from his chair and turned to face his older brothers.

Molly watched Garrett's shoulders stiffen by degrees. The closer his brothers got to their table, the more rigid his stance became. Hunter and Logan appeared far more relaxed than their little brother, and generally pleased to see him. Their big, welcoming Mitchell smiles were firmly set in place.

She wondered if Garrett was smiling, too, or scowling. With his back to her, she couldn't tell.

A sudden, dreadful thought occurred to her. Would the Mitchell brothers misunderstand this little impromptu lunch between her and Garrett? Would they think they were courting?

That's the general idea, a small voice whispered through her thoughts. *All part of the pretense.*

She realized too late that neither she nor Garrett had thought through their plan as well as they should have. Now they had to face two members of his family completely unprepared. And not just any two Mitchells, either. The most perceptive two of the bunch.

From beneath her lowered lashes, Molly followed their progress through the large dining room. They were of a similar height, both over six feet, with the same lean, long-limbed, muscular bodies as Garrett.

Their hair was the same color as Garrett's as well, a rich, sandy blond that stood in stark contrast against their tanned faces. Hunter, the older of the two, had tawny eyes like Garrett. Logan's were a pale, steel-blue.

When they stopped at the table, Molly smiled up into their handsome faces so similar to Garrett's. "Good afternoon Logan, Hunter."

"Hello, Molly. *Molly?*" As if they'd rehearsed this moment on the ride into town, their smiles dropped simultaneously into frowns. They swung their gazes to Garrett then back to her.

Eyes widening in surprise, Hunter found his voice before Logan. "You two are—together?"

"We're having lunch." Garrett spoke with uncharacteristic impatience in his voice. "And, no, it's none of your business how this came about."

"No, it's not." Laughing appreciatively, Hunter slapped him on the back and winked at Molly.

She grinned back, then turned her full attention to Logan when he said, "Haven't seen you at the Flying M for a while."

"I've been busy with my new job."

"So we heard." Making himself comfortable, Logan sat in the chair Garrett had vacated and proceeded to eye the various offerings on the table with interest. Logan lived for food.

"Your father told us about your new position with Mrs. Singletary," he murmured, his gaze zeroing in on a fluffy biscuit.

"You've seen my father?"

"Just left the jailhouse." Logan plucked the biscuit off Garrett's plate and began slathering butter across the top. "We were heading over to see our little brother next." Confirming this with a nod, Hunter pulled up a chair from a nearby table and sat. "Thought we'd grab something to eat first. Fortunate for us we ran into Garrett here." He winked at Molly again. "Two birds, one stone."

Having always felt safe in the company of these two men, Molly settled back in her chair and relaxed considerably. There were several beats of silence as everyone glanced at everyone else. Then, all three at the table turned their gazes onto Garrett, who was still standing.

Sighing, he commandeered a chair from the same empty table as Hunter had and joined them. The waiter hurried over with additional silverware, napkins and glasses.

After the young man took Hunter's and Logan's orders, he left. Molly told the brothers about her position with Mrs. Singletary and then asked about their families. She'd have enjoyed finding out what the entire Mitchell brood was up to, but she sensed the strain in Garrett was growing stronger.

The moment the rest of their food arrived, she decided to give him a moment alone with his brothers. "If you'll excuse me, gentlemen, I wish to secure a few loose pins in my hair."

She rose.

All three stood, as well.

Garrett touched her arm as she passed by him. "Molly—"

"Talk with your brothers. I'll be back shortly."

He nodded, but remained standing until she moved around him. She could feel his eyes on her, but didn't look back.

Not once.

Slipping into the ladies' powder room, she let out a long breath of air and settled on one of the stools placed in front of a mirror that was really quite beautiful in design. The gilded frame added an exquisite, elegant touch.

Hoping to give the Mitchell brothers time to speak openly with one another, Molly let down her hair and began to rearrange the curls into a new style. As she worked, she studied her reflection. She looked unusually pale, a little fragile.

And why not? Her conversation with Garrett had been difficult. Hunter and Logan had arrived at an optimum moment, she realized, saving her from baring any more of her soul.

She'd revealed too much already. Now, she was caught somewhere between the past and the present, when all she wanted was to move straight into the future.

If she was truthful with herself she'd admit that the hole in her heart—in her life—was still there, large and gaping.

She feared only one man could fill it.

Lord, why him? Why Garrett?

It couldn't be right to care for another person this deeply, this strongly, this completely. No, it had to be wrong.

Then again…

How could she understand God's unconditional love for her, if she never allowed herself to experience earthly love in its deepest, purest, truest form? How could she wish to—?

The door flew open and two women tumbled in, giggling.

"Oh. Oh, my! They have to be three of the most handsome men I've ever seen." The smaller of the two, a bubbly, pretty brunette, spoke in a rapid staccato. "I'm all aflutter."

"Quite so, quite so," agreed her companion, a curvy blonde dressed in a pale pink gown cut in the latest fashion. "They look as if they're related."

"Of course they're related, you dolt." The brunette rolled her eyes. "They have the same hair color and features, like brothers. Definitely brothers. I bet the two wearing denim trousers are cowboys, *real cowboys*." She fanned her face with splayed fingers. "I've always had a soft spot for rugged men."

Obviously, the brunette was talking about Hunter and Logan.

"I'm not especially fond of cowboys, too much dust on their boots," the blonde woman stated decisively. "No, I go for a more sophisticated veneer, myself. Take the other man at the table. There was something quite elegant about him, very urbane."

Garrett? Urbane?

Molly stifled a laugh. She supposed he was urbane, especially dressed as he was today in his elegant lawyer attire.

Not particularly in the mood to hear the blonde continue waxing poetic about Garrett's striking eyes and handsome face, Molly headed back into the restaurant. Feeling a bit smug, she rather liked the idea of dining with two *real cowboys* and their *urbane* little brother.

Chapter Twelve

Garrett only half listened as his brothers engaged in a heated discussion over rising cattle prices and what that meant for the Flying M. He had an opinion on such an important matter. One he should probably share, if for no other reason than to insist his brothers consider a different angle altogether.

At the moment, though, his mind wasn't on the Flying M or soaring cattle prices or anything remotely to do with business. His thoughts were firmly ensconced on Molly. She still hadn't returned. Logan and Hunter had already been served, and in true Mitchell fashion had nearly polished off the bulk of their food.

Their discussion turned to branding.

Garrett continued listening with only part of his brain. What was keeping her?

Molly had been gone nearly ten minutes, no—he checked his watch—make that twelve. She'd been gone twelve full minutes, closing in on thirteen.

Frowning, he looked over his shoulder. Had she taken ill? Had she *left?*

"Relax, little brother." Good-natured laughter wove through Hunter's command. "She'll be back."

Garrett said nothing, just sat stiffly in his chair and resisted the urge to look over his shoulder yet again.

After consuming the last dumpling on his plate, Logan let his lips curve into a satisfied grin Garrett had seen often enough. His brother was clearly enjoying Garrett's discomfort as much as the food.

"So, you and Molly." Logan pounced on the source of Garrett's agitation with annoying accuracy. "Something going on between you two?"

Several choice responses came to mind, but Garrett held his tongue and considered his answer carefully. He and Molly hadn't settled on all the terms of their pretend courtship, including the delicate matter of how much—or how little—to tell their respective families.

Where was she anyway?

He gave in and glanced over his shoulder.

Both brothers chuckled.

Swinging back to glare at them, Garrett had to consciously untighten his jaw before speaking. "As I said, now that Mrs. Singletary and I will be working together, it's important I get along with Molly, too."

Hunter snagged the remaining biscuit off Garrett's plate before Logan could get it. "Makes perfect sense to me."

"Me, too."

They eyed Garrett steadily. He tried not to squirm under those astute, all-knowing stares. Not a chance was he giving in to their blatant intimidation tactics. He knew how to wield the weapon of silence just as well as they did.

When neither of them spoke, their stares holding firm, Garrett caved in after all. "Since our paths will cross often," he said in way of explanation. "Molly and I have decided to use this lunch as an opportunity to become better acquainted."

Could he sound any more defensive?

Could his brothers look any more amused?

"You mean reacquainted," Logan corrected.

"Right, then. We're getting *reacquainted*. Two old friends enjoying a brief lunch together. It isn't any more involved than that."

"No?" Logan smirked at him. "You looked pretty involved to me. You were holding her hand and staring at the poor girl with cow eyes."

Garrett ground his teeth together. "You can't possibly know how I was looking at her." He scowled. "You entered the restaurant at my back."

"Just a hunch."

Lips twitching, Hunter chuckled.

Garrett scowled at him next.

Hunter lifted his hands in mock surrender. "All kidding aside, your arrangement with Mrs. Singletary can't be easy." He gave Garrett a sympathetic grimace. "Not with Molly such a large part of the widow's day-to-day life."

Garrett always did like Hunter best. The man understood him. "It's not all bad," he admitted gruffly.

Perhaps the past two days had been more stressful than most. But they'd also been interesting, and surprisingly entertaining. Garrett had actually enjoyed Molly's company more than he'd expected. Much more. "We're finding our way."

"Are you, now?" Hunter and Logan divided a look between them.

Garrett's shoulders instantly tensed. "What?"

"Nothing," they said in unison.

"Oh, it's something."

Logan lifted a questioning brow at Hunter. "You want to tell him, or should I?"

A smile shadowed around Hunter's mouth, right before he put the older, wiser big brother in his tone. "He isn't going to like it coming from either of us."

"No," Logan agreed with his own version of the shrewd

older brother. "But we should tell him anyway. Forewarned is forearmed, or something like that."

"Then, by all means, you do the honors."

"My pleasure." Logan leaned his elbows on the table and waited for Garrett to give him his full attention.

Garrett did so grudgingly, feeling twelve years old again.

"It's no secret that Mitchell men are colossal fools when it comes to love." Logan held up a hand when Garrett tried to interrupt. "We fall fast. We fall hard, and we fall for keeps."

Garrett barely managed to draw in a shocked breath before Hunter picked up the story. "Once we give our heart to a woman we never get it back."

"Romance advice?" Garrett scoffed. "From the two of you?"

"Hey, now." Hunter clearly took exception. "We know what we're talking about. Logan and I are both blissfully married. While you, little brother, are neither blissful nor married."

Garrett let out a low sound that may have been a laugh, maybe a growl. "Don't look so superior." Then he turned to glare at Logan. "You, either. You scoundrels only found happiness by the Grace of God."

"True." Smiling now, Hunter leaned back in his chair.

But Garrett wasn't through. "Neither of you deserve your women."

"Also true," Logan agreed. "Annabeth is a prize jewel. The most exquisite of all gems."

"I'm proud to call her my wife." Hunter lowered his gaze over Logan. "And we all know Megan is worth ten of you."

Logan waved this off with a flick of his wrist. "Not even going to attempt to disagree with that. I thank God for my wife every single day."

Garrett gaped at his brothers in amazement. Hunter, the former bad-to-the-bone outlaw, and Logan, the former by-the-book U.S. Marshal, were acting like a pair of lovesick cows.

"Saps," he muttered, whereby both of his brothers released deep, rolling belly laughs.

"You should try it sometime," Hunter suggested, still chuckling. "Living happily ever after might make you the biggest sap of us all."

Garrett grunted a nonsensical response and then promptly changed the subject. "What brings you two to town anyway?"

"We came to see you," Logan said, sobering. "We need your advice."

Garrett blinked in amazement. "My advice?"

"On a legal matter," Hunter said, tilting his head. "That so hard to believe?"

Actually, yes. "You've never sought my advice before."

"We haven't needed it before." Logan picked up a stray spoon and twirled it around in his fingertips. "We're thinking of acquiring a large parcel of land running along the southern perimeter of the Flying M, but it's complicated."

"Water rights are involved," Hunter explained. "And there's a question over the eastern boundary lines. We need your help wading through the complex language of the contract."

Garrett thrived on combing through complex language and unraveling legal tangles. "You have my attention, but unfortunately not for long. I have an appointment with Mrs. Singletary first thing this afternoon."

Neither man seemed disturbed by this.

"No problem," Hunter said for them both. "We're staying in town overnight. We can discuss the matter in greater detail later this afternoon, or first thing in the morning. You decide."

"My office, first thing in the morning."

"That'll be fine." Logan hitched his chin at a spot behind Garrett. "Here comes Molly."

At last.

Garrett rose to greet her, smiling. The instant she smiled back his heart tripped and his brother's words echoed through his mind. *We fall fast. We fall hard, and we fall for keeps.*

Why did that send a thrill through him? Where was the trepidation? The sheer masculine terror?

He'd fallen for Molly once. And, yes, he'd fallen hard. But had he fallen for keeps?

After all these years, did Molly still have his heart? Was that the reason he'd never been remotely interested in another woman?

The possibility was like a slap to his peace of mind, and just as shocking.

Dear Lord...

He couldn't think what to pray.

By the time she arrived at the table, Hunter and Logan were already standing, tossing down money for their food and saying their farewells. They lingered over Molly, showering her with compliments. Then they took turns hugging her and telling her how great it was to see her again.

She flushed under their attention and returned the sentiment with equal fervor. "I'll make it a point to visit the ranch soon."

"The family will be pleased, especially our folks."

Hunter's comment clearly added to her pleasure and she beamed.

As the two turned to leave, Garrett realized they didn't know about Fanny. "Hunter, Logan. Wait."

They looked over their shoulders, eyebrows lifted.

"You'll want to stop by the boardinghouse and speak with Fanny."

Their previous curiosity morphed into equal expressions of concern.

"Something come up we need to know about?" Hunter asked.

Not sure how much to reveal, Garrett glanced at Molly. She gave him an imperceptible shake of her head. "I'll let Fanny tell you herself."

His response didn't sit well with either brother.

"Well that's certainly cryptic," Logan groused, looking very much like a seasoned lawman set on pulling the rest out of him, one way or another.

Garrett wasn't up for a battle. "Talk to her yourselves."

Both men hesitated, then slowly nodded.

When they turned to go a second time, their footsteps held considerable more urgency.

Garrett waited until they left the restaurant before escorting Molly back to her seat. "Maybe I should have told them about Fanny and Reese."

"It's her tale to tell." Molly shook her head and sighed. "She has a lot of hard questions ahead of her in the coming days."

There was something in Molly's tone, something that had Garrett wondering over what sort of hard questions she'd endured after her breakups.

"Did your family give you a rough time after your engagements ended?"

"What? No. Of course not." She looked at him aghast, seemingly shocked that he would ask such a question. "They gave me their full support."

"Perhaps they gave you a bit too much support?"

Her lips twisted. "You do know the Scotts well."

He knew Molly even better. She would have hated their sympathy, would have preferred their censure. Or so she thought. But had her family given her even a shred of criticism instead of understanding and love she would have been devastated.

She was far more sensitive than she let on.

Feeling softer toward her, understanding her as never before, Garrett offered her a smile. "I seem to remember something about you needing to shop for ribbon. Once we're through eating, we'll head over to the millinery shop."

She stared at him a beat, and then another and still another. "You're going to accompany me?"

"That's right."

"But you *hate* shopping."

"A man can change."

"Not that much."

She had him there. "Let's just say I enjoy spending time in your company."

His statement was met with further suspicion. "What are you up to, Garrett Mitchell?"

He wasn't sure. And, quite frankly, that was a problem. A very large problem. He needed time to think through an idea that was beginning to formulate in his mind. A risky venture he didn't dare act upon until he'd considered all the angles, including the potential hazards and possible gains.

"I repeat…what are you up to, Garrett?"

"I'm practicing my role as the besotted suitor. Ribbon shopping is an excellent start, don't you think?"

"What I think," she said oh so carefully, "is that we may have been a bit hasty in the planning phase of our courtship."

The reminder cast a shadow over his mood. "You're right. We need to decide what we're going to tell our families."

"How far are we going to take this, Garrett?" He heard a trace of panic in her voice. "And what will we tell them when it's time to move on with our separate lives?"

He already had an answer to that particular problem, but he wasn't sure she was ready to hear the particulars.

Garrett wasn't sure *he* was ready to hear the particulars. He was only just coming to grips with the realization that he'd come home for her.

"Don't worry, Molly. When the time comes to reveal the truth, we'll know exactly what to say."

Looking adorably flustered, she blew a tendril of hair off her face. "I don't think I can bear telling my family *a third time* that I've failed at another relationship."

He had no intention of letting her fail. Nor was he going to let her get away a second time. "Then you won't tell them."

"But—"

"Molly, you're overthinking this." He leaned forward, rested his hands on the table and proceeded to use her own words against her. "Where's your sense of adventure?"

It was the perfect thing to say. Her chin shot up and her eyes took on a familiar gleam. "I assure you, Garrett Mitchell, my sense of adventure is fully intact."

"Then what's holding you back?" He leaned in closer still. "Afraid?"

She practically hissed at him. *"Never."*

Biting back a grin, he tossed down enough money to cover his and Molly's lunch then took her hand and drew her to her feet. "We're through here."

"I'm not finished eating."

"Yes, you are." To emphasize his point, he looked at her plate. The untouched food had congealed into an unappealing ball of goo.

Muttering something about high-handed, stubborn, urbane gentlemen, she allowed him to lead her out of the restaurant.

Smiling at her description of him—urbane, indeed—

his plan materialized a little more in his head, one tricky detail at a time.

Once outside, he directed Molly to Mrs. Singletary's carriage and climbed in behind her. Instead of sitting across from her, he made the bold move of planting himself on the narrow seat beside her.

"I think, my dear girl—" he took her hand and placed it against his heart "—we are about to embark on our grandest adventure yet."

"You think so, do you?"

"I know so."

Her hand curled into his shirt. "You are an arrogant brute, and far too full of yourself for your own good."

"Good thing you like arrogant brutes that are far too full of themselves."

"That remains to be seen."

They made the short journey to the millinery shop staring into one another's eyes, neither speaking, neither moving. Garrett could drown in Molly's blue, blue gaze and do so smiling. The moment should have been awkward.

It was glorious.

He inhaled her sweet, floral scent, thinking he hadn't felt this alive, *this awake,* in years. Seven to be exact.

She continued blinking at him, refusing to look away first.

Another detail of his plan slid home.

He might very well be setting himself up for heartache—this one far worse than the first time around. Molly had agreed to marry not one, but two other gentlemen after Garrett had left town. But she hadn't given them her heart.

She'd said as much.

Garrett had to believe she'd held a portion of herself back in her other relationships because her heart still belonged to him.

Was he daring enough to find out for certain?

The alternative would be to let Molly go again. To what end? Another man would attempt to garner her favor almost immediately. And this time, that other man might not care that she held a portion of herself back.

Worse still, her next suitor could actually succeed in securing her love.

Garrett wasn't willing to take that chance.

He was older now. Wiser. Undeniably more patient. That gave him the edge. In a battle this important, he wasn't above pressing his advantage. The poor girl didn't stand a chance.

The carriage stopped just as the last detail of his plan glided into place.

"You're sure you don't mind waiting while I shop?"

Feeling especially generous, he gave her a light kiss on the nose. "Not at all."

She waited until he escorted her inside the shop before turning to him again. "You won't be bored?"

"Not even the slightest. Take all the time you need."

She gave him a long, steady once-over.

He returned the gesture, with an even longer, steadier glance of his own.

"You're up to something."

He merely smiled.

How could he not? She was really quite beautiful with those narrowed eyes, pursed lips and accusatory tone. Garrett had always liked Molly best when she was riled, especially if he'd been the one doing the riling.

"Whatever it is you're planning, you know I'll figure it out eventually."

His smile widened. "I'm counting on that."

Making an inelegant sound in her throat, she spun around and proceeded to shop for ribbon.

Pulse pounding, breath coming fast, he watched her

move through the store. She kept her chin high, her attitude firmly in place.

Whenever she deigned to look in his direction, he added a bit of charm to his smile. To an outsider, he probably looked like a sap.

We fall fast. We fall hard, and we fall for keeps.

So it would seem.

Molly took her time shopping, of course, checking every spool of ribbon in the store. Twice. Garrett knew she was moving especially slow in order to test his resolve.

She was brilliant at testing his resolve.

He excelled at hiding his reaction.

And so, they settled into a familiar battle of wills as if the years of animosity between them had never existed.

All things considered, Garrett thought it a rather pleasant way to spend a portion of his day. He settled in to strategize his next move.

A half hour later, his plan was complete and all but set in stone. No matter how long it took, no matter what tactics he had to use, Garrett would win Molly's heart. And this time, he wasn't giving it back.

Chapter Thirteen

Later that afternoon, Molly paced outside Mrs. Singletary's private office, her mind a riot of thoughts and emotions. She was happy Garrett was working with the widow—truly she was—but, really, how long could they hole up in there and discuss business?

They'd been at it two hours already. Molly knew this because of the wretched chiming of her employer's clocks. They went off every quarter hour, singing their happy, tinny tunes throughout the house.

Mrs. Singletary owned too many clocks.

Giving the door a hard glare, Molly continued her vigil in the poorly lit hallway. She strode along the corridor at a steady pace. Back and forth. Back and forth.

Back. And. Forth.

Her feet were starting to ache.

And she'd been pacing for only thirty minutes. She'd spent the first hour and a half of this incessant waiting more productively, by working on one of Mrs. Singletary's new bonnets. The original design had been singularly uninventive. Molly had seen no other choice than to remove all the adornments and start from scratch. Not that she minded deconstructing the milliner's handiwork. Molly liked nothing better than working with a clean slate.

Swinging her latest creation by the ribbons, she pivoted on her toes and took another pass in front of the door. Having been evicted from the room not long ago, Lady Macbeth looked up at Molly with slanted, broody eyes. "No sympathy here. I've been banished, too."

The cat meowed.

Picking up the overweight bundle of fur, Molly hugged the cat close. "They'll finish soon."

She hoped.

After a kiss to the animal's head, she set Lady Macbeth back on the floor and then pressed her ear to the door. She could hear nothing through the thick wooden barrier. Not even footsteps, which probably explained why she didn't move quickly enough when the doorknob rattled.

One moment she was pressed up against the door, palms and cheek flat against the wood. The next she was tumbling forward.

Straight into Garrett's arms.

"Oh."

"Molly." She could feel the rumble of a laugh moving through him as he steadied her in his strong arms. Then, with a wry smile on his lips, he set her away from him. "If you'd wanted to join us you simply had to ask."

"I…" She fought for composure, fussing with her hair, her collar, then her sleeves. "I was just about to knock when you opened the door."

He spared her a look that clearly said he knew exactly what she'd been doing in the hallway. "Ah, so it was a case of rotten timing." He lowered his voice to a whisper. "Or perfect timing? You did end up in my arms."

He was certainly taking this pretend courtship seriously.

"Molly?" Mrs. Singletary joined them on the threshold. "Did you need something, dear?"

"I…" *Think.* "You've been in there awhile. I thought you

might like me to get you some…" *Think, think, think.* "Tea. Or coffee," she added for Garrett's benefit.

He'd never been a tea drinker.

"I'm afraid I must decline," he said with the utmost politeness and a roughish twinkle in his gaze. "Walk me out?"

"What a splendid idea. Yes, dear, please escort our guest to the door." Mrs. Singletary shooed them along, but then her gaze landed on the bonnet that had slipped from Molly's fingers when she'd tumbled forward. "Oh, look, you've been busy."

The widow plucked up the hat and studied the intricate design.

"It's not complete," Molly warned. "I have a few finishing touches still to make."

"You can tell me about them once you see Mr. Mitchell out." Eyes on the bonnet, the widow waved them along.

Hitting his cue perfectly, Garrett took Molly's arm and steered her toward the stairs. The stingy light in the hallway played off the angles of his face, turning his features into a sculpted masterpiece not seen since the Renaissance period.

As if sensing her gaze on him, Garrett turned his head. He said nothing, simply stared. Yet something shifted between them, something both familiar and altogether new.

Her knees buckled and she lost her balance.

"Watch your step," he said, warm and easy, his grip steadying her as efficiently as the warning. "The footing is uneven here."

He'd uttered the exact same words outside the millinery shop yesterday afternoon. Had that only been yesterday? It felt like a lifetime ago, and yet as if only seconds had passed.

They descended the stairs together. Garrett pulled her close and bent his head toward hers, as if he meant to whisper in her ear. Molly knew this display of relaxed intimacy was for Mrs. Singletary's benefit. Her heart raced anyway.

This isn't real, she reminded herself. *This renewed closeness is only temporary, a ruse.*

But what if their courtship wasn't pretend?

It was a lovely, scary, heart-pounding thought, one she didn't dare allow to take hold. Losing Garrett the first time had been devastating. She couldn't go through that pain again. She wouldn't.

What she needed was a new formula to help her through the coming days, a four-step plan to forestall losing her heart to this man all over again.

When they entered the foyer, he turned to face her, putting his back to the stairs. She glanced over his head and noted that Mrs. Singletary was nowhere in sight.

Garrett took her hands in his. "Is the widow watching us?"

"Not at the moment."

Leading with a grin, he brought her hands to his lips and kissed one, then the other. "Pity."

Her sentiments exactly.

"I would have liked stealing a kiss."

"I wouldn't have objected."

"Don't tempt me." He sounded intrigued, but instead of following through, he merely smiled. The look in his eyes was so sweet and tender and full of promise her breath stalled in her throat.

A deep inhale restarted her lungs.

"My brothers made it clear that they already suspect we're courting. That plays in to our ruse. But, Molly, I won't offer them confirmation unless they ask me directly."

Trying to ignore her disappointment, she forced a light tone in her words. "What will you say if they ask?"

"As little as possible."

What was it she saw in his eyes? A promise? A silent vow?

"Don't look so worried, Molly. I have a plan." He cupped

her face in his palms and held her stare for a long, tense moment. "Trust me."

"But, Garrett—"

"Trust me," he said more firmly.

Will you hurt me again?

She didn't have the courage to ask the question.

"Until next we meet." After pressing an all-too-brief kiss to her cheek, he was gone.

She stared after him, his name a whisper in her heart. Something in his behavior made her believe he cared for her. Was he merely playing a role?

Or was his affection sincere?

She couldn't be sure.

And that made her a little sad.

A sigh escaped her lips at the same moment Winston materialized by her side. "Mrs. Singletary is in the blue parlor. She has requested your company for tea."

Molly nodded. "Yes, thank you. I'm on my way."

"Very good, miss." He sketched a bow.

One last look at the door and Molly set out. Halfway across the foyer, she stumbled across Lady Macbeth. "Well, now, I wasn't expecting to see you here."

The cat gave her a bland look.

Shrugging, she veered around the unmoving lump of fur. A pitiful meow had her looking back down.

"Honestly, you are so lazy." Scooping up the cat, Molly continued on her way. She entered the parlor with a smile on her face and a purring cat in her arms. "Look who I found loitering in the foyer."

"I'd wondered where she disappeared to." Mrs. Singletary reached out her arms.

Molly deposited the cat in the widow's lap. "Did your meeting with Garrett go well?"

"Better than expected." The widow's smile turned smug. "The man has a daring streak camouflaged behind all those fine, tailored clothes and polite manners. He's quite the enigma, isn't he?"

"Quite." Enigma was the perfect definition for the man. Garrett was the most intriguing person Molly knew, and the most confounding. It would take a lifetime to uncover the mysteries in his heart.

"I predict he and I will work very well together."

"That's lovely to hear."

Mrs. Singletary picked up a piece of string and waved it front of the cat. Lady Macbeth batted at the makeshift toy with tempered feline enthusiasm. "Now that my personal fortune is in good hands, I believe it's time I address the charitable arm of my foundation."

Molly smiled. It was no secret that Mrs. Singletary had a large, generous heart when it came to helping those less fortunate. Most of the charities in town wouldn't exist without her liberal support.

"More to the point," the widow continued, "I have a fund-raising idea that will require your assistance."

Intrigued, Molly leaned forward in her chair. So far, her position as Mrs. Singletary's personal secretary had included nothing more taxing than a bit of letter writing and errand running. "What did you have in mind?"

"I wish to throw a ball, a charity ball, with at least a hundred guests in attendance, perhaps more."

Molly sat up straighter, anticipation flowing through her. "I assume you'll want me to help with the guest list."

"No, my dear, I can manage that myself." She gave her arm a little pat. "I'm thinking it's high time you learned how to organize a party on your own."

Apprehension gnawed at her. "I wouldn't know where to begin."

"I'll help you, of course, but only a little."

Her apprehension turned to sheer terror. "I have no experience."

"That is precisely the point, my dear girl." The widow's lips curved into that sly grin Molly was growing to dread. "As the future wife of a talented young lawyer you must learn to entertain properly."

Garrett headed back to his office with his head full of Molly, when he should be drawing up a mental list of preliminary investments for Mrs. Singletary to consider.

The widow had been easy to work with, their thinking eerily similar in terms of taking calculated risks, how far to go, when to pull back. Speaking of when to pull back...

Had he made a tactical error just now in the widow's foyer? Should he have seized the moment and kissed Molly properly? Or had he been wise to do the chivalrous thing and walk away?

Sighing impatiently, he increased his pace, rounded the next corner.

He needed to get behind his desk and put a pen in his hand. The silence, the solitude, the lack of interruptions would provide the perfect ambience for him to work through the cornucopia of ideas he had in mind for Molly.

Mrs. Singletary, he mentally corrected. He needed to draw up a list of ideas for the widow before he allowed himself to think about Molly.

Molly. The Lord had blessed Garrett with a second chance and, this time, he wasn't going to lose her.

She'd looked incredibly lovely in the foyer a few moments ago, with the afternoon light brushing softly across her black hair. The sun had caught her at just the right angle, setting off her blue eyes and creamy, porcelain skin.

He should have poured his heart out to her. He should have—

"Garrett?" A deep, male voice sent his thoughts grinding to a halt. "I thought that was you."

The day only needed this.

Blowing out a slow hiss of air, Garrett squared his shoulders, turned and connected his gaze with Sheriff Trey Scott. For all intents and purposes, Molly's very large, very lethal father.

Dressed in his usual black from head to toe—the only relief in the form of his silver badge—Molly's father looked as formidable as his reputation. "Sheriff Scott."

The lawman's dark, or rather his hard, *black* gaze narrowed. "I don't usually see you on this side of town."

Garrett looked around him, only just realizing he'd taken a wrong turn several blocks back. His mind had been so consumed with wooing Molly he'd failed to pay attention to his surroundings.

Right, he'd been thinking about wooing Molly. This man's beloved, only daughter. Important to keep that in mind.

As if reading his thoughts, Sheriff Scott's eyes narrowed further still. Garrett swallowed. He'd heard stories about this hardnosed, uncompromising man, stories that involved the demise of the most evil outlaws in the country.

As a boy, Garrett had been in awe of the legendary lawman. He'd seemed larger than life and utterly terrifying.

"Something wrong, son?"

Yeah, I'm still stuck on your daughter and all I can think about is winning her heart. "It's been a full day."

"Ah." Sheriff Scott clapped him on the back, held on to his shoulder with a tight grip. "Life as an up-and-coming lawyer has its challenges."

Garrett cracked a smile.

"It's fortuitous we ran into each other."

"Is it?" Garrett was thinking the exact opposite.

"Come with me." The sheriff lowered his hand, his tone brooking no argument. "You look like you could use a cup of coffee."

Yeah, he could. But he'd rather partake in his own office,

alone, without a hawk-eyed lawman watching his every move. "Sounds good."

He followed Molly's father into the jailhouse.

"Have a seat." The sheriff indicated a straight-back, wooden chair in front of a desk overflowing with stacks of papers.

Garrett shuddered at the disorder. "How do you find anything in that mess?"

The other man merely grinned. The gesture did nothing to soften the steely features. "Make yourself comfortable. I'll be right back."

Garrett did as requested and looked around while he waited for the sheriff's return. To say the jailhouse was serviceable was being kind. The one-room structure had a stark, unwelcoming feel. The walls were bare. The black potbelly stove in the far corner spit and belched out only sporadic waves of heat. A mild, if sterile, aroma floated along the dank, chilled air.

The jail cells were empty today, clean, but uninviting with their lumpy cots and threadbare blankets. Not the place he'd choose to spend the night.

Garrett was just finishing his inspection of his surroundings, and trying not to shudder, when the sheriff returned with two steaming mugs of coffee. He handed one to Garrett then placed the other to his lips.

There was something in the other man's gaze, something shrewd and calculating, measuring almost.

Garrett had an uneasy feeling about his *fortuitous* meeting. He took a quick pull from his own mug.

"How are you settling in at Bennett, Bennett and Brand?"

He answered truthfully. "Very well."

"The partners speak highly of you."

"Good to know." And it was. Garrett had spent the past six months proving he'd been hired for his legal mind, not his personal connection to Reese Bennett, Jr. His boss had been a family friend long before he'd asked Fanny to marry him.

Still eyeing Garrett with those hawk eyes, Sheriff Scott sat on the edge of his desk and stretched out his long legs. "You been out to the ranch?"

"Not lately." He put a shrug in his voice. "Work keeps me busy."

Uncomfortable under the sheriff's bold stare, Garrett's eyes tracked through the room, landing on the jail cells to his left. A few wrong decisions, a handful of bad choices, and he could have ended up in one of those as surely as he'd ended up studying the law. Garrett had harnessed an innate wild streak within a strong sense of order, stability and ruthless control.

Most of his life, he'd carefully managed his actions, tamped down any surge of rebellion into the darkest recesses of his soul. In recent years and with a lot of prayer, he'd learned to channel his risk-taking tendencies into business.

"…She seems happy enough, but her mother and I still worry."

Garrett shook his head, realizing he'd missed a vital part of the conversation. He forced his mind to concentrate.

"Mrs. Singletary has been a good influence on her."

Garrett's heart kicked in his chest. Molly. They were speaking about Molly. Or rather, *her father* was speaking about her.

"Her mother and I are praying the widow will have a stabilizing influence on her life."

Garrett's mind went back to their time together in the past few days. The grown-up Molly had been more subdued than her childhood counterpart, with only a spark of her former self showing up in glimpses. "She's certainly matured in recent years."

Was that a good thing, this new restraint he'd seen in her? Wasn't Molly's unpredictable, untamed nature what made her so alluring? Wasn't her feistiness what drew Garrett to her like a bee to honey, a moth to flame, a sap to his doom?

"By your comment, I take it you've spoken with Molly recently?"

Garrett nodded.

With very deliberate movements, the sheriff set his mug on the desk. "When?"

"Yesterday. Last night. And again this morning." Realizing how that might sound to her father, Garrett hurriedly explained Mrs. Singletary's business proposition and the subsequent events of the past two days.

"You attended the opera, willingly?" A look of masculine disgust swept across the sheriff's face. "I can't think of a worse way to spend an evening."

Neither could Garrett. Yet, he found himself saying, "There were enjoyable moments."

The kiss he'd shared with Molly later in the evening had been worth every excruciating, painful moment of bad music and screeching lyrics. Holding her in his arms again had been glorious, an awe-inspiring rediscovery of something he'd thought lost forever.

Caught in the memory, Garrett nearly spoke what was in his heart. Then he remembered who this man was that stared back at him with those merciless, narrowed eyes. The eyes of a protective father who saw far too much.

Garrett set down his mug and cleared his throat.

With the lawman in his eyes, Sheriff Scott leaned forward. "I seem to remember, you and Molly were once very close."

Except for the nodding of his head, Garrett held perfectly still. "Yes, sir, we were."

"And then you left for school."

"That's correct."

Rubbing his hands together, the sheriff's face became a landscape of hard planes and cold, ruthless angles. This was the man who wrung answers out of the hardest criminals in the territory. "Any regrets?"

"I…" Garrett cocked his head. "Sir?"

"I know my daughter suffered when you left. What about you? Any regrets over leaving her behind?"

Under normal circumstances, Garrett would have appreciated the man's direct approach. Right now, he didn't know whether to be horrified or stunned or glad for the chance to explain himself. "Molly was only fifteen."

He said nothing more, as if her age justified his decision. Yet his answer revealed nothing of the agony he'd felt over losing Molly.

Garrett had given his heart to her and, just as his brothers had intimated, he'd never gotten it back.

"My daughter was young, I agree. But that's not what I asked. Let me more specific. Any regrets over your decision to attend school so far away from home?"

Garrett answered from his heart. "I hated leaving Molly. But I made the right decision at the time."

The sheriff's entire body seemed to relax and Garrett felt as if he'd passed a difficult test.

Unfortunately, the exam wasn't over, as evidenced by the man's next question. "Given the same circumstances today, what would you do?"

"I'd ask her to come with me, as my wife."

A rare smile spread across the sheriff's face, this time reaching all the way to his eyes. "You're a good man, Garrett."

Good enough to court his daughter? "I'd like a chance to try again, sir."

"You're going to have be clearer, son."

Garrett's heart knocked against his ribs. But he held the

other man's gaze without flinching. "Sheriff Scott, I request permission to court your daughter."

"So granted."

Chapter Fourteen

Though Garrett wanted to begin his campaign to win Molly's heart immediately, he had to meet with his brothers. At precisely ten o'clock the next morning, he directed them to the large conference table in the corner of his office.

Hunter and Logan wasted no time getting down to business. They laid out their issues with the purchase agreement for the land bordering the Flying M, while Garrett took notes.

He kept silent throughout their discourse, preferring to gather all the information before rendering an opinion.

Winding down, Hunter placed his hands on the table and pushed back in his chair. "Is it as bad as we thought?"

Garrett checked one of his notations with the actual contract then shook his head. "Not if you can talk old man Foley into signing off on your proposed changes to the property lines."

Logan gave an exaggerated snort. "Oh, well, if that's all we have to do…"

Point taken.

Ebenezer Foley was one step on the other side of impossible. Even on a good day, the ancient, grizzled rancher was about as flexible as an iron rod.

"Assuming we can get the old coot to see reason about

the changes to the boundaries," Hunter began in a remarkably patient tone considering who they were talking about. "What about the issue of water rights?"

"Those shouldn't be a problem," Garrett said. "As it turns out, I'm acquainted with the current owner."

"And you think you can get him to sell the rights to us?"

"He'll sell." Eventually. The man in question loved a good negotiation and Garrett was one of his favorite opponents. "I'll speak with him this week."

Hunter's eyebrows traveled to his hairline. "That soon?"

"You're family. That makes this a priority."

Clearly liking what he heard, Logan stood, moved to Garrett's side of the table and slapped him on the back. "Always knew you were the smartest of the Mitchell brood."

"Correct me if I'm wrong." He stood to face his brother. "Weren't you the one who nicknamed me Weasel when I was ten?"

"Hey, it was a compliment." Logan laughed. "Weasels are wily and clever and get into all sorts of—"

Hunter cut him off. "What our brother is trying to say—" he moved directly between Garrett and Logan "—is that we're grateful for your assistance on this."

"Yeah, sure, that's what I meant." Smiling broader, Logan shifted back into view. "All kidding aside, little brother, you're a credit to the Mitchell name."

Until this moment, Garrett hadn't realized just how important proving his worth to his family—these two men in particular—had driven him through the years. Now that he had clear evidence of their respect, he felt somehow lighter, as if a burden had been lifted.

"I won't let you down." He divided a glance between his brothers. "Either of you."

"You're the best of us all, Garrett. You make us all look good." To punctuate his point, Hunter yanked him into a bear hug reminiscent of their big, gruff father.

For a man who'd spent most of his adult life on the wrong side of the law, Hunter was sliding back into his role as the responsible eldest brother with surprising ease.

With family at the forefront of his mind, Garrett addressed another concern. "Have you spoken with Fanny since lunch yesterday?"

The mood in the room turned somber.

"She told us she broke off her engagement and won't reconsider." Hunter's concern was obvious in his unnaturally tense stance. "She wouldn't give us specifics, but she's holding firm to her decision."

Garrett hadn't expected her to change her mind. Nevertheless, he was disappointed to discover Fanny and Reese were truly finished. "Then we stand by her and hope she finds peace in the coming weeks."

Both brothers nodded. "Agreed."

They spent several more minutes catching up on the rest of the family before Garrett escorted them to their waiting horses. Though the air still had a bite, the sun had advanced in the sky.

Blinking past the brightness, his breath misting around his head, he watched his brothers ride due north. Eleven miles and they'd be back on Mitchell property.

He shook his head in wonder at the change in the hard men he used to know, men who hadn't gotten along before a few years ago. Now, they were as close as any brothers could be.

Even more astonishing, if the two had been overly sappy when talking about their wives, they were worse when they mentioned their daughters. Neither man had fathered a son yet, and didn't seem to mind. They doted on the women in their lives and appeared stronger for the experience. They epitomized the Biblical model of spiritual leadership, strength and integrity.

Garrett wouldn't mind following their lead. Nor would

he mind fathering daughters, as long as they favored their mother with her thick, black hair, creamy skin and blue, blue eyes. The fact that he easily put Molly in the role of his wife came as no surprise.

She was the woman he'd always wanted to marry, planned to marry, *would* marry.

No more stalling or putting off the inevitable.

Time to succeed where others had failed.

His first move would be powerful in its simplicity. He prayed she recognized the meaning behind the gesture.

Having cleared off his desk for the next several hours, he made a brief stop that turned into two and then headed over to Mrs. Singletary's house.

The widow's stiff-backed manservant opened the door with the faintest trace of disapproval in his gaze. "Mrs. Singletary isn't expecting you for another hour."

"I'm aware of our meeting time," he said, equally formal in tone. "I've come to see Miss Scott."

Winston acknowledged this with a short nod. "I will see if she is receiving visitors. Wait here."

Obeying the rigid command, Garrett attempted to cool his heels in the entryway. He lasted an entire two minutes before restlessness set in. He impatiently prowled around the foyer, making several passes before a painting caught his eye.

The image of a much younger Beatrix Singletary smiled up at a dark-haired man with laughing eyes and classically handsome features. They were a stunning couple, to be sure, but what struck Garrett was how the artist had captured their love in the bold colors and capable brush strokes.

"That's what love looks like," Molly said from behind him.

Throat suddenly dry, Garrett turned his gaze to meet hers. He felt the impact of her beauty like a blow to his heart.

Words failed him. Coherent thought disappeared. And thus…he simply…

Stared.

Because this was Molly. *Molly.*

The only woman to capture his heart. The only woman he'd ever loved.

Her thick, long eyelashes fluttered softly. And then she smiled.

That smile. He'd seen it once before. A long time ago.

Memories tumbled over one another in his mind, and then her parting vow slid above the tangle.

I will always, always love you, Garrett Mitchell.

He was going to hold her to that.

But for now, he turned back to the painting and narrowed his eyes over the image. "I feel as though I'm eavesdropping on a very private moment."

"I know." Molly's voice held equal parts amusement and awe. "Mrs. Singletary claims he was her soul mate."

Hard to argue that, when the proof was right in front of him.

Molly sighed sweetly, the sound almost wistful. "Is it any wonder the widow believes in true love?"

"None at all." Garrett shifted the bouquet from one hand to the other, surprised to discover his palms had begun to sweat.

Now that the time had come to present the flowers, he didn't know what to say. It was as if he'd morphed into a tongue-tied, love-struck schoolboy again.

Reaching for a calm that didn't exist, he thrust the bouquet between them. "Here."

Charming, Mitchell. Real charming.

"Oh, Garrett." Voice thick and husky, Molly's eyes swam with emotion. "You remembered."

"I did."

As she took the bouquet brimming with all her favorites, a sound escaped her, one that might have been a sigh, maybe a sob.

He had to clear his throat. Twice. "The wild roses and lavender were easy enough to find. But I had to go to two different stores to locate the daises."

Another sound escaped her, this one a gasp of surprise. "You went to all that trouble for me?"

"I know how much you love wildflowers."

"Oh, you wonderful, wonderful man." Clutching the bouquet to her heart, she launched herself at him.

He caught her, wrapped her in his arms and held on tight.

They stood lost in the moment, one foot in the past, the other in the present.

"I've missed you, Molly. I've missed *us*." He whispered the words in her hair, the truth too important to keep to himself any longer. They'd wasted far too much time already. Seven years. "I don't want to lose you again."

She stiffened at that, and then slowly, deliberately stepped out of his embrace. The distance she created was small, barely the length of his arms, but she might was well have dug a ten-foot chasm between them.

His heart stalled in his chest, then sped up again when he saw a spark of hope flicker in her eyes. The moment lasted a split second before her expression went coolly blank. "I'll always be your friend, Garrett. Always."

He didn't want her friendship. He wanted her love.

But she was back to holding a portion of herself apart, keeping her distance as if afraid he'd hurt her again.

Winning Molly's heart wasn't going to be as easy as he'd first thought. For now, he chose a soft, innocuous approach. "I'll always be your friend, too, Molly."

She gave him a shaky smile, then focused on the flowers. "They really are lovely."

"I'm glad you like them."

Her head still bent, she plucked at one of the blooms.

"Garrett, why are you here so early? Your appointment with Mrs. Singletary isn't for at least another hour."

"I came to see you."

Her head shot up. "But *why?*"

She really wasn't going to make this easy on him.

He wanted to be honest with her, to declare his love here and now. To tell her that for him this wasn't a game. It was real. His heart was on the line. But it appeared she wasn't ready to hear those words.

One step at a time, he told himself. Slow and easy.

"Think about it, Molly." He used his most reasonable tone. "If we're to convince the widow we're in love, we must stick to the formula. We start with variable number one, we—"

"Hold nothing back," she finished for him.

He nodded. "Consistency is the key. Mrs. Singletary might not be at home now, but she could show up any moment."

"That's true." She touched her hair, smoothed her palm over the black silk. The slight tremble in her hand told its own story. She wasn't completely immune to him.

Garrett pressed his advantage. "It makes sense I would arrive early in the hopes of running into you."

"Of course." She sighed, fiddled with a stem, sighed again. "All part of the ruse."

"No, Molly. My early arrival is part of the ruse. The flowers…" He knuckled a piece of hair off her cheek. "Are because I care."

Unfair. The man didn't play by the rules. Gritting her teeth, Molly wrapped her fingers around the stems of the bouquet, all but choking the flowers with her grip. Garrett had brought her a beautiful arrangement of roses, lavender and daisies. She knew he was making a statement with the gesture. Maybe even a declaration.

Yet she couldn't allow herself to hope, or dream of something more than friendship with the man. Too much stood between them. Namely their past, or rather *her* past. She'd accepted two offers of marriage in his absence, when she should have remained true.

She should have waited for him, even though he hadn't asked. Maybe even because he hadn't asked. But she'd been so hurt when he'd left for school, so full of anger and pride.

Pride goeth before destruction, and an haughty spirit before a fall.

She'd made so many mistakes.

Because of her impetuousness, the two other men she'd agreed to marry would always stand between her and Garrett. Maybe he could forgive her, maybe he thought he already had. But there would always be the chance that resentment would grow in his heart.

Some mistakes, she'd come to accept, required more than words to repair, more than good intentions, more even than prayer. Some pain could not be undone, or easily forgotten, or perhaps ever fully healed.

No, she didn't dare hope for more than friendship with Garrett.

"Shouldn't you put those in water?" He pointed to the flowers in her hand.

She started. "Oh… Yes. I need to hunt down a vase."

"I'll come with you."

She didn't bother arguing.

When they passed through the open door of the dining room, he stopped. Mouth gaping, his eyes ran over the chaos on the table and she thought she saw him shudder.

"I'm working on several projects." She winced at the defensiveness she heard in her own tone.

He chuckled. "I gathered."

Annoyance hiked up her chin a notch. She tried to take in the table from his perspective. As she did, she found herself shuddering, too. In one section lay a multitude of ribbons, feathers, buttons and bows. Off to the left sat three hats in various stages of production—or destruction, depending on one's perspective.

Underneath all the mess was an array of parchment paper, inkwells and writing utensils.

"Mrs. Singletary is throwing a charity ball next month and has put me in charge," she explained. "I've decided to start with the invitations."

"Seems like a wise first step." He deliberately turned his back on the table, as if deciding it best not to allow the chaos to seep into his brain. "I imagine there's a lot of planning involved in putting together a charity ball."

"You have no idea." She'd quickly discovered an event on the scale the widow had in mind was too much for one person to tackle alone.

She needed help.

"I'm already in over my head," she admitted.

Something of her panic must have shown on her face because he lifted her chin with a fingertip and smiled tenderly into her eyes. "I have no doubt you'll pull it off."

She went still for a heartbeat, having no idea what to do with this grown-up version of the boy she'd once loved. She really shouldn't still care what he thought of her. Or that he knew her so well. Or that his words were taking away the sheer terror as surely as if he'd agreed to plan the party in her stead. "I wish I was as confident as you."

His hand moved to her shoulder. "You know what to do, simply attack this party like one of our former adventures."

"With reckless abandon?"

"No." He laughed, and something shifted in his gaze, something a little dangerous. "Draw up a formula," he said carefully, "and then execute it down to the letter."

"That makes sense." A lot of sense.

"I'm only pointing out what you would have discovered on your own eventually."

He was right. Nevertheless, she wanted him to know how much she appreciated his words. "Thank you, Garrett."

"You're welcome." His other hand took up residence on her other shoulder. Intent filled his gaze.

He was going to kiss her.

At last, she thought. *At last.*

She leaned in closer, a bit closer, one more inch. The sound of her pulse pounded in her ears. She thought she might have heard a door opening and closing in the distance, thought she might have heard voices. Winston's mixed with others.

She thought she recognized one, but her mind refused to focus on anything but Garrett.

He was very slowly, very gently easing her into his arms. His gaze flickered to a spot just over her shoulder. And then…

And then…

His lips brushed against hers.

Her heart sighed. Her head spun. Her resolve vanished.

Had she truly thought she could hold herself apart from this man? That she could keep her distance and maintain a simple friendship?

Absurd.

Just as she settled into their kiss, she heard someone say her name. "Molly Taylor Scott."

Her knees gave out. Thankfully, Garrett's strong hands kept her from falling to the ground.

Another outraged voice raised above the other. "Garrett Mitchell, release that poor girl at once!"

Garrett couldn't have planned this moment any better had he agonized over the details for days. He probably shouldn't be grinning like a sap. He'd been caught kissing Molly, by his own mother. *And hers.*

Yeah, he probably should work up some genuine contrition.

However, he couldn't drum up the enthusiasm. Not when he realized the worst thing that could happen would be an immediate demand for him to marry the "poor girl." Since that was his ultimate goal, he didn't see much problem with that outcome.

Except...

Molly was supposed to *want* to marry him, not be forced against her will.

The thought wiped his expression clean.

But then he caught Mrs. Singletary's gleam of smiling satisfaction as she moved deeper into the room, and had to turn away before his own smile returned.

"Mother? Mrs. Mitchell?" Molly's cheeks turned a becoming shade of pink as she glanced between the two women. "What are you two doing here?"

"You mean, besides watching my son behave in a highly inappropriate manner?"

There was nothing for it, Garrett thought as he smiled at his mother. Oh, she sounded sufficiently mortified. Looked it, too. But her steel-blue eyes, the same color as Logan's, twinkled beneath her fierce scowl.

Molly's mother also had amusement lurking in her eyes, eyes the exact shape and color of her sister-turned-daughter. The two looked so much alike Garrett found himself blinking from one to the other. If the woman standing beside her was anything to go by, Molly would age beautifully.

Garrett looked forward to witnessing the transformation firsthand.

Tread lightly, he warned himself. *No need to put her reputation at risk.*

It was mostly family in the room, but still. He shouldn't

push matters too far. Just a little nudge was all, a slight clarification of where he stood.

"I wanted to make my feelings for Molly clear. Kissing her seemed the best way to avoid any misunderstanding between us."

All four women gasped. Well, three of the women gasped. Molly slapped a hand over her eyes and groaned, with too much gusto for Garrett's way of thinking.

"Let me see if I have this straight." Mrs. Scott glanced from him to Molly then back to him. "You kissed my daughter in order to declare you feelings for her?"

"That's correct, Mrs. Scott. Molly and I are officially courting."

Chapter Fifteen

Molly wanted to respond, needed to respond, tried to respond. But uncertainty held her silent. Garrett had just told her mother and two other witnesses—one of whom was *his mother*—that they were officially courting. Not that he'd had any choice in the matter.

They'd been caught kissing.

No turning back.

It was one thing to continue the ruse for Mrs. Singletary's sake, quite another to lie to their own mothers. They would have to play this pretense out in front of their families, and anyone else in their immediate acquaintance.

All things considered, Garrett seemed awfully complacent over the direction their "pretend" courtship had just taken. In fact, he appeared highly pleased with himself, as if this moment had been part of some master plan of his.

The smug grin on his face reminded her of a time when his mother had caught him teaching Molly how to wield a slingshot on her eleventh birthday. He hadn't been the least deterred when she'd scolded him. Once the storm had passed, he'd increased his efforts tenfold.

That boy—that daring, clever, skillful boy—was the very same one grinning at her now.

What was a former mischievous girl to do but smile at him in return?

She promptly lost herself in his gaze. Shocked at her momentary lapse, she quickly snapped back to attention and glanced first at Mrs. Singletary, then her mother and finally at Mrs. Mitchell. Neither seemed surprised by this turn of events.

Why weren't any of them surprised, especially their respective mothers?

"Aren't you shocked by the news of our courtship?" Molly asked.

"Not in the least." Laughing softly, her mother pulled her into a warm hug. "It was only a matter of time before you two made your way back to one another."

"My only surprise," added Garrett's mother, smiling at Molly as well as her son, "is that it's taken you two so long to get on with it. We've been waiting years."

Shocked at this revelation, Molly looked at Garrett, wondering what he thought of that particularly bold declaration from his mother.

He winked at her. The rascal. He *had* planned this, or at least he'd used the situation to his advantage. He'd heard the women enter the house and had kissed Molly because he'd known they'd had an audience.

This was all a game to him. A grand adventure.

A ruse.

Not sure why her heart twisted with disappointment, Molly focused on her employer.

Never one to hide her reaction, the widow practically beamed at her.

Feeling outnumbered, Molly turned the conversation in a new direction. "Mother, Mrs. Mitchell. You never answered my question." She frowned at the thick rasp in her voice. "Why are you here, in the middle of the day?"

Mrs. Singletary answered the question before they could

respond themselves. "Simple, my dear, I have called in the troops."

"Beatrix told us about the charity ball you're planning for her. We're here to help." Her mother moved to the table, uncovered several pieces of parchment paper previously buried beneath stray ribbons. "By the looks of things, I see we arrived just in time."

Had they offered their assistance an hour ago, Molly would have been grateful for the help. But now, with Garrett's words of encouragement still echoing in her ears, she wanted to plan the party by herself. She wanted to live up to his high expectations of her.

But that was pride talking. What did she know about planning a ball where the object was to raise money for various charitable organizations in town? "Well, then, let's get started."

"We'll leave you ladies to sort this out. Come, Mr. Mitchell." Mrs. Singletary motioned to Garrett to follow her. "We have business to discuss."

Silent throughout this interchange, he strode straight to Molly, took her hands in his and made a daring request. "Have dinner with me tonight."

Not quite meeting his gaze, Molly bit her lip. "I'm not sure I'm free…"

"She's free," all three women said in unison.

Molly shook her head, feeling as though she were an actress in a badly written play. The unaware heroine forced to run through her lines without the benefit of a script.

"Say yes," he urged, then leaned over and whispered in her ear. "We have a few plans of our own to work through."

That was certainly true. This pretend courtship was fast getting out of hand. They needed a new plan. "Yes. I'll dine with you this evening."

He straightened. "I'll pick you up at seven."

"She'll be ready." This came from Mrs. Singletary. Still

holding her hands, proving he knew how to play the gentleman, Garrett pressed a chaste kiss to her forehead.

The room erupted in female sighs, proving the man knew how to play to an audience. He walked over to her mother next, said something that made her laugh and brought out her biggest smile yet.

Smiling himself, he turned his attention to his own mother next. He spoke to her in a low tone. After a moment, he kissed her on the cheek then set out with Mrs. Singletary.

Halfway out the door, he stopped and retraced his steps back to his mother. "I'd like a private word with you before you leave this afternoon."

"Of course, dear."

"It's about…" He paused, turned thoughtful. Then pressed on, "…Fanny."

"I figured as much. She is one of the reasons I've come to town for the next few days."

"Good." He nodded, looking vastly relieved his mother was stepping in. "She needs you. Don't let her tell you otherwise."

He exited the room and several seconds passed before anyone spoke.

Molly shifted from one foot to the other, not sure how to break the silence that seemed to grow heavier and heavier. She didn't want to lie to her own mother. Or to Garrett's. But she didn't want to say more than necessary, either. Too many details would be just as bad as none.

"Garrett and I are still finding our way," she said, speaking the truth as plainly as she knew how. "We haven't actually made any promises to one another." Again, true. "Things might not work out between us, so don't think—"

"Molly, my dear, sweet girl." With a gentle touch to her arm, Mrs. Mitchell cut her off midsentence. "You don't have to explain anything to me."

"Or to me, either." Her mother offered this with the un-conditional love Molly had relied upon through the years. "I, for one, am pleased you two aren't at odds anymore. If this courtship comes to nothing, at least you'll know you gave it one last try."

Not expecting such a bold show of support, Molly twisted her hands together at her waist and addressed her greatest concern. "Aren't you going to warn me about jump-ing in too fast since my last engagement?"

"If it were any other man, perhaps I would. But this is Garrett Mitchell we're talking about." She winked at his mother, who promptly winked back.

Molly sighed in resignation, accepting the truth in the privacy of her mind. Because, as her mother said, this was Garrett they were talking about. Her first love, her only love.

And yet, she'd accepted marriage proposals from two other men who were most definitely *not* Garrett.

His mother couldn't possibly want a woman with Molly's sordid past to dig her claws into her son. "What about you, Mrs. Mitchell? Are you comfortable with Garrett court-ing me?"

The older woman answered without fuss or hesitation. "I'm pleased he's finally made his move. He's dragged his feet quite long enough."

Molly could leave the discussion on that note. The cow-ardly part of her would prefer to say nothing more on the subject. But this was a time for candor, not cowardice. "My history doesn't worry you?"

"Not at all."

She persisted. "I have two broken engagements behind me."

Mrs. Mitchell led Molly to a chair and pressed down on her shoulders until she sat. "There's a logical explanation as to why those other two relationships didn't work out for you."

Molly blinked. "There is?"

"Of course." The woman smiled with a mixture of female solidarity and motherly pride. "Neither of your fiancés was my son."

Garrett ran his finger across the last name on the list. Jonathon Hawkins. The new owner of the Hotel Dupree. Since Mrs. Singletary had seemed most interested in Garrett's suggestion concerning the hotelier, he steered the conversation back in that direction.

"Hawkins is due to arrive tomorrow afternoon. I can set up an appointment with him by the end of the week, if you think you might want to present my proposed venture to him."

The widow considered the idea in silence, her fingernails stroking Lady Macbeth's fur. Having taken up residence on the widow's lap halfway through their meeting, the cat purred in rumbling pleasure. "You think he'll be interested in expanding his operation to San Francisco?"

"He has hotels in Chicago and St. Louis and now Denver, but nothing farther west. San Francisco would be a logical next step."

Which was why Garrett had suggested the idea of recreating the Hotel Dupree brick by brick in San Francisco. Westward travelers who'd stayed in the Denver hotel would feel at home in its counterpart out west.

"It's a daring move," the widow said, tapping a finger to her lips.

"Word is, Hawkins is a natural risk-taker."

"I do like my men bold."

Garrett reserved the right to remain silent on the matter. Instead, he said, "Couldn't hurt to present the idea to him."

Mrs. Singletary nodded. "How quickly can you draw up a detailed proposal for my review?"

"Two days, three at the most."

"All right." She spread her palm over the cat's fur. "Once I review the new draft, I'll decide whether or not I want to proceed."

Garrett made several notations in his leather portfolio.

"We'll meet again in two days at your office, say Friday at ten in the morning."

"Very well." He added the appointment to the previous notations, then looked up. "Anything else we need to address?"

She waved a dismissive hand. "That's enough business for one day."

"Good enough." He closed the portfolio and stood.

"Sit down. I did need to speak with you about that display this afternoon." She gave him a very motherly look. "What are your intentions, Mr. Mitchell?"

At the none-too-subtle shift in topics, Garrett returned to his seat. The widow wanted to know his intentions toward Molly?

Glad for this opportunity to clear the air, he gathered his thoughts. "I've always enjoyed Molly's company, more now that we are both older and a little less—"

"Impetuous? Volatile?"

He chewed on the words, discarded both. No denying that Molly had once been impetuous, and that their relationship had been volatile, at least in the end. But the wild girl he'd once loved had a softness about her now, a maturity and reserve around the edges.

"I've always found Molly's unpredictable nature her best feature," he admitted out loud. "But there are things about the woman she's become that I also find agreeable."

The widow frowned. "Such as?"

"Her poise. Her charm. Her kindness."

Problem was Molly still kept putting up barriers whenever they started to get close. Perhaps she always would if he didn't do something about it now.

Garrett needed an ally. But he wouldn't enlist the widow's aid without confessing his deception first. "I have not been completely honest with you."

"No?"

"My courtship of Molly began as a ruse."

Her hand stilled on the cat's back. "A ruse?"

"The idea was to allow you to think your matchmaking attempts were working, thereby maintaining the control."

"Yes, Mr. Mitchell. I'm fully aware of your initial subterfuge." That slow, sly grin he'd come to recognize—and dread—spread across her lips.

Garrett let out a short laugh. "I should have known you were on to us."

"I did not become a wealthy woman without honing my observation skills."

He sat back in his chair. "How long did you plan to play along with our pretense?"

Her smile turned slyer still. "Until it was no longer a game for either of you."

It hadn't been a game for Garrett from the start. He realized that now, accepted the truth of it. Molly hadn't needed to convince him to play along with her convoluted scheme. Mrs. Singletary hadn't needed to push him to spend time with her companion.

If he was completely honest with himself, he'd admit the rest. He hadn't taken the job at Bennett, Bennett and Brand to prove he was no longer that "other Mitchell boy." He'd come home for Molly.

Every decision he'd made since he'd learned of her broken engagement to Marshall Ferguson had led to this moment. Garrett hadn't been avoiding Molly since returning to Denver—he'd been biding his time, waiting for the right moment to make his move.

And now that he had, he wasn't going to lose her again. He had to be smart in his pursuit, clever. Wily. "Mrs. Singletary, I need your help."

"I'm at your service, Mr. Mitchell." Although she kept her tone mild, Garrett could see the widow struggle not to smile, as if she'd been waiting for this very opportunity since she'd first decided to match her beloved companion with him.

You need an ally, he reminded himself. And there she sat, with that smirk on her face and ridiculously large cat on her lap.

"Molly has always been skittish when it comes to love. I believe that even more true now because of her broken engagements."

"You know her well."

"I haven't always," he admitted. "I once accused her of loving my family more than me."

"Molly's heart is big enough for all of you."

It had taken him far too long to come to that same realization. But he wasn't the one who needed convincing of his change of heart. It was Molly.

One step at a time. Slow, methodical, nothing too aggressive. "I agree she has a great capacity for love, but that's not really the point, is it?"

"No."

He drew in a deep breath. "She's been hurt. By me. And others. She deserves to be wooed, made to feel special and beautiful. I want to show her that I love her for who she is, at the core. I want to court her properly. I want to sweep her off her feet. However..."

He stopped, took a moment to gather his thoughts again.

"Go on, Mr. Mitchell."

"*However,* I won't accept half her heart this time around."

"As well you shouldn't."

"That's where you come in," he said.

She arched a brow. "What can I do to help?"

"How do I convince her I won't ever leave her again?" He heard the frustration in his voice, didn't attempt to apologize for it.

Gaze thoughtful, the widow eyed him for several long moments. "Words won't be enough," she warned.

"No."

"A grand gesture will only serve to make her suspicious of your motives."

Sadly, he'd figured that out, as well. Molly would only think he was acting upon their ruse.

He should have never agreed to her ridiculous scheme.

"You're telling me you think it's hopeless?"

Even as he said the words, Garrett refused to believe all was lost. With God all things were possible.

Molly belonged to him, and he belonged to her. They'd been destined for each other since childhood, drawn by a force bigger than themselves.

"Certainly it's not hopeless, Mr. Mitchell. Quite the contrary." The widow reached out and gave his knee a firm pat. "I can think of several surefire ways to aid you in your quest."

He sat up straighter. "Go on."

"It'll require patience, persistence and the most powerful tool of all, prayer."

"Patience, persistence, prayer." He ticked them off on his fingers, recognizing the value in all three but not exactly what he'd had in mind. "I was hoping for a concrete plan of attack."

"Ah, well, if it's something specific you're looking for…" She crooked her finger at him. "Come closer and I'll tell you exactly what you ought to do…"

When the widow finished mapping out her idea, Garrett sat back and reviewed the outrageous plan in his mind. "You honestly think it will work?"

"It's how my dear Reginald made me his bride." She sighed. "It was terribly romantic."

Garrett firmly disagreed. "Abduction is not romantic."

"The surprise element has its advantages," the widow argued.

Molly did like surprises. And Garrett had plenty of time to plan, to prepare, to—

No.

He would never force her into marriage. Nor would he use underhanded tactics to gain her trust. He would court her the old-fashioned way, not manipulate her feelings for him.

With patience, persistence and prayer Garrett would woo away her every doubt. He would break down every barrier she attempted to erect between them.

He wouldn't stop, wouldn't relent, wouldn't give up until he'd made Molly his bride.

Chapter Sixteen

Over the next three weeks, preparations for Mrs. Singletary's charity ball consumed Molly's every waking hour. With her mother's and Mrs. Mitchell's assistance the planning went smoothly. Now that the invitations had been delivered, and the responses received, only a few details remained before the ball itself.

As she worked on flower arrangements for the party, one small concern nagged at her.

Aside from the occasional dinner and lunch, she rarely saw Garrett. When they did manage a few moments alone, he was courteous, charming and attentive. A near-perfect suitor.

And that was the problem. He was up to something.

The question was what?

Just yesterday, she'd found out—quite by accident—that he'd approached her father to request permission to court her. Considering they were in this ruse together, Garrett should have warned her he was going to take that potentially hazardous step. At the very least, he should have told her afterward.

What if her father had refused his blessing? Why take the risk at all?

Something wasn't right.

Two days before the ball, as she was puzzling over Garrett's behavior, the man himself arrived at Mrs. Singletary's unannounced. He'd been doing that a lot lately, simply showing up when Molly least expected him. She rather liked his spontaneity. The thrill of never knowing exactly when she'd see him again kept her anticipating his next visit all the more.

She heard him tell Winston he'd "find her" himself. Easy enough to do since she'd set up a temporary workstation in the dining room weeks ago.

His purposeful footsteps struck the wood flooring in the hallway with customary efficiency. She could hear him coming closer…

"Take a break," he said from the doorway, "and have lunch with me at the Hotel Dupree."

Molly set aside the flower arrangement she'd marked for the buffet table and turned to face him.

Her heart tripped at the sight he made. There he stood, in all his masculine, urbane glory. He'd propped one shoulder against the doorjamb while his arms were crossed casually over his chest. A roguish smile played across his lips. "You're staring."

"Hard not to as you look very handsome today. Besides, you're staring back."

"Hard not to as you look quite lovely today. And you didn't answer my question."

"I don't recall you actually asking me anything."

Pushing away from the door, he strode through the room and reached for her hands. When he made contact, she caught her breath at the warmth that spread up her arm. Without her gloves, the feel of his palm pressed to hers made logical thought disappear.

She sighed.

"Molly, my love, will you have lunch with me today?"

My love. She resisted sighing again. "I would be honored."

The moment he released her hands, she ran her fingers over her hair and discovered with dismay several loose tendrils.

Proving he could still read her mind, he knuckled a curl off her cheek. "I always did prefer you a little disheveled."

And there went her heart again, skipping a beat. Then tripping back to life with alarming speed. "Give me a moment to fetch my coat and hat."

"Take all the time you need." He waved her off, distracted by something at his feet.

Molly looked down as well, and saw that Lady Macbeth was winding her way through his legs. The cat adored the man. It appeared to be a mutual affection.

As she left the room, Garrett's chuckle followed in her wake. She could hear him talking to the cat in that deep baritone.

He had such a wonderful voice.

In her room, she released the breath she'd held along the way and puzzled over Garrett's behavior. Less than a month ago, he'd avoided her at every possible turn.

Now, he was all easy charm and attentive smiles and witty conversation. Hands shaking slightly, she secured her hat in place. Again, she wondered what he was up to. There was a simple solution to all this confusion.

Molly would simply ask him. She'd learned long ago that direct and to the point was always the best approach when dealing with a man.

Decision made, she donned her coat, slid on her gloves and hurried to the main foyer.

Garrett waited for her near the portrait of Mr. and Mrs. Singletary. He studied the picture with a thoughtful expression, as if there was an answer to some unknown question in the painted image.

"You seem fascinated with that painting," she said, drawing alongside him.

"They look so happy I figure that should make me happy, too. I can't understand why it makes me melancholy instead."

Molly sympathized with his confusion. She'd had the same reaction herself. "It's because they had so little time together." She took a step closer to the painting. The love between Mr. and Mrs. Singletary was nearly painful to witness, knowing how their story ended. "They should have grown old together."

"How long did they have?"

"Fifteen years." She smiled sadly at the painting. "She wanted fifty."

Garrett said nothing, but now his gaze was even more troubled.

"They married against her parents' wishes," Molly explained. "Mrs. Singletary was only seventeen on her wedding day. He was two years older than that. He'd traveled west, penniless and hoping to make his fortune."

"Evidently he succeeded."

"He struck gold a year after they said their vows."

It was a sweet love story, Molly decided, even though Mr. Singletary had died so young. But at least they hadn't wasted any of their time together.

Not like Molly and Garrett. They'd wasted a lot of time. Too much. And she accepted much of the blame. For years, she'd told herself their chance to be together had come and gone.

Had that argument merely been a way to guard her heart through the pain of losing him again? A way to keep her distance from the very thing she craved the most? A life with Garrett.

"Sad tale," he said at last, pivoting to face her. The tender sorrow in his eyes stole her breath. Was he thinking about Mrs. Singletary's loss?

Or theirs?

"Very sad," she whispered.

Eyes grave, Garrett held out a hand to her, and Molly's heart took a quick extra beat.

"Ready?" he asked.

Molly placed her hand in his and smiled. She'd been ready for seven long years.

Garrett escorted Molly through the lobby of the Hotel Dupree. He knew he could have chosen anywhere to dine with her, anywhere other than the restaurant where Callie worked, on a day Fanny was on duty at the registration desk. He wasn't testing Molly's affection for him, nor was he intentionally putting her in a position that would require her to split her loyalty between him and his sisters.

That would be childish.

And beneath him.

Something a seventeen-year-old kid would do.

He'd meant what he said the other day in Mrs. Singletary's private office. He was more than willing to share Molly with his family. He *wanted* to share her with them.

Today was not a test, he assured himself. Not for Molly, at any rate. Was he testing himself, attempting to see if he'd truly let go of the past?

Perhaps.

Halfway through the lobby, he caught sight of Fanny. She stood on the lobby side of the registration desk, head bent, her back to the flow of traffic.

Garrett hesitated approaching her, primarily because she wasn't alone.

A dark-haired gentleman dressed in a superbly tailored, black woolen suit stood beside her. His head was bent over hers as they reviewed what looked like a ledger. Garrett knew the gentleman by name. Jonathon Hawkins, the new owner of the hotel. Garrett and Mrs. Singletary had met with him twice this week already.

"Fanny."

At the sound of her name, she glanced over her shoulder and smiled. "Oh. Hello, Garrett." Her gaze shifted to Molly and her smile widened. "And Molly, too."

Slipping her hand from Garrett's arm, Molly started toward his sister. She'd barely taken two steps when she froze, her gaze riveted on the man beside Fanny.

"Johnny?"

Gaze still fixed on the ledger, Hawkins turned in her direction. A look of recognition crossed his face as his steel-gray eyes fastened with Molly's pretty blue ones.

"Johnny!" She squealed in delight. "It is you."

"Molly Taylor Scott." Hawkins's usually stern features relaxed inch by inch and a slow smile spread across his mouth, the kind that probably devastated women around the world. "Look at you. All grown up."

He opened his arms at the same moment she leaped into his embrace. Wrapping her tightly against him, he swung her off her feet and turned her in a series of dizzying circles.

She giggled like a little girl.

For one black moment Garrett's vision tinged red. He'd been prepared to share Molly with his family. He was *not* willing to share her with another man.

Fanny didn't look any more pleased by this laughing display of affection than Garrett. He didn't have time to wonder at his sister's reaction before Molly bounced out of Hawkins's embrace and dragged him over to Garrett. "Garrett, this is Johnny. Johnny, meet Garrett Mitchell."

"We know each other." Though he'd only met with Hawkins twice, he'd come to respect the man's business acumen, admired his sound judgment and had even thought he could like the man. Until now.

"Hawkins," he said in a flat tone.

"Mitchell." A frown settled over the already serious features and his sharp, narrowed eyes cut from Molly to Garrett, then back again. Clearly, he didn't like what he saw.

"Molly?" Fanny's voice broke through the charged moment. "Do you know Mr. Hawkins?"

"Mr. Hawkins?" Eyebrows pressed together, Molly's gaze darted around the lobby. "Who's Mr. Hawkins?"

"That would be me." Smiling, he bent over her hand and pressed a kiss to her knuckles. "Jonathon Hawkins, at your service."

"Hawkins," she repeated, her bafflement more pronounced than before. "Why don't I remember that name?"

Something shifted in the man's eyes, just for a moment, then went away. "Because you only ever called me Johnny."

"And you used to call me Peanut." She sent him a quick, lovely smile. "I can't believe it's really you."

Garrett tightened his jaw so hard he thought it might crack. Dark, slick emotion threatened to spill over. He cleared his throat. "How do you two know each other?"

Hawkins turned his attention to Garrett. He had a quiet, aloof edge to him now. This was the man who'd turned a fledgling men's boardinghouse in St. Louis into a hotel empire.

"We were children at Charity House together," Hawkins said with no inflection.

"His mother worked with my real mother before she died," Molly added, which was to say Hawkins's mother had been a prostitute along with Molly's.

At this revelation, Fanny scanned her boss's face, a look of transfixed interest in her gaze. "Your mother worked in a brothel?"

"She was one of Mattie Silks's girls." He showed no shame over the fact that his mother was a prostitute, other than his slightly stiff posture. "I was among the first to leave with Laney O'Connor and move into the…orphanage."

He'd hesitated over the term, proving that he hadn't been a real orphan at the time. His mother had probably sent him to Charity House to better his lot in life.

She'd gotten her wish.

With far too much affection in her tone, Molly gushed over the other man. "Johnny was everyone's big brother."

As if to prove her point, Hawkins smiled down at her with an indulgent look similar to the one Garrett and his brothers bestowed on their sisters. "I remember dragging you out of a few tough spots."

"More than a few," she admitted, half wincing, half laughing. "I wasn't always an obedient child."

"All part of your charm, Molly."

"My parents would disagree." They laughed over that, then launched into a retelling of childhood tales Garrett had never heard before. Most were from before he'd known Molly.

Fascinated, he rocked back on his heels and let the two reminisce.

This Jonathon Hawkins—or rather, *Johnny*—was a different man than the one Garrett and Mrs. Singletary had met with during the week.

Hawkins was more relaxed with Molly, quicker to smile, laughing easily and without pause. He seemed comfortable around her, in a brotherly sort of way. Whenever he shot a glance in Garrett's direction, his gaze was full of quiet warning, as if he sensed Garrett had intentions toward Molly.

The man was proving perceptive, too.

"Garrett, may I have a quick word?" Fanny asked.

"Now?"

"Yes…now."

Giving him no chance to argue, she tugged him aside

while Molly and Hawkins continued reminiscing about their days at Charity House.

After issuing his own silent warning at Hawkins, Garrett turned to his sister. The look in her eyes had him sighing. "What's happened now?"

"Callie means well, I know she does, and I love her for worrying about me. But, Garrett, she won't let up." She blew a strand of hair off her face. "She's convinced I should reconcile with Reese."

"Tell her she's wrong."

"You think I haven't tried?" Fanny shoved at the same, stubborn lock of hair as before. "I told her Reese and I have come to an understanding. She won't listen. If she keeps it up I...I'm going to leave town."

"Don't you think that's a bit drastic?"

"Mr. Hawkins has other hotels, and when I mentioned a possible desire to relocate, he said I can work at any of his properties in Chicago or St. Louis."

"Fanny, running away isn't the answer."

Closing her eyes a moment, she drew in a careful breath. "I'm not running away."

"Aren't you?"

"Maybe I am. But, Garrett—" she fisted her hands by her sides "—I can't think of any other solution."

"Let me talk to Callie."

"It's not just her—it's the whole family." Frustration rang in her voice. "And that includes you."

"What have I done?"

"You've been absolutely wonderful." Her head fell forward and several locks of her hair curtained her face. "The whole family has been remarkably supportive."

Though her words were spoken with affection, he'd never seen his sister look so defeated. "You're saying we've been too nice to you over this business with Reese?"

"That's exactly what I'm saying." She grimaced. "And don't think I don't appreciate it."

"I can hardly stand this vast outpouring of your gratitude."

"Don't be snide. You know what I mean. You're all killing me with kindness. Even Reese is treating me as though I'm the one who needs comforting."

"Reese is a good man."

"I know." She practically shouted the words and drew Hawkins's narrow-eyed gaze her way. Sighing, she cast an apologetic look at her boss, and then lowered her voice. "Reese is a very good man, but he's not the man for me."

"Yes, you've made that clear."

Again, she glanced at her boss. Something flickered in her gaze, something Garrett couldn't quite decipher. She shook her head. "It would be a mistake to backtrack now."

"Then don't." Garrett considered his sister's bent head and her tight fists. He knew she was hurting. He just didn't know how to ease her pain. And that made him feel helpless.

He hated feeling helpless.

"If I only had to deal with the family, things might be bearable," she said, her eyes still focused on the floor. "It's the speculation, the whispers, the open criticism that hurts the most."

Garrett had never put much stock in what other people said, but he'd never had to endure the kind of censure Fanny described. "Has it been bad?"

"You have no idea." She visibly shuddered. "I'm not strong like Molly. I can't pretend I don't care what people say about me."

He felt his blood run cold. "What do people say about Molly?"

"Don't you know?"

"I don't engage in gossip."

Fanny glanced discreetly at her friend, cleared her throat. "She's known as the girl who loves to be engaged almost as much as she loves the Lord."

Instant fury bubbled up from the bottom of his soul. Molly deserved better. So did Fanny. From this moment on, Garrett would ensure neither suffered any more criticism, even if that meant he had to personally stop the gossip himself.

"Don't you see, Garrett?" Fanny gave him a wobbly smile. "Mr. Hawkins's offer to work in either of his other hotels comes at a perfect time."

If his sister wanted to leave Denver for a while, Garrett wouldn't stop her. But he hoped she made the decision for the right reasons. "Have you prayed about this?"

A little of her old self reared in her impatient snort. "Give me some credit, would you? I've done it without ceasing."

"And you think moving away is the answer?"

She glanced at her boss again, released a soft breath. "I do."

Garrett could present several arguments to deter his sister from leaving town, but he knew that would only serve to push her away quicker. If Fanny wanted to leave town, she would find a way. Either with his support...or without.

"I'll miss you," he said.

She laughed at that. "Oh, I think you'll find some way to fill the void in my absence. Or should I say *someone*." She hitched her chin at Molly. "You two seem to be getting closer."

He caught Molly's eye.

She winked at him. His blood scrambled through his veins. "We're definitely getting closer," he said.

"I'm glad. Oh, Garrett, I'm so very glad you're friends again."

"Make no mistake, Fanny. Molly's not simply my friend." He winked back at her, smiled at the answering blush that spread across her cheeks. "She's my soul mate."

Chapter Seventeen

The day of the charity ball blew in on the heels of a cold, westerly wind canopied beneath dingy gray clouds. Despite the dismal weather, and the threat of snow, Molly woke with a heart full of joy.

She'd never felt more vital, more alive. And this renewed confidence wasn't solely due to putting together a grand party. No question, Garrett was pursuing her. Whether his efforts were pretend or real—and she was beginning to believe the latter—she'd never felt more cherished or more beautiful in the sight of a man.

As was true most mornings this week, he was scheduled to meet with Mrs. Singletary at ten o'clock sharp. Knowing Garrett's penchant for punctuality, Molly positioned herself in the foyer two minutes prior to his arrival time.

At the same moment the clocks began chiming the hour, Garrett strode through the entryway. He greeted her with a brief kiss to her cheek. "Good morning, my love."

"Good morning, Garrett."

He didn't linger, didn't try to turn the innocent greeting into something more romantic. But he didn't wait until they were alone to demonstration his affection for her, either.

He'd walked straight up to her and presented the chaste kiss right in front of Winston.

Garrett's casual, open display of affection spoke of long-term familiarity between them, while the flicker of tenderness in his eyes told anyone who cared to look that he adored her. Another kiss to her cheek, a promise to see her later, and he headed up the stairs to the widow's private office. Sighing breathlessly, she watched him move with that confident, long-legged effortlessness she'd always admired. At the top of the stairs, he glanced over his shoulder and smiled down at her.

Her heart dipped to her toes.

Containing the rest of her response until he disappeared around the corner, Molly placed her hand on her throat and collapsed in a nearby chair.

Oh, my.

The way Garrett had looked at her just now it was, well, it was quite wonderful.

The adoration in his eyes reminded her of another time, another day and something…else.

She dug through her memory, came up blank.

Her gaze tracked through the foyer, landing nowhere in particular, sliding over the painting of Mr. and Mrs. Singletary.

The painting.

Of course.

She hurried across the marble floor. Rising onto her toes, all but touching her nose to the painted image, she squinted at the truth staring back at her.

Garrett had looked at her just now in the very same way Mr. Singletary smiled down at his wife in the portrait. It had been love in Garrett's eyes.

He loved her.

She'd been too scared to understand, too hesitant to see what had been in front of her all along. Nothing had changed in seven years. If anything his feelings for her seemed to have grown stronger, as hers had matured for him.

The Lord had blessed them with a rare second chance.

But, oh, how they'd wasted so much time.

She'd wasted so much time.

Instead of trusting that the Lord was in control, instead of believing that He had a bigger plan for her life, Molly had taken matters into her own hands.

Would she ever be able to overcome the mistakes of her past? Would she ever be able to forgive herself for not waiting for the only man she'd ever truly loved?

She was spared from answering the disturbing questions when the doorbell chimed. Happy for the distraction, she waved off Winston and went to open the door herself.

"Johnny." A smile lit her face.

He grinned back at her. "We have to quit meeting like this."

She laughed. "You're here to see Mrs. Singletary."

Although she hadn't posed it as a question, he nodded in answer. "I have an appointment with the widow and her attorney, Mr. Mitchell."

"I'll take you up." She started through the foyer.

Johnny fell in step beside her.

Smiling up at him, she looped her arm through his. "I can't believe you're back in Denver."

"I should have returned long before now."

On the surface, his answer sounded nostalgic. But there was more to the story. When Johnny had left town he'd been a penniless orphan with a bad attitude and a large chip on his shoulder. He was now a wealthy, successful businessman who'd created his own hotel empire. There were a lot of missing years in between.

"I seem to remember you making a solemn vow never to return."

He didn't exactly cringe, but he definitely looked uncomfortable at the reminder. "At the time, I meant every word."

Searching her memory, she tried to recall his final days in town. She'd been young, but not so young she hadn't sensed something terrible had driven him away. Her father had just taken over as county sheriff and had hauled him into jail for...something.

She couldn't remember what he'd done, or maybe she'd never known. What she did remember was Johnny's attitude toward everyone who cared about him, God most of all. "You were pretty angry the last time I saw you."

"I hated the world."

"What changed?"

"Me." She heard so much in that one word. Regret, resignation. Pain.

She stopped on the stairs and turned to face him. "Whatever brought you back, I'm really glad you're home."

"Me, too." He angled his head and studied her a moment, his eyes full of admiration. "You look the same, Molly, still so pretty, your features nearly as perfect as a porcelain doll. But you've changed, too."

"I've grown up."

"It's not that." He continued to study her, his eyes narrowing over her face. Then he touched her cheek. "You seem happy, but I sense an underlying sadness."

He'd always been perceptive, always saw too much. They had that in common, a skill that had been learned from the unstable years in their childhood when the future held only uncertainty. "No, I'm not sad. Not anymore."

She was healing. At last. Time and prayer had started the process. Turning to the Lord had helped as well, as had her position with Mrs. Singletary.

And then, there was Garrett.

His reentry into her life was turning into the greatest blessing of all. She was determined to put the past behind them, and reach for the future. A future she hoped to share with her one true soul mate.

But if Garrett walked away a second time, how would she ever survive? Could she really trust he was being sincere? Did she have the courage to take a leap of faith, or would she let her past stand in their way?

A jolt of fear stole her breath.

"Anyone you want me to beat up for you, Peanut? Just say the word and he's pulp."

She laughed, her mood instantly lighter. "I thought you were a changed man."

"I don't lead with my fists anymore. But if anyone hurt you—" his eyes turned dark "—I'd reconsider."

She fluttered her eyelashes at him. "My very own big brother."

"Always."

Eight years older, Johnny had always been protective of her. Not just of her, but of all the kids at Charity House. She'd been ten years old when he'd left town. She remembered crying for days.

"Come on." She took his arm and pulled him along with her. "Mrs. Singletary is waiting."

They stopped in front of the shut door. Before Molly knocked, she swiveled her head to look at him again. "I forgot to ask if you've been out to Charity House since returning home."

"Twice." A distant look filled his gaze, something a little frustrated and…bitter? No, that couldn't be right.

"They've made a lot of improvements since you've been gone," she said. "God has blessed Charity House beyond imagining."

A muscle ticked in his jaw. "So it would seem."

What was that odd note she heard in his voice? Suspicion? Resentment?

She touched his arm, nearly asked him what was wrong

then decided against it. Now that he was in Denver again, there would be plenty of opportunities for serious conversations. "It really is good to have you home."

"Thanks, Molly." He gave her the crooked smile she remembered so well. "I think I needed to hear that."

Looking slightly embarrassed he'd admitted such a thing, he broke eye contact, lifted his hand and knocked on the door. At the command to enter he turned the handle and walked inside the room.

He didn't look back.

She was only slightly hurt by the silent dismissal.

Her mind full of last-minute details she had to address before tonight, she turned to go. She was hurrying down the hallway when the door swung open again. She looked over her shoulder in time to see Garrett step out and make his way toward her.

It wasn't until he was right beside her that she noted the look in his eyes. Something had upset him. "Garrett? What's wrong?"

"Mrs. Singletary has asked me to finish drawing up an important contract before the ball tonight."

Not sure why that upset him, she angled her head and waited for him to explain.

"I could possibly be late in my arrival."

"Oh."

He stepped closer, towering over her. "I don't want to be late, not tonight."

She had to tilt her head to see into his eyes. He was truly upset over this turn of events.

How…sweet.

"It's all right, Garrett. I'll probably be too busy to partake in the festivities anyway."

He ignored this. "With our family and friends assembled in one room, I thought tonight would be the perfect opportunity for us to take our courtship to the next level."

Her stomach fluttered. He looked so determined, so steadfast, as if he was about to make a very important declaration. Was he planning to proclaim his love for her? Here? Now?

She wasn't sure she was ready.

A little thread of panic wove through her joy, enough to have her stepping back. She was suddenly worried he might still be playing a role. She was equally worried he was not.

She hated this uncertainty.

"You mean our *pretend* courtship," she clarified.

"No, Molly. I mean our courtship. No more pretense, no more make-believe, I want us to—"

"Mr. Mitchell? Ah, there you are." Mrs. Singletary leaned her head in the hallway. "We need your assistance over a particular matter in the contract."

"I'll be right there." He continued staring down at Molly. Gaze intense, he caught a wisp of her hair between his fingers. "Your first dance is mine."

"No one else's."

According to the invitation Molly had sent to one hundred of Mrs. Singletary's closest friends and business associations, the ball was to begin promptly at seven o'clock. That gave Molly precisely one hour to address any last-minute glitches that may have arisen since she'd come upstairs to dress.

Working quickly, she stabbed the last pin into her hair and stepped toward the full-length mirror to eye her handiwork.

"I suppose you'll do," she said to her reflection. Pale, shimmering moonlight streamed through the window, spreading fingers of silver over her dress.

She glanced out the window; thankfully the clouds had disappeared hours ago, taking the snow with them.

"Are you ready, dear?" The widow came up from behind her, her exquisite face appearing in the reflection beside Molly's.

"Oh, Mrs. Singletary, look at you." She spun around. "You're beautiful."

The widow wore an emerald gown made from the finest silk imported from Paris. The gold trim captured the light and highlighted her pale green eyes and caramel-colored hair. An intricately designed diamond necklace added a touch of elegance to the already splendid picture.

"And you, my dear, dear girl are absolutely gorgeous." The widow stepped back and studied Molly, her gaze running from her head down to her toes and back again. "That color suits you perfectly."

Molly smoothed her hand over the crimson bodice, then flattened her palm against her nervous stomach. "I feared red might be too much. But you were right, as always. The bold color makes a statement."

"You simply glow, Molly. And I don't think it's due solely to the color of your dress."

"I'm happy," Molly admitted.

"Your Mr. Mitchell has been very attentive these past few weeks."

Her Mr. Mitchell. Yes, Garrett was hers. Completely, irrevocably hers. "He's been wonderful."

If only she had the courage to take the final step and tell him she loved him still, always, forever.

In unison, the clocks began their incessant chiming. Molly shut her eyes and counted off the hours in her head. Six. "I better get downstairs. I must make sure the flower arrangements I put together make it to the buffet table."

"Before you go…" Mrs. Singletary reached into a pocket in her skirt and pulled out a ruby pendant hanging from a thick, gold chain. "I want you to have this."

Molly gasped. The large gemstone was the size of her thumbnail and had to be worth a small fortune, the gold equally valuable. "I couldn't possibly accept such a generous gift."

"Of course you can. Think of it as a token of my appreciation for all you did to put this party together."

Molly was shaking her head before the widow could say anything more. "I was only performing my duties."

"Duties you were not hired for. Now, stop arguing and accept this gift with the grace I've come to expect from you."

How was Molly supposed to argue with that without appearing ungrateful?

Taking her silence as acceptance, Mrs. Singletary walked behind her and draped the pendant around her neck. A bit of fumbling and the closure snapped into place.

"There. Have a look."

Heart in her throat, Molly turned to face the mirror. She covered the ruby with trembling fingertips. "It's lovely."

"It's perfect," the older woman declared. "*Now* you may go downstairs."

"Not before I do this." With quiet abandon, Molly kissed her employer on the cheek. "Thank you, Mrs. Singletary. Thank you for the necklace, for believing in me, for…for…"

How did she put into words the depth of her gratitude for all this blessed woman had done? The widow had given her both a job and a purpose when she was at her lowest. She'd even smoothed the way for Garrett to come back into Molly's life again. "Thank you for…*everything*."

"You're quite welcome. Now go away before you make me cry."

"Yes, Mrs. Singletary." With her own tears threatening, Molly hurried out of her room.

Heart full, emotions brimming over, Beatrix watched her sweet companion rush down the hallway, her slipper-clad feet light as air. She would have to say farewell to the girl soon. For all his organization and attention to detail, Garrett Mitchell was not a patient man.

He'd be asking Molly to marry him soon.

Perhaps even tonight.

What a splendid, validating thought.

With the Lord as their guide and their love for one another binding them together, they'd have a strong, happy marriage.

Oh, but Beatrix would miss Molly dreadfully.

The thought made her sigh. A bit overwhelmed, she sank to the edge of the bed and looked around the room.

Molly was everywhere, having made the space her own almost from the start. She'd chosen the wallpaper herself, the floral pattern a perfect complement to her personality. The design was both bold and sweet, impossible to ignore yet warm and welcoming.

Beatrix would have a hard time replacing Molly. Another pang sliced through her heart. The girl had left her mark not only in this room, but on Beatrix, too.

Lady Macbeth sauntered into the room, her narrowed feline gaze full of accusation. Too much activity below stairs and a change in her nightly routine had put the cat in a foul mood. Yet instead of pouting, she'd come in search of Beatrix.

"Ah, my pet, you always manage to find me when I need you most."

The cat jumped on the bed and collapsed beside her. With a heartfelt sigh, she bumped her head against Beatrix's open palm.

"Cheer up," she said, scratching the cat's silky head. "We'll be planning a wedding soon."

The cat purred in response.

Beatrix smiled.

"As much as I enjoy your company, I need to head downstairs myself." She stood, brushed off her hands and rolled her shoulders. "It's time to finish what we started."

Chapter Eighteen

The majority of party guests arrived on time, much to Molly's relief. Within an hour, a hundred voices clamored for supremacy, each trying to be heard above the loud din.

Although she thought she'd grown used to the opulence of Mrs. Singletary's home, she was still struck by the beauty before her now. Standing just inside the ballroom, cloaked in the shadows behind a candelabrum, she watched the festive scene.

Her decision to stick to a simple color pallet of silver and gold was a good one. The elegant decorations, abundant with greenery and simple flowers, were a perfect accompaniment to the long row of crystal chandeliers hanging from the high ceiling.

The candlelight she'd insisted upon provided an old-world feel. An added touch of glamour came from the guests themselves. The ladies wore lavish, colorful ball gowns. The men were clad in formal black and white.

Smiling to herself, Molly scanned faces, seeing many dear friends both old and new. Garrett had not yet arrived, though every member of his family was already in attendance. Everyone, that was, except Fanny. She'd left for Chicago early this morning.

Molly sighed.

She would miss her friend.

She sighed again, wishing Garrett was here to share this moment with her. He'd warned her he might be late; nevertheless she felt the disappointment of his absence.

Ducking out of the ballroom unnoticed, she made her way to the dining room and the overflowing buffet tables. The hordes of guests partaking in the plentiful fare appeared sufficiently satisfied with the variety of offerings.

Smiling, Molly continued surveying her handiwork throughout the house. She paused periodically to speak with friends and acquaintances along the way. When she entered the foyer, she told herself she was merely checking to ensure the flow of arriving guests was moving at a steady pace.

But that wasn't precisely true. She really wanted to be near the door when Garrett arrived.

The couple hovering in the entryway caught her notice. For a moment, Molly simply stared at them. They were both so beautiful, the handsome man and his lovely wife. The woman was dressed in a midnight-blue gown that highlighted the rich, pale color of her eyes. Her entire being glowed as she smiled up at her husband.

Dressed in formal attire, gone was the bad-to-the-bone lawman's glower. In its place was a tender expression Molly had seen him bestow on his wife countless times through the years. She never tired of watching the two interact. Tonight was no exception. Trey and Katherine Scott were as deeply in love today as they'd been seventeen years ago when they first gave in to their feelings for one another.

Molly had been five at the time, and had just moved into Charity House to live with her sister. She'd like to think she'd had a hand in their romance. After all, she'd specifically chosen Trey for her older sister, and he'd happily fallen in line.

Perhaps she wasn't remembering that correctly. She didn't much care, they were her family now. The only parents she'd ever truly known. She loved them to distraction, admired them immensely and desperately wanted what they had—a happy, faithful marriage filled with laughter, joy and steadfast support.

Her father saw her first.

The smile that spread across his face was full of love and affection. He whispered something in his wife's ear. Her head shot up and her gaze fixed on Molly.

If she'd ever doubted her parents' love for her, evidence to the contrary radiated back at her now.

She hurried to greet them.

"Oh, Molly." Her mother pulled her into a warm embrace. "You've done a lovely job with the party. I see a little of you in every detail."

Reveling in the compliment, she hung on to her mother for several moments, uncaring that her gown was being crushed in the process.

As soon as they separated, her father clamped his hands on her shoulders and turned her so he could study her face. "You look beautiful, kitten."

The endearment brought her back to her childhood, when life had been easy, her future finally secure after being shuffled from one broken-down hovel after another. This man, this woman, together they'd rescued Molly from a tragic life and had provided her a safe, loving home in which to thrive.

"You look happy, too," her mother added.

Throat burning, eyes stinging, her response was a little shaky. "I am happy. Very happy."

He fill thy mouth with laughing, thy lips with rejoicing.

Smiling now, her father released her shoulders and visibly relaxed. "You look like your old self, kitten."

"I feel like my old self."

"Praise God," her mother said.

Molly absolutely agreed. *Praise God.*

"The dancing will commence any minute," she told them, glancing from one to the other.

Her father's face scrunched into a frown. "I'd rather explore the food options first."

Molly laughed with Katherine. She kissed them both, lingered in her mother's arms a moment beyond necessary, then sent them in the direction of the buffet tables.

Garrett caught sight of Molly immediately upon arriving at the ball. He let out a sigh of relief when he saw she was talking with her parents, and not one of her many suitors.

Molly laughed at something her father said, then hugged her mother. She was so lovely Garrett's breath hitched in his throat. The shock of her beauty never ceased to call forth a strong visceral response in him. He let it come, gave in to the sensations coming on top of one another as his heart pounded wildly in his chest.

The gown she wore shimmered, taking on the same hue as the rich flames all around. Molly should always be bathed in candlelight, he decided. Delicate, fragile, with unexpected flares of fiery mischief lurking beneath the doll-like beauty.

After all these years, she still dazzled him. Captivated him.

Called to him.

There was only one solution to these profound feelings threatening to overwhelm him. Secure her as his bride.

Soon. Very soon.

Perhaps even tonight.

He took a step in her direction and nearly combusted when another man approached her first.

* * *

"Miss Scott. May I have the honor of escorting you into the ballroom?" Giles Thomas stood before her, hands hanging stiff by his side, gaze unbending.

Molly tried not to wince. She'd lingered too long watching her parents depart the foyer. Now she was stuck.

Forcing a pleasant smile on her face, she attempted to send Mr. Thomas on his way with as much grace as possible. "I'm afraid I am not yet ready to head in. I still have a few matters to address in the—"

"I shall not be deterred."

No, she could see the truth of the sentiment in his narrow-eyed glower. It was not the most attractive look for him.

Hoping to avoid a scene, she relented. Without further argument, she took his offered arm and allowed Mr. Thomas to lead her into the ballroom.

Thankfully, the music hadn't begun yet. She may still have time to separate herself from the man.

"Will you dance the first dance with me?"

Shielding her discomfort behind heavy lashes, she wondered at Mr. Thomas's persistence. She'd never given him any encouragement, other than the kindness she afforded all her male acquaintances. "I have promised the first dance to Mr. Mitchell."

"The man you were with at the opera?"

"The very same."

Mr. Thomas glared harder at this, then took her arm as if to lead her onto the dance floor despite her refusal. Or the fact that the music hadn't started. "I suppose you believe I will retreat in the face of opposition, but no. I am more resolved than ever to win your affection, Miss Scott."

Shocked at such a forthright speech, and his surprisingly tight grip on her arm, she attempted to free herself from his grasp.

She tugged too hard and promptly lost her footing.

Strong, capable hands steadied her from behind, then carefully, gently, resolutely wrenched her away from Mr. Thomas's hold.

"If you wish to dance with Miss Scott, you are in for a large disappointment, my good man." Garrett's severe voice fell over their unhappy little group. "She has already promised to dance with me."

Oh, my.

Garrett looked positively furious as he glared at the other man. Molly had never seen him this, this…formidable.

Mr. Thomas eyed him just as coldly in return.

Oh, my.

Surely they wouldn't come to blows over her.

As if sensing her unease, Garrett took a slow, deep breath and visibly pulled himself together. "Forgive my tardiness. I am here now, ready to dance with the most striking woman in the room."

On cue, the orchestra began playing the melodic strains of a waltz. Even as Garrett reached to her, Mr. Thomas refused to concede. "I asked her first."

"Oh, honestly." Lifting her chin, she scowled at the man. "I am not a toy to be fought over."

"Indeed, you are not." Garrett's mouth gentled and his gaze warmed. "You are, however, the belle of the ball."

She felt her cheeks flood with color at the appreciative look in his eyes.

"You were born to wear bold colors," he continued. "That particular shade of red is a favorite of mine."

Smiling debonairly now, the rascal was suddenly full of charm and perfect manners and tender affection, when mere moments before he'd appeared more than ready to engage in fisticuffs with Mr. Thomas.

"Molly." His entire demeanor softened even more. "Please forgive my previous boorish behavior."

"Oh, Garrett." Her heart melted and the rest of the room disappeared.

He reached out his hand. "Dance with me, my love."

My love. The endearment whispered across her cheek like a caress. *My love.*

"I would like nothing better."

"Now, see here," Mr. Thomas sputtered in outrage, his voice taking on a churlish note. "You cannot swoop in at the last minute and steal Miss Scott away like this."

Having forgotten that she and Garrett still had an audience, a rather irate audience at that, Molly bit back a sigh. "Not to worry, Mr. Thomas. I will dance the next waltz with you."

"We'll see about that," Garrett muttered, twirling her onto the dance floor without further delay.

They fell into the steps of the waltz as if they'd danced it a thousand times together, when there'd been no such opportunity to do so in the past.

This was their first dance ever.

A sense of rightness filling her, Molly settled into Garrett's embrace. *This* was where she'd always belonged. "What with the unpleasantness before, I failed to greet you properly." He gently stroked her cheek, seemingly uncaring they were in front of half of Denver. "Good evening, Molly."

"Good evening, Garrett."

"You've done an excellent job with the details of this ball. Beautiful," he whispered. "Beyond compare."

She felt her cheeks grow warm again. He was speaking of her, not the decorations. "I took your advice and applied one of my formulas."

"I'm proud of you." His words were spoken with infinite confidence, but she could feel the tension in the muscled shoulder beneath her hand.

Why was he on edge? "Garrett—"

"Molly—"

They laughed and the tension in him disappeared.

"Molly," he began again, his tone unusually formal. "I wish to ask you something extremely important."

What sort of question could put such a serious look in his gaze?

Nervous now, she almost lost track of the waltz steps. Recovering quickly, she forced a sweet smile onto her lips. "All right. Go ahead, then. Ask me whatever you like."

"Not here." He glanced around them, seemingly only just becoming aware of the crowded dance floor. "Somewhere more private."

That sounded interesting.

A flutter of anticipation shimmied through her as they turned as one to leave the dance floor.

Pausing, Garrett looked around a moment. His gaze tracked to the doors leading into the garden and he started in that direction. "This way."

They'd barely made it to the edge of the dance floor when her father swooped into view. "I believe this is my dance."

Molly's eyes widened at the unprecedented request. "You want to dance with me?"

"That's what I said." He nudged Garrett aside with nothing more than a look.

Before Molly could take a breath, she was twirling once more across the dance floor in perfect, three-step rhythm.

The sheriff was surprisingly light on his feet.

"Where did you learn to dance so beautifully?" she asked, amazed at his skill.

"I wasn't always a lawman, kitten." He gave her ear a tweak. "I learned how to dance nearly as early as I learned how to walk."

She remembered now. A member of the elite Southern gentry, her father had grown up in New Orleans before the War Between the States. Given the circumstances of his childhood, he probably had learned to dance at a very young age.

Proving his expertise went beyond the basics, he spun her in an array of complicated steps that had her gasping for air and coming up laughing.

"I've missed this," she said.

He didn't pretend to misunderstand her meaning. "You haven't laughed enough in the past year."

"No."

He changed directions, backpedaling once, twice, spinning her around again. "You were made for joy, kitten, it's one of blessings the Lord has bestowed on you."

"I lost my way for a while, but I believe I'm finally back on the right path."

"I believe you are, too."

She cut a quick glance around the ballroom, caught Garrett's eye and felt a sigh rustle up from her toes.

He wore his evening attire with natural ease, looking as comfortable in the formal clothing as he did in rancher garb. Gilded by the light of a hundred candles, the aura of power and strength emanating out of him was as natural as his hair color. He looked exactly what he was, a successful attorney of godly character making a name for himself in his chosen profession.

To Molly, he was simply Garrett. Her Garrett.

The love of her life.

"I've found where I belong," she told her father, her gaze still locked with Garrett's, as if she were speaking the truth of her heart to him directly.

"What's changed, kitten?"

How did she respond? *With the truth,* whispered a still, small voice in her head, giving her the courage she needed to continue. "I could say my position as Mrs. Singletary's companion has made all the difference. And that would be true, but only partially so."

"So there's another reason for your contentment," he mused, glancing at Garrett now, too.

Her father knew her well.

"Garrett and I have become…" Friends, she nearly said, but that wasn't the full truth, either, and perhaps not even accurate. There was so much more to her feelings for the man than mere friendship. "We're courting."

"I know, kitten."

She shook her head, giving in to the urge to laugh at herself. Of course her father knew. Even if Garrett hadn't gone to speak with him about her, this was Trey Scott. The man knew everything.

Nevertheless, she found herself saying, "I understand Garrett has asked your permission to court me."

He nodded. "As any respectable man should."

A strange sensation took hold of her, one full of hope. "When did he make his request?"

Her father gave her an odd look. "Does it matter?"

She thought that it might. "I believe so, yes."

Smiling softly, her father guided her expertly into another series of turns.

"It was the same afternoon his brothers came to town. Logan and Hunter had stopped in to see me just hours before Garrett and I spoke." He shook his head in wry amusement. "I remember the day well because I'd gone months without seeing a single Mitchell, then three of them crossed my path within a matter of hours."

Molly did a quick mental calculation. Garrett's brothers had come to town the same day he'd taken her to lunch at The Brown Palace. That meant he'd gone to speak with her father after they'd agreed to a pretend courtship. After they'd discussed their turbulent past, and *after* she'd told him the truth about her broken engagements.

Had he been playing his role as the besotted suitor? Or had he been sincere in his request?

She thought back to that day and forced her mind to think logically, rationally.

Garrett had treated her differently ever since their conversation that day at the restaurant, his attention seemingly more real than pretend.

Dare she hope?

Dare she open her heart to him at last? Dare she become vulnerable enough to accept his suit without reservation?

"He's a good man, kitten."

"The very best man I know," she agreed. "Aside from you, of course."

"Of course." His lips twisted at an amused angle. "Do you love him?"

"I...yes. I love him." She was through lying to herself about something as essential to her as air and water. "I have always loved him."

Seemingly unsurprised by this, her father nodded.

"Daddy?" she asked, using the name she'd called him as a child. "Did you give Garrett your permission to court me?"

"I did, kitten." Her father drew in a sharp breath. "Of all the men who've come to me with that same request, Garrett Mitchell is the only one I fully trust with your heart."

Chapter Nineteen

From Garrett's position beyond the dance floor, it looked as though Molly and her father were having a serious conversation. Satisfied she was in the best hands possible, he went in search of Mrs. Singletary.

He found her holding court on the opposite side of the room.

She waved him forward, then surprised him by meeting him halfway.

"I have been remiss in greeting my lovely hostess properly," he said, bending over her hand. "Forgive me."

"You're late, Mr. Mitchell. Embarrassingly so." She drew her hand free of his. "Tell me where you've been and I'll decide if you're forgiven."

Recognizing the amused twinkle in her eye, he nonetheless gave her a solemn answer. "I was tying up loose ends on the contract between you and Mr. Hawkins. The wording is nearly where I want it, with the overall agreement leaning in your favor."

"In that case, I am sufficiently appeased."

"You are also one of the most breathtaking women in attendance this evening."

Swatting at his arm, she laughed in feminine delight. "And now I am sufficiently charmed."

They fell into a general discussion about the ball, the guests and the decorations in the room. "My companion has proven gifted at planning large parties."

"Very well, indeed."

"Although gauche to talk of such things," she said. "I predict when it's time to pass the baskets we will come away with sufficient funds to build a new wing on the hospital."

"That would be quite a coup d'état." Garrett scowled when Marshall Ferguson approached Molly and her father at the edge of the dance floor.

The smile Molly bestowed on the other man had Garrett scowling harder. And then she was no longer holding on to her father, but ensconced in Ferguson's arms, spinning into the center of the parquet flooring.

After only an initial hesitation in the man's arms, Molly's smile widened.

Ferguson smiled back.

Garrett frowned at them both.

They seemed to be getting along a bit too well considering their history.

Mrs. Singletary's amused voice added to Garrett's overall discomfort. "You don't like seeing her with other gentlemen."

"No, I don't."

The widow stepped in front of him, cutting off his view of Molly and her dance partner, who were now laughing together.

"There is a way to end your agony, once and for all."

He heard the provocation in her tone, saw the challenge in her eyes and knew the widow was attempting to incite his jealousy in order to force his hand. He refused to rise to the bait. "I like seeing Molly happy."

"When another man is the source of her pleasure?"

Garrett's heart squeezed. *"No."*

"I thought not." Mrs. Singletary gave him that sly, far-too-sweet smile he'd first seen in his office when she'd made her initial business proposition to him.

But again, Garrett chose to pretend he didn't know where she was leading him, or why. He might have enlisted her help with securing Molly's heart, but he wasn't going to allow the woman to force him to act before the proper time had come.

The music stopped—*Praise God*—and Garrett thought to make his excuses with the widow. But Molly was back on the dance floor. In yet another man's arms.

This time it was Jonathon Hawkins spinning her in circles, making her laugh.

"Would you look at that?" Mrs. Singletary's tone filled with innocent glee. "Molly and Mr. Hawkins seem to be enjoying one another's company beyond a recent acquaintance would indicate."

Garrett gritted his teeth. "They are old friends."

The aggravating woman's voice practically hummed with delight. "Our Molly certainly has a lot of friends."

He chose to remain silent.

"At the risk of sounding redundant, Mr. Mitchell—" she patted his hand with obvious condescension "—there is a way to stake your claim."

"Stake my claim?" He snorted. "Molly is not a prize to be won."

"Forgive my choice of words. What I meant to say is that you can end this now, tonight, in front of family and friends."

"I could." *He would.*

When she wasn't dancing with one of her many…friends.

The widow ambled oh so casually out of his line of vision. "I see you have come to the proper conclusion at last. I'll leave you alone, then, to strategize your next move."

"I don't need—"

He was talking to Mrs. Singletary's back.

Garrett remained alone for a maximum of three blessed seconds before another feminine voice fell over him. "You're brooding, brother dear."

He let out a rough laugh. "Go away, Callie."

"When annoying you is so much more fun?" Her voice held just a touch of irony. "Not a chance."

Garrett arched a brow at her, then stiffened at the melancholy he saw lurking in her eyes. "What's wrong, Cal?"

She attempted a bright smile and failed miserably. "Would you believe me if I claimed nothing?"

He took her hand and squeezed gently. "No."

"I was afraid of that." She sighed. "If you must know, as frustrated as I've been with Fanny lately, I already miss her."

"She's been gone half a day."

"Yes, but she's always been my best friend. We've never been apart more than a day or two at a time."

"You haven't?" Garrett hadn't realized, hadn't even thought about it until now.

Blinking rapidly, Callie stared up at the ceiling. "We attended school together, toured Paris together, returned home to Colorado together. We even took positions at the same hotel so we could be—"

"Together?"

She sighed again, twisted her hands at her waist. "I still can't believe she went through with her threat and took the position at Mr. Hawkins's Chicago hotel."

"She needed to get away."

Looking even more miserable, Callie lowered her gaze. "You mean she needed to get away from me."

"From all of us," he corrected.

"She should have stayed and worked things out with Reese."

"She needed to get away from him most of all." Garrett

touched her arm, nearly sighed himself when she jerked out of his reach. "Callie, she doesn't want to marry him. And I'm not sure he truly wanted to marry her."

"They were perfect for one another."

"Fanny didn't think so." He remembered Molly's words in the hallway outside Reese's office a few weeks ago. *He's not heartbroken.* "Reese will recover."

He said the last part absently, because Molly was thanking Hawkins for the dance. This was Garrett's chance, one that vanished before he could make a move. A group of men were already gathering around her.

Garrett felt something tighten in his chest. He'd allowed himself to forget that Molly was never without a handful of suitors vying for her attention wherever she went.

A brief conversation ensued and she was back on the dance floor, spinning in yet another man's arms.

This one Garrett didn't know.

He was getting extraordinarily tired of standing off to the side while other men monopolized her time, her attention. Not only this evening, but at every other occasion when their paths had crossed in the past six months.

Molly's current dance partner was a bold reminder that if Garrett didn't act quickly, another man would attempt to claim her heart.

Unacceptable.

Callie hitched her chin to a spot off to their left. "Look at him, Garrett."

Oh, he was looking.

"He's brooding, too."

No, the man dancing with Molly was smiling, one of those big, toothy, wolfish grins that meant nothing but trouble.

"He misses Fanny," she said almost wistfully.

Reese. His sister was talking about Reese, not Molly's dance partner.

Garrett shook his head, but kept his gaze on Molly. "If you're that worried about Reese's well-being then go talk to him."

"I couldn't." Her hand flew to her throat. "I wouldn't begin to know what to say."

"Ask him to dance."

She gasped, the sound drawing his attention back to her. Her look of mortification made him realize his mistake a shade too late.

"I can't ask *a man* to dance. Why would you suggest such a thing?" She lowered her voice to a soft jeer. "There are rules concerning proper behavior, Garrett."

Of course there were rules. He'd been so caught up with watching Molly and her assortment of suitors that he hadn't been thinking properly. "Right. Sorry, Cal. Ignore what I said."

His gaze drifted to the dance floor again. Molly had been passed on to yet another partner. Enough.

Enough.

Garrett set out.

Callie stopped him with a hand on his arm. "Where are you going?"

He glared at the dance floor. "To stop this madness once and for all."

"You mean all the men dancing with Molly?"

"Of course that's what I mean." He pried her fingers from his arm. "Now, if you'll excuse me."

She opened her mouth to argue—Callie seemed to be doing that a lot lately—but clamped her lips tightly shut when he shot her a speaking glance. "Not a word," he warned.

"Not a word," she repeated, her eyes dancing with sisterly affection. Then she wiggled her eyebrows at him. "Be sure to give Molly my love."

It was *his* love he planned to give her. Now, tomorrow, always.

He approached the dance floor then stopped cold when Giles Thomas stepped up for his turn. Garrett might have been willing to allow the man one dance, *one,* but Thomas had the nerve to shoot him a smirk over his shoulder.

"The man's spoiling for a fight," he murmured to the gentleman coming up beside him.

Reese's eyebrows shot up. "Pardon me?"

"Nothing worth repeating." Garrett released a mirthless laugh and forced himself to concentrate on his boss. "How are you holding up?"

Hands clasped behind his back, Reese sighed in a philosophical manner. "As well as can be expected, I suppose, given that today was supposed to be my wedding day."

Right. Garrett had forgotten the date. No wonder the man was standing outside the festivities, brooding. "That's got to be rough."

Reese shrugged. "I'm coping well enough." His gaze fixed on a spot across the room. "I suppose you spoke with Fanny before she left this morning?"

"Indirectly." His parents had taken her to the train station and then reported back this afternoon. "She's nervous about leaving family and friends, but looking forward to the challenge of learning a new city."

Reese absorbed this information in silence. "I wish her the best."

"I'll make sure she knows." Garrett studied his boss more closely. Although he wasn't in the best of moods, he didn't appear as distraught as a man should be on a wedding day that would never come to pass. "Not dancing tonight?"

"No, and I see you aren't, either."

"The only woman I want to dance with is currently occupied."

Reese followed the direction of Garrett's gaze. "Miss Scott is a popular young woman."

"A little too popular," Garrett grumbled. Mr. Thomas had no business gazing down at her so possessively. "Excuse me."

Reese nodded his approval. "By all means."

Wading through the spinning couples, Garrett strode purposefully onto the dance floor.

No better time than the present to make his intentions clear.

Ever since their one and only dance, Garrett had never been far from Molly's thoughts. His eyes had held such a look of open adoration as he'd spun her around the dance floor that she'd felt an answering twist of emotion in her own heart.

She was having a lovely time tonight and Garrett was the main source of her joy. She'd kept him in sight since their waltz. She couldn't help but notice he'd danced only with her, and no one else, not even his sister or mother.

Now, with her heart in her throat, she watched his very determined approach through the crush of dancers. He was coming for her.

She was ready.

Only this moment mattered. Only this man.

Their eyes met over the sea of twirling couples. A silent promise spread across the tiny divide. A lasting, eternal vow that couldn't be put into words.

"Miss Scott? Is something the matter?"

She hadn't realized she'd stopped dancing and pulled out of her partner's arms. "I'm sorry, Mr. Thomas, but our dance is over."

Confusion crossed his features. "The music is still playing."

Her eyes remained locked with Garrett's. Oh, my. He looked like a man on a mission. "Nevertheless..."

Forgetting what she was saying, the rest of her words trailed off.

Mr. Thomas glanced over his shoulder and snorted audibly. "*Him?* You are throwing me over for him?"

"Don't take it personally. My heart has always belonged to Garrett." Only him.

Unappeased, Mr. Thomas huffed out an expletive, one Molly thought quite rude for mixed company. Then he stomped off, leaving her to stand by herself in the center of the dance floor.

She wasn't alone for long.

Garrett took her hands in his. "Molly. My love."

"Garrett." She could say nothing more.

He seemed equally tongue-tied now that they'd exchanged greetings. And so they simply stared at one another in captivated silence, neither moving, neither speaking.

A thousand promises passed between them, enough to fill a lifetime.

He took a step closer and his voice dipped to a husky whisper. "I love you."

"I love you more."

"I love you most."

They'd recited the same words, in the same order, seven years ago, when they'd first fallen in love. The declarations, though somewhat juvenile in nature, were just as real today. And just as life-altering.

"I don't have a ring, or a fancy speech prepared."

Her heart sighed. "I don't need either."

Talk around them didn't cease all at once, nothing so dramatic, but rather the chatter slowed by degrees.

Then, as if realizing they were about to witness a memorable moment, the dancers began forming a makeshift circle around them.

"You're everything good in my life," he said, his voice strong. "Everything beautiful and pure."

Tears filled her eyes. "Oh, Garrett."

He dropped to one knee and a collective hush fell over the room. "Molly Taylor Scott…" The crowd pressed in closer.

"Will you marry me?"

The tears spilled down her cheeks. This proposal, *this* was the one she'd been waiting for all her life. "Yes. Yes, I'll marry you."

Smiling, he bowed his head over her hand, and placed a reverent kiss on her knuckles.

"Oh, Garrett."

He barely had time to rise to his feet before they were surrounded by family and friends. Everyone talked at once, the noise hitting earsplitting levels.

Molly lost track of Garrett almost immediately.

Next thing she knew, she was being pulled into her mother's arms. Then her father's. Then Mrs. Singletary's.

Garrett's mother moved in next. His father took a turn. Each one of his brothers swooped in, then their wives.

Molly's head spun. Her vision grayed.

A loud roaring filled her ears.

Another pair of arms encircled her—Callie's—and then someone else hugged her. The gray in front of her eyes turned darker still. Molly steeled herself against the dizzying sensation taking hold of her, refusing to let the darkness consume her on this happy, blissful occasion.

She was passed around to more family and friends.

Finally, she wound her way back to her mother. "Are you happy, my dear?"

"The happiest I've ever been," she managed to say, her voice echoing in her ears and sounding far, far away.

"He'll make you a good husband."

Her mother's words were the last she heard before her world went black.

Garrett watched Molly fall to the ground, helpless to stop her descent. With every step he took toward her, he was thrown two in the opposite direction. A hard jostle from the right sent him farther back. The sea of bobbing heads parted, just a bit, and he pushed through.

He had to get to Molly.

But the crowd closed in around her again, cutting off his view. Helplessness clogged in his throat. The sensation felt as though a noose had been cinched tightly around his neck.

He twisted around. And around again, searching for the familiar cloud of black hair.

There she was.

Rising to her feet again, supported by her father while Mrs. Singletary and her mother shooed aside gawking on-lookers.

Once the way was clear, their entire party set out.

Where were they taking her?

Garrett redoubled his efforts to get to her, careening up-stream against the tide of determined well-wishers.

By sheer determination, he caught up with his future bride on the opposite side of the room. "Molly."

Leaning heavily on her father, she rolled her gaze to his. "Oh, Garrett, there you are." She laughed, even as she listed dangerously to her right. "I was trying to get to you and I lost my balance."

"You fainted," her father corrected.

"I did? How odd. I never faint." She shook her head in bemusement. The gesture sent her wobbling again.

Pushing into a room just off the kitchen, her father helped her to a chair.

Once she was settled, Garrett rushed to her side and cupped her cheek. "You're pale."

"I merely need a little air."

"Step back," Garrett shouted over his shoulder. "Everyone just step back."

"Garrett, darling." His own mother touched his shoulder, her voice gentle but firm. "You're crowding the poor girl."

"Come with me." Trey Scott's hand clamped on his arm. "We'll let the ladies take care of her for now."

Garrett dug in his heels. "I'm not leaving Molly."

"She's not going anywhere," Katherine said gently. "But we need to loosen her corset and you cannot be in the room when we do so."

"We'll just be outside," her father said, dragging Garrett to a door. "A mere holler away."

"I'm not leaving—"

"Outside, Garrett." Sheriff Scott's tone brooked no argument. "Now."

Chapter Twenty

Garrett paced the perimeter of the kitchen's enclosed garden. His footsteps crunched in the hardened snow. His breath swirled around his head.

Eyeing his every move, Molly's father leaned a shoulder against the brick and mortar of Mrs. Singletary's house. "You certainly know how to propose to a woman."

"She fainted." He scrubbed a hand over his face, changed direction, exhaled sharply. "And I wasn't there to catch her."

"It won't be the only time you'll fail her."

Garrett's feet ground to a halt. "I'm not going to fail her, Sheriff Scott."

"You can't make that promise."

Holding her father's gaze with an unwavering one of his own, Garrett set his shoulders. "Oh, but I can."

"Let me give you a piece of marital advice, son." Trey Scott shoved away from the wall, his expression unrelenting but not completely unkind. "No man can be everything to his woman."

"I don't want to be everything to Molly."

Don't you? He drew in a tight breath. "All right, maybe I do. I want to stand by her in good times and bad. I want to love her without condition, grow old with her and protect her from every harm."

"Noble, to be sure, and I don't doubt you'll do your best to live up to your wedding vows. I even trust you'll protect her—"

"With my life."

Her father nodded. "I wouldn't have given my blessing if I believed otherwise. But, Garrett, you can't be her savior. And she can't be yours."

His shoulders went rigid at the blasphemous suggestion. "There's only one Lord and Savior."

"Good to know you have that straight in your mind." The other man continued holding his gaze. "You and Molly will be good together. She'll inspire you to become a better man. You'll bring out the best in her. But at the end of the day, the only place either of you will be able to get true validation is from the Lord."

Garrett knew this, believed it, lived it as best he could, but he wasn't sure why Molly's father was so insistent on the matter. "Why are you telling me this, sir?"

"Molly has always held a special place in my heart, even before she became my daughter." He shoved at his hair, the only sign this conversation was hard for him. "She came to Katherine and me after being subjected to unspeakable pain in her life, some of which she's never shared with anyone."

Garrett closed his eyes a moment. He didn't like hearing that Molly had suffered as a child, didn't like knowing she held a secret pain in her heart she'd shared with no one, not even her parents.

"When she first arrived at Charity House she refused to talk to anyone—not to her sister, not to me, no one. For months she didn't utter a single word."

What sort of trauma had Molly endured that would steal her ability to speak?

"Katherine and I made every effort to create a safe home for her. Over time, she became the gregarious, charming girl you've always known." He took a step toward Garrett.

One lone, menacing step that made a louder statement than his words. "There has been only one other time in her life that I've seen her caught in despair like that."

Garrett swallowed back a surge of guilt, but held the other man's gaze without flinching. "When I went away to school."

"That's right." Her father took another step forward, closing the distance to mere feet. "I'm only going to say this once, Garrett, so listen very closely."

Bracing himself, he nodded and silently prepared for the warning to come.

"Follow through with your promise to marry my daughter."

"Yes, sir, as soon as possible."

It was the easiest promise he'd ever made.

Molly returned to the ballroom a half hour after fainting—*fainting!*—her head clearer, her balance all but restored. Her mother stood beside her as they silently watched the dancers glide past.

She noted with great pleasure that Reese Bennett, Jr. was finally out on the dance floor, with Callie Mitchell as his dance partner. Neither looked comfortable, nor did it appear they were attempting to talk to one another.

No wonder, tonight had to be difficult for them. Fanny had played such an integral role in both of their lives.

"I'm happy for you, Molly." Her mother hooked her arm through hers and tugged her close. "God has brought favor into your life. Garrett will make you a fine husband, indeed."

"I love him, Mother, so very much." The words flowed from her lips with ease, words she'd never said about another man.

"Yes, dear, I know."

A movement in the far corner of the ballroom announced

Garrett's return to the party. Her father strode along beside him. Much to Molly's relief, both men were smiling.

Her father stopped to speak with Garrett's brothers, while Garrett continued making his way through the crowd. He was heading straight for her. But when he stopped, he acknowledged her mother first.

They spoke briefly about the exciting events of the evening. At last, he turned to Molly. "We've only danced once tonight."

"Then I'd say it's time we did so again."

"We're in full agreement."

He drew her into his arms and spun her away. A few steps later, everything in her simply stopped and sighed.

"Molly." His expression turned somber. "Whatever comes our way we'll see it through, together. And I promise, to the best of my ability, to never hurt you again."

"Oh, Garrett, of course you're going to hurt me again. And, sadly, I'll hurt you, too. This isn't heaven. We're going to fail one another. But we'll also have great triumphs."

He angled his head at her. "Have you been talking to your father?"

"My mother, actually. Why?"

"Your father said nearly the same thing to me when we were outside just now." His hand flattened on her back and he tugged her a little closer. "Molly, I know I'll make mistakes through the years. I'll frustrate you at times. I'll let you down. But I'll honor you, always. I'll protect you with my life and love you until the day I die."

"You know." She tangled her fingers in the hair at his collar, her eyes filling. "That sounds like wedding vows."

"Feels like wedding vows."

Hope blossomed in the darkest corners of her soul, the burst of emotion stinging in her eyes. "You might want to write that down, because I expect to hear every bit of what you just said again at our wedding."

"I won't forget a word."

"Nor will I."

They stared into one another's eyes, the steps of the waltz an afterthought as they clung to one another and spun across the dance floor. Around and around and around, the perfect start of a grand adventure.

"You look in desperate need of a kiss," he whispered.

She pressed a tiny step closer. "Hold that thought until the end of the night. We'll steal a moment alone once all the guests have gone."

"Only a moment?"

She laughed. "Maybe two."

"I like the way you think, Molly Taylor Scott."

Unfortunately, a moment alone eluded them over the next several hours.

Mrs. Singletary pulled Molly away from Garrett as soon as they left the dance floor. Apparently, it was time to pass the baskets and collect whatever donations they could. Thus, Molly returned to her duties the rest of the evening.

Meanwhile, she noticed that Garrett was accosted by well-meaning family and friends wanting to congratulate him. Even Marshall Ferguson approached him and they spoke for quite a while. They both walked away smiling.

By the time Garrett made his way into the foyer, the guests were leaving the party in droves. As official hostess, Molly was required to stand beside Mrs. Singletary and thank everyone for attending. She'd rather let Garrett spirit her away and seal their engagement with a kiss as promised.

He stayed on his side of the foyer.

Watching him from her vantage point, she was overwhelmed by her good fortune. *Thank you, Lord.*

The prayer was simple yet sincere.

Once the majority of the guests were gone, Garrett finally approached her. With Mrs. Singletary looking on, he gave Molly a chaste kiss on the cheek. "Good night, my love."

She sighed into him, mourning their moment alone that had never come.

"Good night, Garrett." She lifted on her toes and whispered in his ear, "I can't wait to marry you."

"And I you."

It took every bit of willpower not to wrap her arms around his neck and insist he kiss her properly, regardless of their audience. For years she'd told herself they could never be together again, that their time had come and gone. Now, she wondered why she'd ever doubted.

"I'll stop by tomorrow." He paused as the clocks began chiming the hour. One, two, three. He smiled. Tomorrow had arrived hours ago. "Correction, I'll come by later today."

"Yes, yes." Mrs. Singletary stepped between them and turned his shoulders toward the exit. "Take your leave, Mr. Mitchell. Molly needs her sleep."

A brief bow of his head and Garrett left the widow's home.

Molly watched him go.

He'd acted on impulse tonight, perhaps for the first time in his life. He was a thinker by nature, a planner, but his feelings for her had inspired him to take a chance, to propose in front of a hundred of Denver's most influential people.

That not only took courage, it took unspeakable love. Garrett loved her. He really, truly loved her.

Why then, wasn't she melting into a puddle of happiness? Why did she feel as close to tears as to laughter?

Fear, exhaustion, something far darker tickled the edges of her joy. The staggering complexity of her emotions didn't fit the exultant mood of the evening.

A soul-searching moment later, Molly knew why.

It wasn't that she didn't trust Garrett. It was that she didn't trust herself. What if she allowed fear to enter her heart again one day, and she found a reason to step back from Garrett?

Would he let her?

Unlike her other fiancés, he knew her. Really knew her. Surely, if she attempted to hold a portion of herself back from him, he would break down whatever barrier she erected between them?

Or would it be up to her to fight for what she wanted this time around? If it came to that, she prayed she had the courage to make a stand.

Under Mrs. Singletary's strict orders, Molly slept late the next morning. It was nearly noon when she finally rolled out of bed. A decadent way to start the day, but a small amount of decadence wouldn't hurt just this once.

As her mind slowly awakened, so did her memory.

Garrett had asked her to marry him.

And she'd said yes.

Under normal circumstances, their whirlwind courtship of three weeks, two days and four hours would be considered suspect. But the man in question was Garrett. The only man Molly had ever loved. Not for the first time, she realized the Lord had blessed them with a rare second chance.

Better rested, head clearer than when she'd gone to bed, Molly was determined not to allow fear to get in the way of what she wanted this time around. She wanted Garrett. And soon he would be her husband.

With that happy thought, she finished dressing for the day. One look in the mirror told her the events of the previous evening were no dream. She practically glowed.

The doorbell rang, announcing a visitor. Molly rushed downstairs just as Winston escorted Garrett into the main foyer.

"I thought it might be you." She all but glided across the marble floor to meet him.

His eyes traveled over her. "You look rested."

"I slept in."

"I'm glad." Although he didn't attempt to touch her, the smile he gave her was full of promises.

She waited for him to take her hand, *needed* him to take her hand, to prove last night hadn't been a dream, that this new happiness between them was real.

Why wasn't he touching her? They were engaged. Surely her reputation could stand a bit of public affection.

Old worries reared, working unwelcome nerves through her bliss. Perhaps he hadn't come to see her, after all.

"Do you have an appointment with Mrs. Singletary?" Her voice sounded as nervous as she felt. Why was she allowing anxiety to creep in?

This was Garrett. *Her* Garrett.

The man who'd asked her to marry him last night.

She forced herself to relax.

"I'm not meeting with Mrs. Singletary until tomorrow." He clasped his hands behind his back. "I've come to take you to lunch. Unless you have other plans…"

"Mrs. Singletary insisted I take the entire day for myself." She couldn't bear it. She reached out and touched him, a tentative grip on his arm. "I'm all yours."

"Yes, Molly." He smiled rakishly down at her. "You're all mine."

A shiver skittered down her spine. "I…I'll get my coat."

"I'll wait here."

Refusing to allow thought in her head, good or bad, she ambled upstairs, retrieved her coat, then rushed back down the hallway.

She skidded to a halt at the top of the stairs, her breath backing up in her lungs. Garrett was cradling Lady Macbeth like a baby.

Rather than squirm or resist the vulnerable position, the smitten cat gazed up at him with big green eyes and a look of complete adoration. He spoke softly to the animal, nonsensical words Molly couldn't make out from this distance.

Not that it mattered. What settled her nerves and made her heart beat in quick, hard bursts of hope, was the picture Garrett made holding the animal. He was the very image of masculine strength, even as he tenderly stroked the animal's head with an exquisitely gentle touch.

Their children would receive the same attention. Molly could see Garrett with them in her mind's eye. He would speak softly to them, as he did with the cat now. He would listen to them, *hear them,* stand between them and harm. They would flourish under his love and protection.

As would Molly.

She had no business allowing fear to color her perspective.

Eager to start their life together, she banished any remnants of doubt in her heart and started down the stairs.

Smiling, Garrett set the cat down on the floor, and offered her his arm.

She took it without hesitation.

Outside, he guided her to a waiting carriage.

The joy and acute satisfaction of loving this man made her voice a bit husky. "Where are we dining?"

"It's a surprise."

"I like surprises."

He chuckled. "I know."

They already knew so much about each other. And yet, there was so much more Molly wanted to learn about Garrett. Seven years was a long time to be apart. A lot of life had been lived by them both. A lot of choices had been made.

So many questions sprung to mind that she had no idea where to begin.

Casting a quick glance in his direction, an awkward sensation came over her. She wasn't supposed to feel uncomfortable around him, not with their history. Or perhaps their history was the very reason she felt so ill at ease now.

They might be engaged but their relationship was still so new, held together by fragile threads.

They needed to strengthen the cords.

She'd shared her pain, her humiliation, even parts of her wounded heart with him only weeks ago. He'd not done the same. Oh, he'd spoken of his early days at school, but not the years since.

"Garrett, why did you never marry anyone else?" She blurted out the question, then quickly clamped her lips closed. That wasn't what she'd been meant to ask him, or at least not in such blunt terms. "What I meant was—"

"I know what you meant." A tender smile flitted across his face, giving him the boyish look she held so dear.

She felt herself relax, but just as quickly stiffen with concern. "You didn't answer my question."

"Molly. My sweet, amazing, beautiful girl." He took her hand and brought it to his lips. "I never married because I never found a woman who made me forget you."

Her mouth formed a perfect *O*. She hadn't expected him to be quite so, so…honest.

"I've rendered you speechless."

"I…yes, I suppose you have." She stared into his amber eyes and noted the hint of vulnerability there. He hadn't meant to speak so plainly and now he was regretting his honesty.

Of all the things she wanted in her marriage with this man, regret was not one of them.

It was her turn to provide comfort. "Do you know why I never fully gave my heart to Marshall or Bart or any other man of my acquaintance?"

He shook his head, his gaze wary now.

"Because they weren't you."

Surprise and pleasure filled his eyes, but he remained silent, as if waiting for her to say more.

He deserved to hear the rest. "You once asked me if I would have followed through with either wedding if my fiancés hadn't called them off."

A frown marred his handsome features. "I remember."

"Do you also remember what I said?"

The groove between his eyes dug deeper. "You said yes, you would have gone through with your promise to marry them."

"I was wrong." She reached out and lovingly cupped his cheek. "Truth is, I wouldn't have married any other man but you."

His features relaxed little by little, until he wore the boyish grin again. "Let's set the date."

"Is tomorrow too soon?"

Laughing, he kissed her lightly on the lips. "Tomorrow would be perfectly fine with me, but I think our parents might have something to say about that."

The mention of their individual families spread a wave of joy through her darkest worries. She was marrying the man of her dreams, and getting the extended family she'd always wanted.

"Molly Taylor Scott Mitchell." She tried out her new name aloud, grinning at Garrett as she did. "It has a nice ring to it, don't you think?"

"The very best."

Chapter Twenty-One

With his hand on the small of her back, Garrett escorted Molly into the dining room of The Brown Palace. He ushered her to the table he'd reserved specifically for them.

Although his brothers had arrived unexpectedly the last time they'd eaten together in this restaurant, Garrett would forever mark that lunch—that day—as the official beginning of their second chance.

Smiling down at the woman he loved, he held out her chair then took the seat across from her. She filled the moment for him. Her scent, her smile, her very presence.

Gaze full of delight, she glanced around, smiled wider. "This is where we sat the last time we dined here."

"I'd hoped you would remember."

Big, blue eyes blinked up at him. "I remember every moment I spend with you."

A sentiment he shared, but the waiter's arrival prevented Garrett from speaking the truth in his heart.

As the young man took their orders, Garrett kept his eyes on Molly. A dozen thoughts ran through his mind, a thousand promises poised on his tongue. He wanted to tell her he was sorry he'd left her behind all those years ago, sorry he'd walked away from her, from them, out of stupid, foolish pride. But looking back he realized that he'd needed to leave home. Had needed to go alone, to work out his convictions on his own. To fail or succeed away from the comfort of family and loved ones.

He was home now, his beliefs and principles worked out. His faith in God secure. His path set. Best of all, the Lord had brought Molly back into his life. Garrett didn't take that blessing for granted.

Waiting until they were alone, he took her hand, clutching it protectively in his. Their stares connected across the table with a force that nearly immobilized him.

Molly gave him a sweet, shy smile and all the pretty speeches he'd prepared scattered from his mind.

"You do realize," she murmured, "that Mrs. Singletary will claim victory for all of this."

He lifted an eyebrow. "All of this?"

"You, me. Us." She waved a hand between them. "She'll assert we never would have found our way back to one another without her nudging us in the proper direction."

"I say let her gloat a little."

"I was thinking we would let her gloat a lot."

Laughing at that, he let go of Molly's hand and leaned back in his chair.

Now, he told himself. *Give it to her now.*

"I have something for you." Slipping his hand inside his jacket, he wrapped his fingers around the tiny jeweler's box and pulled it free. "I was a little impetuous with my proposal last evening."

"I liked it."

Because she sounded sincere, he felt his heart flip over in his chest. "Nevertheless, I skipped several steps." He was only mildly surprised by the hoarse timbre of his voice. This was a big moment. "I'd hoped for a more sophisticated delivery when I asked you to marry me."

"Oh, Garrett." She gave him a soft, dreamy smile, erasing any doubts in his mind as to whether he'd disappointed her. "Your proposal was perfect."

"I left out one key element." He set the black velvet box on the table between them. "Molly, my love, will you—"

"Garrett? Molly?" a familiar female voice called out their names from across the restaurant.

Then another, equally familiar voice added, "What a pleasure running into you two here!"

Sighing inwardly, Garrett quickly palmed the box. He barely had time to tuck the ring back into his jacket before his brothers' wives arrived at their table.

Molly was out of her chair in an instant. Garrett rose a bit slower, a complicated mix of pleasure and frustration warring inside him. It wasn't that he didn't love Megan and Annabeth. He did. Beyond measure. But presenting Molly's ring to her was an important moment he didn't want to share with anyone but her, not even their loving family.

By the time he and Molly had each been pulled into one embrace then another, and then passed around a second time, Garrett resigned himself to the interruption.

Family was, well, *family*.

Both women had been instrumental in his young life, having married his brothers when Garrett was more boy than man.

Megan, with her blond hair, blue eyes and willowy figure, looked so much like the rest of the Mitchell brood she could have been a sister. Annabeth's dark Mexican coloring and pale blue eyes could never be confused as a Mitchell, but she was just as attractive as her sister-in-law and just as special to Garrett.

It didn't take him long to discover how much they adored Molly, and she them.

"We never had a chance to welcome you into the family properly." Annabeth, Hunter's wife, beamed at Molly. "So, welcome."

She hugged Molly again, holding on longer than last time.

Megan, Logan's wife, added her own words of welcome, her gaze including Garrett. "We're so happy for you both."

"Please, join us."

He offered the invitation with only a brief moment of hesitation, but Megan must have sensed his initial reluctance. She touched his arm. "Are you sure? We don't want to intrude…"

"You aren't intruding," he said, regretting his earlier hesitation. There would be plenty of time to give Molly her ring. A lifetime.

Smiling, Garrett motioned the waiter back to their table. While his brothers' wives settled in and ordered lunch, he gave Molly a stoic lift of one shoulder.

She mouthed her thanks, though an apology was in her eyes just behind the gratitude. Looking closer, he saw a hint of frustration beneath the other emotions. Like him, Molly was torn between wanting her new sisters to join them and having Garrett to herself.

The revelation that she wanted time alone with him, as much as he did with her, settled any lingering doubts in his mind. He and Molly were going to have a good, happy life together.

Over the next few days, Molly recognized the tension growing in Garrett, tension born of frustration, impatience and annoyance.

She suffered similarly. Every time he attempted to present her engagement ring to her, a member of his family, or hers, interrupted them.

Although the ring was merely a symbol, she hoped, wished—*prayed*—these constant delays weren't a sign of things to come. She loved both their families, relied on them even, but Garrett was the man she'd pledged to marry, to love all her days. Rather than sit back wondering when the next opportunity to be alone with him would come, she decided to act.

With Mrs. Singletary's blessing, Molly took the carriage across town. In her eagerness to take matters into her own hands, she arrived at Bennett, Bennett and Brand before the start of business. Before, it seemed, any of the lawyers themselves had arrived, including Garrett.

Settling in to wait, she positioned herself on the front stoop and glanced up at the regal building that housed the law firm. The brick and mortar were of the finest quality, the glass and bronze of the door as elegant as any she'd seen in town.

The wind moaned shrilly behind her, indicating a turn in the weather. She huddled deeper in her coat.

Despite the cold nipping at her cheeks, she found her mind wandering to Garrett and the way he'd looked at her when he'd asked her to marry him. She wasn't quite so cold anymore.

"Good morning, Miss Scott." Reese Bennett, Jr. joined her at the door. "You're here bright and early."

"I…" For a moment, she felt unmoored, disoriented, even a little silly. "I've come to see Garrett, er…Mr. Mitchell."

"He won't be in for several hours," he said. "He's at the courthouse, filing documents for Mrs. Singletary."

"Oh." She blinked. It hadn't occurred to her that Garrett wouldn't be at his office this morning.

A cold breeze kicked up, slipping icy fingers under the collar of her coat. She shivered, wrapped her arms tightly around her waist.

"Would you like to come in from the cold and wait for him inside?"

"Goodness, no." She shouldn't have come. Embarrassed, she considered her options. Decided returning home was the best solution. "I'll see him another time."

"Would you like me to give him a message for you?"

"No. I mean, yes. Or rather, no." She shook her head at her ridiculous indecision. "If you could just tell him I stopped by this morning?"

"Consider it done."

"Thank you."

He nodded, but didn't head inside building. "Miss Scott?"

"Yes, Mr. Bennett?"

"Congratulations on your engagement." The smile on his face and the sincerity in his tone had her relaxing. "You've made Garrett a very happy man."

She took a long breath of air. "You're kind to say so."

"It's not about being kind." His smile lifted the corners of his mouth. "It's the truth."

"Then I *truly* thank you."

He laughed, the gesture giving him an almost boyish appeal. He should laugh more often, she decided. The transformation to his stern features was nothing short of remarkable.

"If there's nothing more you need from me, I'll say good day, Miss Scott."

She sighed, feeling very much alone and foolish for having made the trip across town for nothing. "On second thought, if Mr. Mitchell asks where I am, will you tell him I'm at the county jailhouse?"

"The jailhouse?"

"I've a mind to speak with my father." She suddenly wanted, *needed* to see her father.

The attorney's smile returned. "Of course. I'll be sure to tell him."

"Thank you."

"My pleasure." He tipped his hat in silent farewell.

As he disappeared into his law offices, Molly shook her head. Reese Bennett, Jr. was such a nice man, courteous, charming. Handsome, too. He would have made Fanny a fine husband.

Apparently, it was not in God's plan for either of them. At least they'd found that out before they'd married.

Across town, Molly had better luck finding her father. He sat at his desk, buried beneath a pile of paperwork. His frown told her what he thought of the task.

"Am I interrupting?" she asked from the doorway.

"More like rescuing me." Tossing down his pen, he came around the desk in three quick, long-legged strides and pulled her into a bear hug.

She held on to him, allowing his strong arms to comfort her.

Sensing her unease as only a father could, he placed a kiss on the top of her head. "What's wrong, kitten?"

"Who said anything's wrong?" She pressed her cheek into his shirt. "Can't I visit my father without a hidden agenda?"

He smoothed his hand over her hair. "A jailhouse is no place for a woman."

"I'm not a woman. I'm a daughter."

"Who sounds excessively unhappy." He set her away from her and searched her face. "Has Garrett done something to hurt you? Has he—"

"It's not Garrett." She drew her bottom lip between her teeth. "Not in the way you mean."

"Come. Sit." He guided her to a hardback chair, then pulled up another one and sat beside her. "Now tell me what's going on."

Where did she begin? *How* did she begin? "I don't even know what's wrong."

He chuckled. "That's quite the female response."

She swiped at her cheeks, surprised to discover they were damp. When had she started to cry? "It's just…oh, Daddy, Garrett hasn't given me my ring yet."

Thankfully, her father didn't scoff at her ridiculous, *female* response.

"Ah," was all he said. Then, "I'm sure it's nothing to worry about, kitten. He's probably just taking his time picking out the perfect stone."

"No, you don't understand. He's already purchased the ring. He's tried to give it to me in every possible way imaginable." She swiped at her cheeks again. "He's tried at lunch, on a stroll through the park, during dinner last night…"

Her father said nothing.

She continued, her words tumbling out fast now. "He begins with this lovely speech, and I get all fluttery inside. But when he attempts to present the ring, we're interrupted, either by a well-meaning family member…" She gave him a pointed look. Her father had been one of those well-meaning family members just last night. "Or a friend, or one of Garrett's business associates."

Again, her father didn't condescend, or patronize, or tell her she was being foolish. "That must be frustrating."

Very. "This morning, I decided enough was enough. I went to his office, in the hope of catching him before the start of business." She balled her hands into fists. "But he's at the courthouse, doing lawyerly stuff."

Her father's lips twitched. "Lawyerly stuff?"

She lifted a shoulder. "Something to do with filing documents, or something."

"Kitten, God's timing isn't always on our schedule. You'll get your ring soon."

"When?" She huffed out the word. "How? If we can't find a private moment soon, I'll be tempted to do something drastic."

As if to mock her frustration, the door flew open and a blast of cold air shot into the jailhouse.

Frowning, she hunched her shoulders against the added chill. Would the interruptions ever stop?

Her father nodded at the newcomer over her shoulder, then returned his gaze to hers. A smile was in his eyes as he patted her knee. "Take off your gloves, kitten."

"What? *Why?*"

"You're about to get that private moment you've been wanting."

Just as she opened her mouth to reply, a familiar, rich baritone addressed her father. "Sheriff Scott, could I speak with your daughter alone?"

"Certainly." Her father stood, then leaned over her and whispered in her ear, "God's timing, kitten. Always better than our own."

After shaking hands with Garrett, her father turned back to Molly and hauled her to her feet. "I'll be on the other side of the door."

She launched herself into his arms. "You're the best father ever."

He chuckled, pressed a kiss to her forehead, then left her alone with Garrett.

Blinking at the closed door, Garrett shoved at his hair. "What was that about?"

"Just a private moment between a father and his daughter."

His well-sculpted lips curved. "Ah."

"Speaking of private moments…" She moved around him, gazed up into his eyes. "Notice how we're completely, *absolutely* alone?"

"I noticed." He pulled off his gloves, then went to work on hers, starting with her right hand first.

"Did you also notice how my father is guarding the door for us?"

"I most certainly did. Remind me to thank him later." He tossed the glove over his shoulder, smiled tenderly down at her.

She offered her other hand. "Word around town is that my father is very good at his job."

"I'd heard that rumor." Focusing diligently on his task, Garrett freed one gloved finger at a time, slowly, deliberately.

"No one's getting past him," Molly added.

"No one." He tossed her other glove over his shoulder and took her left hand in his. "Molly, my love, I've given you a lot of words in the past three days."

"They've been really great words."

He stared deeply into her eyes. "Each one came straight from my heart."

Her own heart dipped to her toes. "I'll remember them always. To the end of my days."

Nestling her hand in his, he inhaled slowly. "I want to give you a token of my love, a reminder of my commitment to you always."

She sighed at that, a big, shuddering pull of air. Garrett Mitchell was some man when he set his mind on a task.

"Molly Taylor Scott." He let go of her hand and reached into his jacket. "Will you accept this ring as a promise and reminder of my love?"

With a flick, he opened the lid.

"Oh. Oh, Garrett. It's…" She gawked at the perfectly oval, exquisitely beautiful, blue, blue sapphire winking up at her. "It's breathtaking."

"The color reminded me of your eyes."

With trembling fingers, she reached out to touch the stone then whipped her hand back as if it might bite her.

"Allow me." He plucked the ring from its nest, and then slid it on her finger. His eyes never left her face.

"It's a perfect fit," she whispered.

He tugged her against him and kissed her tenderly. "You're mine, Molly. Now and forever."

Two words echoed in her head. At last.

At last.

Chapter Twenty-Two

The next two weeks flew by in a whirlwind of activity. Garrett spent most of his days with Mrs. Singletary, securing the details of her business venture with Jonathon Hawkins first, then helping her set up a benevolent fund for the hospital. In between the two, he presented several more business ventures for her consideration.

His evenings were spent wooing Molly. He was falling in love with her more and more every day, discovering facets to her personality he'd never known before. She shared her hopes and dreams with him, while he confided his.

He hadn't been surprised when she'd confessed that she wanted to own a millinery shop. In turn, he'd told her about the law firm he'd hoped to start one day, business acquisitions his specialty.

With each revelation came more intimacy between them. What had once been childhood infatuation was becoming mature love.

When I was a child, I spake as a child, I understood as a child, I thought as a child: but when I became a man, I put away childish things.

Garrett couldn't imagine his life without Molly in it. The more time he spent in her company, the more he wanted to be with her. If that made him a sap, then, yeah, he was a sap.

He took Molly out to dinner most nights, attended the theater with her when a play caught her interest. He even suffered through two evenings at the opera with his future bride and her employer.

"Must be love," he muttered.

Chuckling at himself, he retrieved his mail from his clerk's desk before retiring to his own office. Garrett relished the fact that he was getting to know Molly on a more intimate, personal level. He believed she was beginning to trust him, to open her heart to him.

She still held a portion of herself back, but not nearly as much as she once had. Each day she let down a little more of her guard. He had no doubt, in time, she would give herself to him fully.

One concern still plagued him, though. He never had her to himself.

At first, he understood the interruptions, accepted them with quiet resolve. But he and Molly had been engaged for three weeks now and the intrusions weren't stopping.

When would their well-meaning family and friends leave them alone? Surely, once they were married, everyone would step back. Except, Garrett feared that might never happen.

Was he being selfish, possessive even?

Brooding over this problematic matter, he absently sorted through his correspondence. A letter with a St. Louis postmark caught his eye and his hand froze.

For only a moment.

He tore open the seal and read the words quickly, not stopping—or thinking—until he reached the end of the page. He set the paper on his desk and leaned back in his chair. Was this a solution?

Or an escape?

What if it was both?

He picked up the letter and read the words again. And again. And one more time for good measure.

Instead of reaching clarity, he came away more confused than ever.

Setting the letter back on his desk, he looked up to heaven. "Lord, is this from You? Or am I searching for a sign that fits my needs and alleviates my reservations?"

He thought of Molly, and the promises he'd made her over the past few weeks, one in particular. *Whatever comes our way, we'll see it through together.*

He couldn't keep this from her, couldn't pretend he didn't want what was offered in a few paragraphs of ink on parchment.

This could change his life.

It had the potential to destroy his life, as well.

He closed his eyes and prayed for guidance. *Lord, grant me the wisdom to know what to do.*

"Miss Scott, you have a visitor."

Surprised, Molly looked up from the bonnet she'd been working on. "I do?"

Winston gave a short bow of his head. "It's Mr. Mitchell."

"Oh?" Garrett was hours too early for their evening at the opera. A wave of foreboding washed through her. Why was he here? Why now?

Her hand went reflexively to smooth her hair, which was undressed and hanging loose down her back.

"I…" She was being silly. Garrett wouldn't care that her hair was a mess. "Please, send him in."

She quickly rose to her feet.

He entered mere seconds later and, of course, his gaze went immediately to her hair.

"Garrett, I wasn't expecting you." She resisted the urge to run her fingers over the disheveled waves. "I would have taken more care with my appearance had I known you were coming."

"You're lovely just the way you are." Two long strides brought him to her side, whereby he cupped her face in his hands. "I'm reminded of the wild, impetuous girl I used to know, the one who was willing to take on any adventure for the sheer fun of it."

"Oh, she's still inside here." She tapped her heart, smiling at the love she saw in his eyes.

"Good to know." He laughed, the sound coming out a little forced. "I wouldn't want you changing for me."

"Not even a little?"

"Not even a little," he confirmed.

She relaxed. Then felt her spine stiffen when he didn't do the same.

"Garrett?" Her legs suddenly felt like jelly. "What's wrong? Has something happened I should know?"

He turned away from her, took a step toward the door, then swung back around. His expression was guarded now and her stomach rolled inside itself.

"I have something to tell you," he said.

He looked so serious. He sounded so serious. A fresh spurt of panic tickled in her throat. "I'm listening."

He strode back to her, reached out, stopped from touching her, then stepped back again.

"What's wrong?" She'd never seen him so agitated.

"It's nothing bad." He laid a hand on her arm in a show of quiet comfort. "At least not if you look at it from a certain perspective."

For an instant, fear paralyzed her. And then she knew— *she knew*—whatever he said next, her life would be changed forever.

"What is it, Garrett? What's happened?"

He struggled to pull in a tight breath. "I thought this would be easier."

Dread burned a trail down her throat.

Holding her gaze, he dug a letter out of his coat pocket. "This will explain everything."

Molly stiffened her spine, slowed her breathing, then took the letter between her thumb and forefinger. She held it away from her, eyes locked with his.

"Go on, read it."

She lowered her gaze and read the letterhead aloud. "'Mead, Tyler and Hoyt.'" Confused, she lifted her gaze to Garrett's. "Should I know them?"

"Mead, Tyler and Hoyt are the senior partners of a law firm in St. Louis. They specialize in tax law and business acquisitions."

No. *No.* She could hear nothing but the drumming of her heart. She looked back at the letter and began to read.

The tears came on the heels of the first paragraph. She held them tightly in check through the second. And the third. But when she came to the end, her control snapped and the tears fell unrestrained down her cheeks.

She couldn't speak, couldn't move.

The law firm of Mead, Tyler and Hoyt wanted Garrett to work for them. With them. They wanted him so badly they'd offered him an unprecedented partnership.

How could he consider taking the job?

How could she ask him not to? By all accounts, the position was tailor-made for his particular skills.

A sob crawled up her throat, begging for release. She quickly swallowed it down.

The despair remained. This was their past all over again.

Her knees buckled.

Garrett was by her side in a flash, cradling her in his arms, holding her tightly against him. "Say something." He breathed the request in her hair, his voice desperate.

"It's a wonderful opportunity for you," she said, keeping her head lowered, her voice even, her heart cold.

"For *us,* Molly. It's a wonderful opportunity for us. Every decision I make from here on out affects you, too. Tell me what you think."

Her head snapped up. "You want my advice?"

"We're getting married. Your opinion matters."

He'd come to her with the letter, was willing to discuss it as a couple. For a long moment, she looked into his eyes, saw the truth staring back at her. The horrible, awful truth. He wanted to take the job, but he would sacrifice the opportunity if she asked it of him.

She choked back another sob.

How could she ask him to turn down the job?

How could he ask her to leave everything she knew?

A terrible quandary lay before them. *Lord, why are You testing us like this?*

"You already have a job here in Denver," she whispered.

"Yes, Molly." He guided her to a chair, waited for her to sit. "I have a job here in Denver. But a better one awaits me in St. Louis."

He was handsome, even now, in this dreadful, agonizing moment. Lean, muscular, a strong slash of cheekbones, the boy she'd always adored inside the man she would always love. "Denver is our home," she said simply.

With careful, deliberate movements, he pulled out a chair and sat beside her. "Yes, this is our home. Where I'm just another Mitchell boy and, you—"

He broke off, looked away, but not before she saw his pained expression.

"Go on, Garrett. Say it."

He swallowed. "Denver is where you're the girl who loves to be engaged nearly as much as she loves the Lord."

She drew back as though he'd slapped her, but she couldn't deny his words. She knew what people whispered about her, knew they thought she was frivolous and self-centered, incapable of keeping her promises. "We're both more than what others say about us."

"I know we are." He dragged a hand through his hair, his emotions carefully contained. "Molly, my love, don't you see? This is our chance to make a fresh start. We can begin our lives together with a clean slate, in a city where no one knows us."

"But, Garrett, that's just it. We'll be in a city where no one knows us. There will be no family, no friends, not even the passing acquaintances we've made over a lifetime."

"We'll have each other."

He wanted the job.

"You'll have your work," she said. "What will I have?" Nothing. Nothing but endless hours of waiting for him to return home to her every night. That was no way to live.

He glanced at the table, picked up one of the unfinished bonnets. "This. You can have this."

"You want me to make bonnets all day long?"

"No. Yes. I mean, what about your dream, Molly? The one you told me about the other night? You could start your own millinery shop in St. Louis."

A spark ignited deep within her, one she didn't dare fan into a flame because she was afraid. Deathly afraid. She knew what it meant to be left alone all day, knew the fear of not knowing if he would come home at night. "What do I know about starting a business?"

"I'll help you." He rose, pulled her to her feet. "You're talented, Molly. Gifted, creative. I don't know much about women's hats, but I see how you take ordinary bonnets and turn them into pieces of art. A shop run by you would be a smashing success."

She loved him for his confidence in her. But she was still afraid, and didn't have the courage to tell him why. She'd never told anyone why she feared leaving Denver. "Garrett, this is a big decision for us both."

"Molly, think of what we can accomplish. Together. The possibilities are endless, the potential triumphs immeasurable."

Hand shaking, she picked up the letter from the St. Louis law firm and tried to read the words again. They blurred in front of her eyes. One big, black smudge over white.

The paper slipped from her fingers.

"I love you, Molly."

"Oh, Garrett." She practically leaped into his arms. "I love you, too."

They held one another tightly, as if if they dared to let go the other person would vanish right before their eyes. She'd only ever felt so desperate, so afraid one other time in her life. They'd been here before, at this same impasse where one of them would win, and one of them would lose.

The stakes were higher now. The potential for pain unparalleled.

Why, Lord? Why put us in this position again?

She clung to Garrett. Instead of feeling comfort in his arms, she felt nothing but sorrow, bone-deep sorrow. Because this moment felt like goodbye.

She wanted him so much, wanted to be his wife, the mother of his children. But she didn't want to leave Denver, didn't want to leave *family.* His or hers.

"I want our children to know their grandparents." She spoke into his shoulder. "I want them to know their aunts and uncles, their cousins."

He buried his face in her hair. "St. Louis is only a train ride away."

"It won't be the same."

"That's not to mean it can't be a good life for us." He stroked her hair. A gesture so sweet, so gentle, so full of love her heart broke a little more.

And then the trembling began. Bone-rattling, teeth-chattering shakes.

Garrett's arms tightened around her, keeping her from falling. This was getting them nowhere.

As she'd done so many times before, she locked her fear deep inside her and stepped back from him.

His eyes searched her face. "Tell me what you want."

Afraid to respond, afraid to beg him for something that could potentially destroy his love for her, she broke eye contact.

"Look at me, Molly." When she merely shook her head, he took her chin in his hand and gently urged her to do as he requested. "Ask me to stay."

She couldn't. "I can't ask you that." She jerked her chin free. *"I won't."*

The frustration on his face morphed into hurt, such hurt her own face burned. "Why not?" he demanded.

"I can't ask you to sacrifice your future for me."

"So we're back to that. You play the martyr. I play the man unwilling to compromise." He gripped her shoulders, his hands so gentle she thought she might weep. "Molly, my love, ask me to stay."

"You'll only come to resent me if I do."

"Ask me to stay."

"No." She stepped back and his hands fell away. "Ask me to come with you."

"I can't."

Now she demanded an answer. "Why not?"

"For the same reason you won't ask me to stay. I couldn't bear waking up one day and confronting nothing but resentment in your eyes, resentment toward me because I took you away from home."

Tears threatened again. She let them come, let them spill down her cheeks in a river of sorrow. "What are we going to do?"

"I don't know." He reached for her, his hand shaking ever so slightly, and wiped away her tears with his thumb.

"I guess we haven't settled our differences after all," she choked out.

He cupped her cheek. "We're good together, Molly."

She closed her fingers around his wrist. "I don't want to lose you."

Eyes a pale amber-gold, he dropped his hand. "You're giving up on us."

No. No. She shook her vehemently. *"No."*

"All right, then, consider this. A very wise woman once gave my sister judicious advice when she was confused about her engagement. She gave her a four-step formula to help her decide what to do."

She gave him a shaky smile. "You think I'm wise."

He nodded. "You told Fanny to start with prayer, spend time in the Bible, trust the Lord's guidance. And, finally, most importantly, follow your heart."

Follow your heart.

Did she have the courage? Did she trust Garrett enough to leave everything she knew behind and rely solely on him?

You won't be alone. You'll have the Lord.

Did she have a strong enough faith to truly believe that?

Needing a moment to gather her thoughts, she turned her back on Garrett, took a deep breath and forced her mind to think through the situation calmly, logically, without emotion.

"You're pulling away from me." He laid a hand on her shoulder. "I can feel it. I can *see* it. You're distancing yourself from me, from us."

"I...no, Garrett." She spun around to face. "I'm not pulling away. I love you with all my heart. I want to marry you and spend the rest of my life with you."

He stuffed his hands in his pockets.

"I love you," she repeated.

"I've scheduled a meeting with the law firm in St. Louis

to discuss the position in greater detail. After reaching out to me as they have, I owe them the chance to make the offer in person."

Molly felt his words like a blow to the heart.

"You're going to take the job." She saw it in his eyes, heard it in the firmness of his voice.

"I'm going to gather more information."

A formality, nothing more.

"All I ask while I'm gone is that you decide if you love me enough to put your complete trust in me, in us."

"I love you," she insisted.

He took her hands, his eyes full of pain. "I know what I want, Molly. I want you. But if you can't give me your whole heart it doesn't matter if I stay or go. You have to decide if you trust me completely. If you gave me that assurance, I'll stay in Denver. If you can't, I'll take the job in St. Louis."

Without her. He was telling her that if he took the job in St. Louis he would do so without her.

"It's all or nothing this time around, Molly."

Accepting his right to issue the ultimatum, she nodded, even as her heart shattered. "I understand."

He kissed her on the temple, the forehead, then lingered over her mouth. "Follow your heart, Molly."

If only she knew how.

Chapter Twenty-Three

Garrett made the trip to St. Louis with a heavy heart and a mind full of conflicting thoughts warring inside his head. He hadn't wanted to leave Molly, even for a day, but emotions had been high between them. They'd both needed to step back, to regroup, to decide what they really wanted.

Garrett already knew what he wanted.

Thus, as he sat in Robert Hoyt's office, listening while the three law partners took turns selling him on the position they'd created specifically for him, he came to two separate and distinct realizations at once.

He wanted the job.

He was going to turn down the offer.

Losing Molly wasn't worth any opportunity, no matter how tailor-made it was for him. He'd let his pride rule his heart seven years ago. He wouldn't do so again.

When Robert Hoyt, a man with a balding pate and a large girth, finally came up for air, Garrett had his response prepared in his mind.

"Well, Mr. Mitchell?" Hoyt asked, eyebrows lifted, face alight with expectation. "Will we be adding your name to the letterhead?"

"Gentlemen." He eyed each of the partners in turn. "While I admit, I want this position—"

"That's good news. Good news, indeed." Hoyt clapped him on the back. "When would you like to start—"

Garrett held up a hand. "While I want this position," he said again. "I'm afraid my answer is no at this time."

Seemingly stunned by his refusal, the three lawyers looked from one to the other, then back at him.

Hoyt spoke for the group. "You want the job, but your answer is still no?"

He nodded. "My home is in Denver."

Silence met his words.

When both Hoyt and Mead continued staring at him, clearly speechless, Richard Tyler, the senior partner, took hold of the reins and plowed through his objections. "Mr. Mitchell, you once indicated a desire to make a name for yourself beyond your family's influence. Is that no longer true?"

"I can accomplish that task in Denver." In truth, he was already on his way now that he was working with Mrs. Singletary. Even his older brothers had turned to him for advice.

"You will have better success in St. Louis," Mr. Tyler argued, his kind, agreeable features holding an earnest expression beneath a shock of full white hair. "As a partner, you will have unprecedented autonomy for a young man your age."

True. But he wouldn't have Molly.

"You are young, unmarried and—"

"I'm engaged."

"Ah." Understanding dawned in the man's eyes. "Your fiancée doesn't want to leave Denver."

"It's her home."

Eyes carefully blank, the older man steepled his fingers beneath his chin. "You would put her wishes above your own, above your career, above your very future?"

Garrett answered without hesitation. "Yes." He sat up

straighter, his gaze unwavering. Absolute conviction filled his heart, bringing with it great power, great strength. "Molly is my priority. She always will be. Her happiness and our life together are more important than any job. I would be remiss to allow you to believe otherwise."

To Garrett's surprise, respect filled the other man's eyes. "I can't fault your answer, sir. Although we regret losing you, you must follow your conscience."

Garrett let out a slow exhale, liking the senior partner more and more. "I believe I would have liked working here."

"You would have been a great asset." Reluctantly, Tyler rose.

Following the man's lead, Garrett did the same, then proceeded to make his way through the room as he shook each of the partners' hands.

Richard Tyler escorted him to the door. "I'll walk you out."

"Thank you."

Out in the hallway, the lawyer fell in step beside Garrett. At the door leading onto the busy St. Louis street, he paused. "I want you to know, Mr. Mitchell, if you change your mind, the offer is always open."

He scanned the man's face, saw only sincerity staring back at him. "But I just turned you down."

"For all the right reasons." He clapped Garrett on the back in a paternal gesture. "Any man who puts his future wife's interests above his own is the kind of man I want working by my side."

"I consider that a great honor, sir."

"Go back to Denver, Mr. Mitchell. Marry your girl and live a good life together." He reached around Garrett and opened the door. "You're making the right decision."

Yes, he was. "Goodbye, Mr. Tyler."

"Goodbye, Mr. Mitchell. And Godspeed."

* * *

Molly spent the majority of the day crying in her room. She hated giving in to such weakness, but it couldn't be helped. Her heart was breaking.

After several attempts to talk to her through the closed door, Mrs. Singletary left Molly to wallow in her misery alone.

Flat on her back, tears leaking out of the sides of her eyes, Molly stared at the ceiling over her bed. Garrett had left town without her. He'd walked away from her, from them, just as he had seven years ago.

And you let him.

They'd learned nothing in their seven years apart. She'd let him leave town without a fight. And he'd gone without a backward glance.

There still hope, she reminded herself. Garrett had only traveled to St. Louis for an interview. He hadn't accepted the position.

Yet.

A thick blanket of despair fell over her. She let it come, let it consume her. For five full minutes. Then she scrambled out of bed, lowered to her knees and took her pain to the Lord.

By the time the sun dipped beneath the horizon, Molly was finished feeling sorry for herself. She would not allow fear to hold her in its sinister grip.

"Now faith is the substance of things hoped for, the evidence of things not seen," she whispered in the darkening room.

She desperately wanted to rely on faith, not fear. She wasn't sure she knew how. She needed wise counsel. Thus, when Mrs. Singletary knocked on her door and suggested she "come out and eat something," Molly padded across the floor and let the widow in the room.

One look at her red, swollen face and Mrs. Singletary

pulled Molly into her arms. "My dear, dear girl, you can't give up hope like this. Mr. Mitchell isn't gone forever. He'll be back tomorrow."

Sighing, Molly pushed away from her employer and went to look out the window. The setting sun had strung ribbons of color above the snow-tipped mountains, a remarkable melding of pink, orange, red, purple and blue.

Unable to stare at God's beautiful artistry when her heart was breaking, she squeezed her eyes shut, tipped back her head and breathed deeply. "He'll take the job."

"You don't know that."

"I won't let him turn it down."

"I see." Mrs. Singletary touched her back, her voice but a whisper and full of sorrow. "I'll miss you when you're gone."

Molly opened her eyes, but didn't turn around to face her employer. "I'm not going with him."

"Of course you're going with him." The widow gripped her shoulders and gently turned her around. "Your place is by his side."

Molly waited until she was certain she could speak without her voice breaking. "He doesn't want me to come with him. He says I'll resent him if I do."

"Will you?"

"Why does he have to go to another city to prove his worth?" The anger in her words surprised her, but now that she'd unleashed the dark emotion she couldn't pull it back. "Why can't he be happy here?"

"The opportunity is in St. Louis, Molly." The widow spoke calmly. "Besides, if he stays here there's a very real chance he may spend the rest of his life wondering if he'd really made it on his own. That kind of doubt can destroy a man."

"Doesn't he understand how much his family loves him?"

"Of course they love him, so much that they helped him acquire a position at one of the best law firms in Denver."

All right, yes, perhaps he'd been given his start because of his family name. Why was that so terrible? "Anything they've done to help him in his career has been out of love, not to keep him in his place. He's only ever been 'that other Mitchell boy' in his own mind."

"Molly." Mrs. Singletary drew her to a chair. "This isn't about Mr. Mitchell. It's about you. Why are you so afraid to leave Denver?"

"I'm not afraid."

The widow simply stared at her. Then, in silence, she went to Molly's dressing table, picked up a hairbrush and returned.

As the widow brushed her hair, Molly closed her eyes. Perhaps it was time to reveal the source of her fear, a memory that was buried so deep in her heart she'd not shared it with anyone, not even her own family.

"I don't want to be left alone again."

Mrs. Singletary's hand paused, then resumed brushing an instant later. "Again?"

"When I was a five, my father—my *real* father—took me away with him after my mother died in her brothel." Cowardice came with the words. Shame. Humiliation. She could stop her story here, leave the rest unsaid. She pressed on. "He wasn't prepared to care for a child, didn't know what to do with me. So he left me alone in our tent all day while he went searching for his fortune in the hills."

"You must have been so scared."

"Petrified."

"I'm sorry, dear, so very sorry." Mrs. Singletary hugged her from behind.

"Every morning before he left for the day, he would issue strict orders for me not to leave our tent." She shuddered at the memory, at the fear that still gripped her today. "He left me no toys to play with, no food. But he always, always came home at night."

The brush paused, then stroked through her hair again.

Molly squeezed her eyes shut, hating the tears stinging behind her lids. "He would sing me to sleep every night. He had a deep, rich, lovely voice, and for a few moments, I wasn't afraid or sad. But then he would get up the next morning and—" she choked on a sob "—leave me again."

"How long did this go on?"

"Weeks, months, I don't remember." She shrugged carelessly, refusing to feel anything, anything at all. "Then, one night, he didn't come back."

"Oh, Molly." The widow set down the brush and came around her chair. Tears of sorrow swam in her eyes. "Listen to me. You're not that helpless five-year-old anymore. And, God forbid, if something ever happened to Garrett in St. Louis you would only be a train ride away from family and friends."

"I know that. In here." She tapped her head. "But the little girl still trapped in that tent, still trapped deep inside me, is afraid."

There. She'd spoken her secret aloud.

"So you would choose the comfort and safety of home over being with the man you love, the man who would never leave you alone in the way your father did?"

"I want both Garrett and family."

"Of course you do." Mrs. Singletary knelt in front of Molly, took her hands. "But God may have a different plan for your life, one that will require you to take a bold leap of faith."

Knowing the widow was right, Molly drew in a shuddering breath. "I don't know if I have that much courage."

"What's faith, my dear, if it doesn't endure when we're most afraid?"

Closing her eyes, Molly absorbed the question.

"Are you courageous enough to take a leap, to trust that the Lord will catch you if your man doesn't?"

Molly squared her shoulders. She'd spent her entire life holding a portion of her heart back from the rest of the world. Some part of her had stayed hidden inside that tent in an effort to protect the frightened, lonely child she'd once been.

But somewhere along the way, her safe place had become a prison. She must free that little girl, or risk living enslaved to fear forever.

Picking up her Bible, she read the verse she'd marked in Ruth the day before. *For whither thou goest, I will go; and where thou lodgest, I will lodge: thy people shall be my people, and thy God my God...*

"Mrs. Singletary." Molly cleared her throat. "I believe it's time you found yourself another companion."

A watery smile spread across the widow's face. "I already have the young woman picked out."

Garrett jumped off the train before it came to a complete stop in the Denver station. His feet barely hit the platform before he took off at clipped pace. A movement out of the corner of his eye had him switching directions.

Set a little apart from the rest of the passengers hurrying to catch their train, Molly stood smiling at him. Sheltered under an awning from the wind, she twirled her parasol.

The mischievous curve of her lips, the ever-present twinkle in her eyes, the slight tilt of her head, drew him a step closer. Stunning from every angle, he'd always thought her beautiful.

Now, she stole his breath.

Lost in the moment, lost to the girl from his past that had turned into the woman of his future, he paused and simply stared.

Big, expressive, clear blue eyes connected with his. With two fast strides he closed the distance.

For a moment, they said nothing while unspoken promises flowed between them.

Molly broke the silence first. "Do you remember what I said to you the day you left for school?"

Needing to do something with his hands, he stuffed them in his pockets. "You said, 'I will always, always love you.'"

A laugh tinkled out of her. "Well, yes, I did say that. And, Garrett, I meant it. I will always, always love you."

"I will always, always love you, too." He reached toward her, touched her face.

She smiled tenderly at him, closed her hand over his wrist. "What else did I tell you that day?"

He dropped his hand to his side, and forced his mind to relive the worst day of his life. He drew a blank.

Taking mercy on him, she gave him the answer. "I said, you might think we're through, Garrett Mitchell, but the Lord will bring us together—"

"Again someday."

"And so He has," she said.

"And so He has."

"Garrett—"

"Molly—"

They shared a laugh.

"I want to go to St. Louis with you."

At the same time she made her declaration, he made his. "I'm staying in Denver with you."

"I...wait a minute." He blinked, shook his head, blinked again. "Molly, what did you just say?"

"You're taking the job in St. Louis and, Garrett, my love, my heart." She set down her parasol, grabbed his lapels and tugged him to her. "I'm going with you."

Holding on to his coat, Molly scanned the face of the man she loved, understanding the mixture of shock and hope in his eyes. The same emotions braided through her heart, healing her past once and for all.

"I turned down the job."

"Tell them you've changed your mind."

"You're more important to me than any job." He smiled down at her, his love shining in his molten amber eyes. "I'm staying in Denver. With you."

She dropped her hands from his coat, then reached to him again and shook him slightly. "Garrett Mitchell, you have to take that job."

He covered her hands with his, drew his brows together. "Why? What's different now than when I last saw you?"

Swallowing back her nerves, banishing any last remnants of fear, she took a giant leap of faith and told him about the months she'd spent in the mining camp with her real father.

When she finished her tale, his eyes were filled with sorrow, sorrow for her.

"I never suspected, Molly, never realized you experienced something so unspeakably traumatic. No wonder you don't want to leave Denver." He stroked her face tenderly. "That settles it. We're staying here, where you'll always have the safety of family."

"Garrett, no." She pressed a fingertip to his lips. "I'm no longer a scared little girl. I'm a grown woman. I want to be your wife, in every sense of the word." She thought of the Bible verse that had pushed her in the proper direction and recited the verse from memory. "'For whither thou goest, I will go, and where thou lodgest, I will lodge: thy people shall be my people, and thy God my God.'"

"I'll take care of you, Molly. I won't leave you, or forget about you, or put you in a position to be afraid or feel alone." Tightening his arms around her, he bent down and kissed her forehead. "I love you."

"I love you, too. My heart is yours."

A smile crossed his lips. "I like the sound of that."

"We're getting married, immediately, this week if possible. Our families will adjust."

He beamed with pleasure. "You'll get no argument from me."

"But if you think I'm going to let you sacrifice your future for me, think again." She planted her fists on her hips. "You're taking the job in St. Louis, and that's the end of it."

"No, Molly. I'm not, I'm—"

"And," she cut him off midsentence, "you're going to help me start my own millinery shop. We're going to do great things together, Garrett. In St. Louis."

Something shifted in his eyes, something that looked very much like the hope she herself felt. "Anyone ever tell you your bossy?"

She laughed. "Only every person who meets me."

"I love you, Molly Taylor Scott." He pulled her to him, evidently uncaring that they were in a busy train station where anyone could see them. "I'll make you a good husband."

"I'll make you a better wife."

"I have no doubt, my love." He pressed his lips to hers, retreated, pressed again. "Absolutely no doubt."

Epilogue

Their wedding was one of the most well-attended events in their individual families' history. The mother of the bride cried. The father of the bride came close.

The bride remained perfectly dry-eyed, until she entered the church and saw her groom waiting for her at the end of the aisle, in all his masculine glory. She was finally a bride—*Garrett's bride*. He was the only man she'd ever loved.

God's perfect timing. Worthy of a few tears, she decided, and then let several fall.

"Ready, kitten?"

She nodded.

Without another word, her father guided her down the aisle. He looked nothing like the tough lawman of legend today, but more like the father she'd come to know and love, the one who adored his daughter to distraction.

She adored him in return.

Halfway down the aisle, Mrs. Singletary caught her eye and winked. Two full months after Garrett's marriage proposal at the charity ball, the widow was still gloating.

Seemed fitting, somehow.

Molly winked back.

At the end of the aisle, her father kissed her on the cheek, and then handed her off to Garrett.

From that point forward, the ceremony proceeded without a hitch. After the traditional vows were spoken, Garrett took her hand and recited the same words he'd professed the night of their engagement.

"Molly, I know I'll make mistakes through the years. I'll frustrate you at times. I'll let you down. But I'll honor you, always. I'll protect you with my life and love you until the day I die."

She sniffed delicately. "Oh, Garrett, you remembered."

"Word for word."

"I love you," she said through her tears. "I'll always love you, through good times and bad, to the end of our days."

They stared into one another's eyes, this moment of quiet solidarity the most precious one they'd shared so far.

"Yes, well." The preacher cleared his throat. "I, uh…I now pronounce you husband and wife."

The congregation cheered when Garrett swept his bride into his arms for a soul-searing kiss.

There was no traditional reception planned because the newlyweds had a train to catch. A collection of their most treasured family and friends joined them on the platform immediately after the wedding ceremony.

With her new husband's arm wrapped around her waist, Molly surveyed the assembled group.

Some of their loved ones smiled at them, while others— namely their parents—attempted to hide their teary-eyed sorrow behind handkerchiefs and booming words of wisdom. All were there to say goodbye in their own way.

Knowing it could be a very long time before she smelled the scent of Colorado pine, Molly drew in a deep breath of cool mountain air. She would miss Denver, the only home she'd ever known. She would miss her family and friends even more.

But her life was with Garrett now.

They needed to take this next step together. Nevertheless, her eyes filled with bittersweet tears. She blinked them away, determined to maintain a small degree of dignity in these final moments with her family.

She would not cry. She would not cry. She would not cry.

She would, however, indulge in one, lone, heartfelt sigh.

Misinterpreting the sound, Garrett pulled her closer still. "It's not too late, Molly. You may still change your mind. We don't have to go—"

She kissed the rest of his words away.

"We're making the right decision," she whispered against his mouth, then drew back and smiled into his beautiful amber eyes. Mitchell eyes. She prayed every child she bore him inherited that stunning characteristic.

"Molly—"

"I'm not going to change my mind, Garrett. It is my greatest joy and honor to take this leap of faith with you. Whatever comes our way we'll see it through—"

"Together," he finished for her, kissing her once, twice, three times.

Another bout of tears threatened, this time tears of joy.

As soon as she and Garrett boarded the train to St. Louis, the next chapter of their life together would begin. Or, as Garrett had whispered in her ear in the carriage ride over, they were about to embark on their next Grand Adventure. Their first as husband and wife.

He fill thy mouth with laughing, thy lips with rejoicing.

The backs of her eyes stung. Blinking away the dampness, that was quite enough crying for one day, she smiled up at her husband. The wind had tousled his hair, giving him a very roguish appeal. He was so handsome, so strong, so…*hers*.

A train whistle split the air.

Garrett pulled his arm away from her waist and took

hold of her hand. "This is it, time to say a final goodbye to our family and friends."

"I'm ready."

Chin lifted high, Molly walked across the train platform, her husband by her side.

Garrett's nearness gave her the strength to kiss her mother goodbye, and then her father and all the rest of their family and friends.

His earlier vow to protect her with his life gave her the courage to board the train without an ounce of fear or regret.

His ever-abiding love gave her the surety to know that she would never be alone again. It had taken them seven long years to find their way back to one another, but God's perfect timing had prevailed.

* * * * *

Dear Reader,

Thank you for choosing *Finally a Bride,* the seventh book in my Charity House series. Molly has always held a special place in my heart. She first showed up in book one of the series, *The Marshal Takes a Bride,* as a five-year-old orphaned scamp in desperate need of a loving mother and a father.

With her willful disregard for bath time and her refusal to follow most rules, Molly stole the hero's and heroine's hearts from the moment she skidded on the page. It was a joy to give that rambunctious little girl a happy ending of her own. That her hero was the only man she's ever loved made the journey all the sweeter.

This book has many themes I love—reunion, runaway bride, first love, a nosy matchmaker. Add the Old West in the mix and, well, this story has turned out to be one of my personal favorites to date. From page one, Garrett and Molly didn't stand a chance, especially with Mrs. Singletary nudging them along.

I love hearing from readers. You can contact me through email at renee@reneeryan.com, or at my website: www.reneeryan.com. I'm also on Facebook and Twitter.

In the meantime, Happy Reading!

Renee

Questions for Discussion

1. In the opening of the book, Molly is surrounded by several potential suitors vying for her attention. What is it about Molly that draws men to her? How does Garrett show himself to be a cut above the rest?

2. What is Mrs. Singletary up to in the opening scene? Does she have a hidden agenda for offering her business proposition to Garrett? What? How do Garrett and Molly act toward one another in his office? What's behind the tension between them?

3. What advice does Molly give Garrett's sister about her engagement? Do you think this is good advice or bad advice? Why? When Garrett discovers his sister has broken her engagement to his boss, whose help does he seek and why?

4. Why is Garrett trying to prove his own worth at the law firm? What name is he given by the townspeople who know his brothers? Have you ever been in someone else's shadow? If so, how did it make you feel?

5. Why didn't any of Molly's previous engagements work? What secret has she been harboring about her breakups? Why do you think she's perpetuated this pretense? What did her former fiancés claim was the reason they couldn't marry her? Were they right?

6. What event does Mrs. Singletary ask Garrett to attend with her and her companion? Why is attending this event a problem for him? Why do you think he agrees to go anyway?

7. What was the source of Molly and Garrett's first argument when they were together seven years ago? How did that argument end? Does the memory of this cause tension between them? Why or why not?

8. When Molly and Garrett figure out Mrs. Singletary's agenda for them, what do they decide to do in response? Why do they only draw up three variables to the formula at first? What interrupts the process? Does this bring them closer or push them further apart?

9. Where do Molly and Garrett go after leaving the law firm? Why? What do they discuss at this lunch? What does Molly reveal about her past engagements? Have you ever made decisions during a vulnerable emotional state? What happened?

10. Why does Mrs. Singletary put Molly in charge of the charity ball? Why is this new duty a problem for Molly? What happens at the ball that changes the course of Molly and Garrett's relationship?

11. What arrives at Garrett's office from St. Louis? Why does this letter change his life forever?

12. What secret pain from her past makes it difficult for Molly to leave Denver? Who has she shared this information with before now? Why does she share it with Mrs. Singletary?

13. Who's waiting for Garrett at the train station when he returns from St. Louis? What happens at this rendezvous? How is the St. Louis problem resolved?

REQUEST YOUR FREE BOOKS!

2 FREE INSPIRATIONAL NOVELS
PLUS 2
FREE
MYSTERY GIFTS

Love Inspired.
HISTORICAL
INSPIRATIONAL HISTORICAL ROMANCE

YES! Please send me 2 FREE Love Inspired® Historical novels and my 2 FREE mystery gifts (gifts are worth about $10). After receiving them, if I don't wish to receive any more books, I can return the shipping statement marked "cancel." If I don't cancel, I will receive 4 brand-new novels every month and be billed just $4.74 per book in the U.S. or $5.24 per book in Canada. That's a saving of at least 21% off the cover price. It's quite a bargain! Shipping and handling is just 50¢ per book in the U.S. and 75¢ per book in Canada.* I understand that accepting the 2 free books and gifts places me under no obligation to buy anything. I can always return a shipment and cancel at any time. Even if I never buy another book, the two free books and gifts are mine to keep forever.

102/302 IDN F5CN

Name   (PLEASE PRINT)

Address   Apt. #

City   State/Prov.   Zip/Postal Code

Signature (if under 18, a parent or guardian must sign)

Mail to the **Harlequin® Reader Service:**
IN U.S.A.: P.O. Box 1867, Buffalo, NY 14240-1867
IN CANADA: P.O. Box 609, Fort Erie, Ontario L2A 5X3

Want to try two free books from another series?
Call 1-800-873-8635 or visit www.ReaderService.com.

* Terms and prices subject to change without notice. Prices do not include applicable taxes. Sales tax applicable in N.Y. Canadian residents will be charged applicable taxes. Offer not valid in Quebec. This offer is limited to one order per household. Not valid for current subscribers to Love Inspired Historical books. All orders subject to credit approval. Credit or debit balances in a customer's account(s) may be offset by any other outstanding balance owed by or to the customer. Please allow 4 to 6 weeks for delivery. Offer available while quantities last.

Your Privacy—The Harlequin® Reader Service is committed to protecting your privacy. Our Privacy Policy is available online at www.ReaderService.com or upon request from the Harlequin Reader Service.

We make a portion of our mailing list available to reputable third parties that offer products we believe may interest you. If you prefer that we not exchange your name with third parties, or if you wish to clarify or modify your communication preferences, please visit us at www.ReaderService.com/consumerchoice or write to us at Harlequin Reader Service Preference Service, P.O. Box 9062, Buffalo, NY 14269. Include your complete name and address.

LIH13R

Whitfield Calder, Earl of Danning, would much rather spend a fortnight tending to his estate than entertaining three eligible young ladies. But when his valet insists that marriage is an earl's duty, Whit agrees to the house party. He has no intention of actually proposing to anyone…until flame-haired Ruby Hollingsford declares she'd never accept him anyway.

Ruby has been tricked into attending this charade, but she certainly won't compete for the earl's attentions. Yet, Whit isn't the selfish aristocrat she envisioned. And with a little trust, two weeks may prove ample time for an unlikely couple to fall headlong into love.

The Master Matchmakers

The Wife Campaign

by

REGINA SCOTT

*is available December 2013 wherever
Love Inspired Historical books are sold.*

Find us on Facebook at
www.Facebook.com/LoveInspiredBooks

www.Harlequin.com

LIH82992

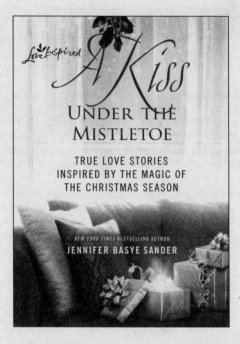

Christmas has a way of reminding us of what really matters—and what could be more important than our loved ones? From husbands and wives to boyfriends and girlfriends to long-lost loves, the real-life romances in this book are surrounded by the joy and blessings of the Christmas season.

Featuring stories by favorite Love Inspired authors, this collection will warm your heart and soothe your soul through the long winter. *A Kiss Under the Mistletoe* beautifully celebrates the way love and faith can transform a cold day in December into the most magical day of the year.

On sale now!

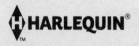